PLEASE LEAVE ALL VALUABLES AND
EXPENSIVE PERSONAL EFFECTS
HERE SO THAT THEY CAN BE, UM,
STORED AND GIVEN BACK TO YOU
AT THE END OF ETERNITY.

ALSO BY DALE E. BASYE

Heck: Where the Bad Kids Go

DALE E. BASYE

ILLUSTRATIONS BY BOB DOB

RANDOM HOUSE  NEW YORK

RAPACIA

THE SECOND CIRCLE OF ~HECK~

Text copyright © 2009 by Dale E. Basye
Illustrations copyright © 2009 by Bob Dob

All rights reserved.

Published in the United States by Random House Children's Books,
a division of Random House, Inc., New York.

Random House and colophon are registered trademarks of Random House, Inc.

Visit us on the Web! www.randomhouse.com/kids
www.wherethebadkidsgo.com

Educators and librarians, for a variety of teaching tools, visit us at
www.randomhouse.com/teachers

Library of Congress Cataloging-in-Publication Data

Basye, Dale E.

Rapacia : the second circle of Heck / by Dale E. Basye ;
illustrations by Bob Dob. — 1st ed.
p. cm.
Summary: Formerly dead Milton Fauster tries to save his older sister
Marlo from "eternal darnation" when she is sent to
another level of the underworld reform school known as Heck.
ISBN 978-0-375-84077-7 (trade) — ISBN 978-0-375-94077-4 (lib. bdg.) —
ISBN 978-0-375-85387-6 (e-book)
[1. Brothers and sisters—Fiction. 2. Future life—Fiction. 3. Greed—Fiction.
4. Reformatories—Fiction. 5. Schools—Fiction. 6. Humorous stories.]
I. Dob, Bob, ill. II. Title.
PZ7.B2938Rap 2009   [Fic]—dc22   2008019115

Printed in the United States of America

10 9 8 7 6 5 4 3 2 1

First Edition

THIS BOOK IS DEDICATED
TO MY SON, OGGI,
AND MY WIFE, DIANA,
WHO MAKE ME FEEL THAT I CAN ACHIEVE ANYTHING
WHILE LEAVING ME WANTING NOTHING

◆ CONTENTS ◆

RAPACiA

THE SECOND CiRCLE OF
~ HECK ~

FOREWORD

As many believe, there is a place above and a place below. But there are also places in between. Some not quite awfully perfect and others not quite perfectly awful.

One of these places is so shiny with glittering desire and itchy can't-live-without-it-ness (which is amusing considering the life-challenged state of its inhabitants) that you can't help but see yourself in its dazzling reflection. Only this reflection is as warped as a fun-house mirror.

Thousands of years ago up on the Stage, there was a king named Midas who had the power to turn everything he touched into gold. He had a lot of fun at first, but then—after turning his wife and children into golden statues—the king viewed his gift as a curse. His story comes with a valuable lesson: Never touch your wife and children if you turn things into gold. *I mean, duh. How tacky.*

In this place, self-gratification rarely results in self-satisfaction, even though they sort of rhyme. See, where there's rhyme, there isn't necessarily reason.

The mysterious Powers That Be (and any of its associated or subsidiary enterprises, including—but not limited to—the Powers That Be Evil) have stitched this and countless other subjective realities together into a sprawling quilt of space and time.

Some of the patches on this quantum quilt may not even seem like places. But they are all around you and go by many names. Some feel like eternity. And some of them actually are eternity—at least for a little while. . . .

1 · BLiND AS A BRAT

"OWW ... YOU FLIPPIN' maniac!" Marlo Fauster shrieked. The demon driver, after untying Marlo's hands, had jabbed his pitchspork in a place just south of cordial. Marlo fell to her knees outside the stagecoach and fumbled to remove her blindfold.

The driver, his shape smudged and cloaked in the murky darkness, stood atop the stagecoach and struck a match across his fangs. The bright flare of light felt like an explosion in Marlo's eye sockets.

The driver's nightmarish features burned themselves into the back of Marlo's retinas. Like most of the demons she had met in Heck, he was a creature turned inside out. But this one was even *more* inside out somehow: a lanky, walking pizza with everything on it held together by a network of pulsating veins and arteries.

"On second thought"—Marlo gulped—"maybe the blindfold wasn't so bad."

A pale horse with shiny pink eyes clomped nervously in place in front of the stagecoach. The demon driver pompously puffed out his disgusting chest.

"*Snatched away in beauty's bloom, on thee shall press no ponderous tomb,*" he recited in a wet, snooty tone, like a butler with a bronchial infection.

As if things weren't bad enough, Marlo reflected, *now I have to hear his poetry.*

Her eyes adjusted to the light, and she saw she was in some kind of subterranean tunnel. She stood up, brushing gravel off her baggy, sequined #1 GRANDMA sweatshirt and sagging turquoise stirrup pants.

After her brother Milton's unprecedented escape at the Gates of Heck, Marlo had been forced at sporkpoint into this ugly Rapacia uniform, blindfolded, and shoved into the stagecoach of some poetic cadaver.

The next thing Marlo knew, she was here—wherever "here" was. "You are *so* not getting a tip," she said.

The demon folded his arms together smugly. The mesh of winding red and blue capillaries made him appear as if he were a living, throbbing road map. Watching the creature's pulse made Marlo's own pulse quicken.

"My, aren't we a brave little girl?" the demon mocked before suddenly leaping to the ground.

Startled, Marlo jumped back, hitting something with a clang. *"Dang!"* she cursed, rubbing the back of her skull. The demon laughed.

She turned to glare at what had connected with her head so painfully.

UNWELCOME TO RAPACIA, read a sign atop an ornate metal gate. Twin wrought-iron fleurs-de-lis were welded against a gleaming brass serpent, double curved into a shiny letter "s." At the side of the gate, attached to a crisscross of iron bars, was a large metal box, with a message etched across it: PLEASE LEAVE ALL VALUABLES AND EXPENSIVE PERSONAL EFFECTS HERE SO THAT THEY CAN BE, UM, STORED AND GIVEN BACK TO YOU AT THE END OF ETERNITY.

Marlo peered down the tunnel past the open gate. The passage grew darker in progressively blacker rings that formed a big, black, fathomless eye. She shivered.

"You'd better pick up the pace," the demon jeered. "The Grabbit doesn't like to be kept waiting."

Marlo turned back toward the exploded, over-microwaved Hot-Pocket-of-a-man.

"The Grabbit?" she asked. "What's a *Grabbit?*"

The demon laughed. "The Grabbit is your new vice principal. It's what makes Rapacia such an . . . *interesting* place of torment for greedy, grasping little moppets such as yourself."

The demon turned toward his stagecoach. The creepy white horse "nayed" with a deranged titter.

A wave of panic washed over Marlo.

"What am I supposed to do, you . . . you . . . *freaky carcass thing?*" Marlo shouted into the dark, her chest tight with fear.

The demon sneered over his sinewy shoulder.

"The name is Byron . . . *Lord* Byron," he replied haughtily, his inside-outside body flushed with indignation. "I once wore my heart on my sleeve and now must wear it draped outside my chest, a palpitating medallion for all to see."

The demon chuckled.

"But at least I'm not a naughty little girl—alone—*in the dark.*"

Marlo could practically hear Lord Byron's uncaring shrug as the demon stalked back to the stagecoach, muttering another depressing poem.

After a few long seconds of complete silence, Marlo's ears were suddenly assaulted with the sounds of hooves clacking, wheels squeaking, and monstrous snorts. Slowly, the noises flattened into fading echoes, leaving behind nothing but Marlo's frantic panting. The darkness and silence seemed to grip her around the midsection, squeezing out every ounce of her usual bravado.

"*This sucks!*" Marlo shouted to herself, kicking the wall.

"This sucks!" Her words echoed back at her, whiny and afraid. Marlo tried in vain to hold back the twin gushes of hot, salty tears streaking down her cheeks.

At least there was no one around to see what a total chicken nugget she was, Marlo thought—down here, submerged in darkness, alone, en route from one terrible place to another.

She sighed and tugged straight her sweatshirt—an acrylic travesty the color of old dentures—and hiked up her stirrup pants.

Might as well get this over with, Marlo reasoned as she felt along the tunnel with her hands, reading the walls like braille.

After Marlo's brother, Milton, had escaped from Limbo—using the buoyant power of freed souls to lift him up, up, and away back to the Surface, the Stage, the land of the living, whatever you wanted to call it— things had gotten a little *tense* down in the Netherworld.

Bea "Elsa" Bubb, Heck's hideous Principal of Darkness, had gone ballistic. She had been so angry that she couldn't so much as *look* at Marlo due to her sheer *Fausterness*—those hereditary bits of Milton the principal saw mocking her in Marlo's face.

Now, here she was, told to scurry in the darkness to meet her new vice principal.

After groping her way along for several minutes, Marlo felt a prickly wave of electricity creep under her skin. She stopped. There was a shimmer of . . . *something* . . . in the distance. A glint of garish green. A flash of cruel metal. A beguiling glimmer that drew Marlo closer like a moth to a lightbulb. She drifted toward the beckoning twinkle.

Marlo moved forward, the burrow narrowing steadily until, after a few hundred yards, it constricted into a dark, open portal. She sniffed the air. It smelled like ozone, like dust and electricity, like the smell just before lightning strikes.

Closing her eyes, Marlo breathed deeply to calm her frazzled nerves and then crossed the threshold into a humming chamber. Deep rumbling waves rattled her bones. Although she still couldn't see, Marlo sensed the presence of something even darker than the darkness, a shadow in a nest of shadows waiting patiently for her to come one fatal step too close. Her heart galloped like a rabid, three-legged racehorse.

Dim neon bathed a shape that towered before her at the core of the chamber. A gorgeous spectrum of far-away light leaked faintly from a grate in the ceiling beyond the shadow, daring Marlo to come closer. Its color danced along the edges of the dark shape, making the shadow seem even more sinister in contrast.

"What the bloody heck *is* this place?" a voice boomed in the blackness.

Marlo jumped with shock.

"This is like that lame haunted house in the mall," a familiar voice whined like a slow helium leak, "where they hire bums to dress up as monsters and pass out samples—"

"Pause it, Bordeaux," another familiar voice snapped. "Let the dumb demon do its 'oogie oogie' thing so it can get its costume back to the shop before—"

Suddenly, harsh light and screams flooded the chamber. Marlo gasped.

At the center of the great, rounded burrow was a colossal, full-metal . . . *rabbit*. It was Frankenstein as imagined by Beatrix Potter, a carnival of grinning steel, painted in aggressively cheery pastels. At least nine feet tall, the freakish mountain of leering metal was perched atop a nest of barbed-wire grass. The creature, sculpture, object . . . *whatever* . . . shimmered softly, vibrating so fast that its edges blurred.

Marlo gulped. She fought to free her eyes from the rabbit's blank, smiling eyes and the cold smirk that wrapped around its humming head. Once she tore her gaze away, she noticed five more tunnels branching out from the chamber and five terrified girls clad in awful sweatshirts and stirrup tights.

To Marlo's left were skinny, bleach-blond Lyon Sheraton and her skinny, bleach-blond fashion-accessory-in-crime, Bordeaux Radisson. Figured that Lyon would be shipped off to Rapacia to make Marlo's stay as excruciating as possible, Marlo thought. Lyon had been the bane of her nonexistence in Limbo and was primed to grow even . . . *banier* here in Rapacia. Lyon leveled a withering, fierce blue gaze at Marlo while Bordeaux, a few dippy seconds later, followed her lead.

Marlo and the other girls checked each other out with quick, darting glances. To her right an African-English girl with cornrows peeking out from beneath her scarlet head scarf; a lumpy girl whose hair looked as if it had been cut with a food processor; and a Japanese girl with shocking pink bangs framing a chalk-white face.

Marlo scratched her arms. Her flesh felt like it was crawling with frozen fire.

The African-English girl shook her head and turned to leave. "This is barmy," she said with a sneer of crooked white teeth. "I'm clearing off. *Cheers.*"

At that instant, golden gates shot down like gilded guillotines from the entrances of the six tunnels. The girl looked down at her orthopedic shoes, which were only an inch away from being open-toed sandals: *hold the toes.*

A voice erupted from the metal monstrosity:

"Welcome, all you greedy girls,
now don't be so naive.
You're my latest batch of grubby pearls,

I'd never let you leave.
So much for you to long for;
the rub is you can't have it.
Feeling empty 'cuz you want more?
That's my job, for I'm the Grabbit."

The creature's maddening smile somehow promised exhilaration and contentment. But it also creeped Marlo out.

Her heart pounded with longing. She wanted to get closer to the Grabbit, to embrace it, to please it, to become part of it. Yet her stomach was filled with molten dread. Marlo's extremities tingled with terror and excitement. Even her ankles stung and throbbed, as if they were covered with tiny cuts. . . .

Marlo looked down and realized that she was now, inexplicably, standing in barbed-wire grass, inches away from the Grabbit, her ankles scratched and bleeding. *How long have I been standing here?* she wondered in a haze. *How did I get here?* Marlo backed away and looked around her.

The chamber was a gaudy green-and-gold lair, overstuffed with opulent furnishings jumbled in incomprehensible heaps. It was like the estate sale of an old movie starlet who hadn't left her Hollywood mansion for decades.

Lyon stepped alongside Marlo, not out of any kind

of sisterhood or solidarity but to send a message to the other girls that *she* was the alpha deb around here, not the creepy little Goth girl.

"And what exactly is a *Grabbit*?" Lyon asked, her eyes narrowing into cold, twinkling sapphires. The eerie, ancient voice again thundered through the chamber:

> *"Pleased to meet you, one and all.*
> *You'll make fine inventory.*
> *Now that you are in my thrall,*
> *I'll share a little story. . . ."*

2 · THE TAKING TREE

"**ONCE THERE WAS** an oleander bush that loved a little boy. Every day on his way to school, the boy would pass by the poisonous shrub, trembling with fear. The bush would sway its pointy, spear-shaped leaves coquettishly, and the boy would blanch, clutching his inhaler.

"One day, the boy hobbled past the bush. The bush waved its branches, stretching its blooms, which, if ingested, cause vomiting and fierce abdominal pain. The boy, shambling with terror, tripped on one of the bush's lower branches and fell. He lay on the ground, crying. The oleander bush drank in the boy's tears through its roots. The bush was happy. But it wanted more. Much more."

Rapacia, the circle of Heck reserved for greedy kids, wasn't exactly what Marlo had expected, she thought as she and the girls sat at the Grabbit's cast-iron feet. Marlo had prepared herself for some kind of a haunted nunnery, a deathly dull place devoid of anything worth wanting.

But, instead, she found herself trapped in a dazzling treasure trove, like that cave in *Ali Baba and the Forty Thieves*—not that Marlo had actually *read* the book, per se, but she *had* skimmed the report she'd tricked Milton into writing for her.

"The boy grew older. One day, he shuffled quietly past the bush, praying it was dormant, when it shook itself awake.

" 'Give me some money,' the oleander hissed.

" 'But I have no money,' the boy croaked in reply. 'Just allergies.'

" 'Get me some money or I will rub you with my jagged, prickly branches.'

"So the boy fetched the bush some money. And the bush was happy. But it wanted more. Much more."

During the course of the Grabbit's horrible fable, Marlo stared at a sparkling crystal chandelier above her that grew fainter and fainter with each passing moment. In fact, all the long-eared vice principal's prized possessions were steadily evaporating into nothing.

Several burnished brass chutes supplied fresh valuables for the creature to covet, but as soon as they appeared, they began their slow fade into nothingness. It was as if the whole warren were caught in a state of pointless, perpetual *vanishment*.

"And time went by and the boy came back, now an old sagging sack of withered flesh draped casually over a skeleton

of brittle bones. The oleander bush perked up as it smelled the boy approach.

" 'I want—'

" 'I have nothing left to give,' wheezed the ninety-year-old boy.

" 'Then I have a gift for you,' the oleander bush replied coolly.

" 'What?' the boy whispered, clutching his tightening chest.

" 'Release.'

"The boy smiled a weary smile and stooped down, grabbing a fistful of leathery leaves in his arthritic hands.

" 'Come, boy,' the bush said. 'Sit down and rest . . . forever.'

"And the bush was happy."

The Grabbit stopped, its maliciously merry expression expressing nothing. The silence made Marlo uneasy. Awkward. Anxious. She traded looks with the other girls, seated cross-legged just beyond the Grabbit's metal feet.

"So, I take it that you're the nasty bush and humanity or something is the little boy," Marlo hypothesized aloud. "Always feeding something that will never be full until someone else is all used up. Right?"

"How good of you to fathom
my happy little tale.
Bubb, she said that you were dumb,
assuring me you'd fail."

The girls eyed Marlo with amusement.

"Ooh . . . *snap!*" Lyon snickered to Bordeaux.

Even more than she disliked being reprimanded in rhyme by a large, freaky metal rabbit thing, Marlo *loathed* Lyon Sheraton.

Coveting, wanting, grabbing things she didn't pay for—this was Marlo's domain. But Lyon practically ate greed for breakfast—after her chef had prepared it, of course. With the Sheraton billions to fund her every whim, Lyon had barely had a chance to feel a desire before it was met. Marlo, on the other hand, had been forced to work hard to take what didn't belong to her. It wasn't fair.

Now the Grabbit, having concluded its sick story, resumed its previous state of eerie inactivity, rumbling in subsonic ripples that made Marlo's flesh crawl. Perhaps it was in "sleep" mode, or whatever, Marlo thought as she slowly rose and feigned a stretch while the other girls—after sharing an uncomfortable silence—chatted among themselves.

A beckoning, shimmering gleam had snagged Marlo's eye like a fishhook. The lurid glow trickled into the warren from the gilt ceiling grate above and beyond the Grabbit.

Marlo grazed the wallpaper with the tip of her finger as she made her way nonchalantly around the Grabbit. Upon closer inspection, she realized that the intricate wallpaper was a collage of international currencies lacquered against the warren's walls. After a futile attempt to peel off a cool-looking French franc, Marlo sidled along the chamber's edge until she was just beneath the grate.

Marlo climbed up on a lushly upholstered antique love seat. She stretched up onto her tiptoes, scrunched one eye closed, and squinted through one of the grate's ornate wrought-iron loops as if it were a telescope. Marlo couldn't believe her eye.

Above her was a gargantuan, spiraling structure that blinked, buzzed, and hummed with frantic activity. Marlo gasped and gave her eye a quick rub with her fist. It was a *mall*—a grand, majestic, and stupefyingly wondrous shopping complex that made the Mall of Generica back home in Kansas seem like an Amish garage sale.

Marlo's mind could barely process the assault of information pounding into her eye. The mall was like the inside of a massive electric wedding cake—indulgently filled with hundreds, maybe thousands, of stores—and iced with a glittering, stained-crystal ceiling. Marlo counted ten, eleven . . . thirteen tiers, until her own tears blurred the sight into a kaleidoscopic smear.

Her ring finger stung as if she had plunged it into a beehive. She held it up to her face, expecting it to be pricked and swollen. It was fine. *That tingle,* she thought as she scrutinized her undamaged hand, *it's like when I see a primo shoplifting opportunity . . . only this time the feeling is off the charts.*

The sensation branched out through her body like slow, creeping lightning.

Right above her was . . . *everything.* It was heartbreakingly beautiful. It was mind-bogglingly exciting. It was sticky-finger-lickingly good.

It also seemed tormentingly out of reach. If only she could think of some way to get up there, some artful ruse, even a somewhat convincing excuse . . .

"Excuse us, our Miss Fauster,
we'd welcome your attention.
I think, girls, that we lost her.
She must want some detention."

Marlo stumbled off the love seat with shock.

Lyon snickered into Bordeaux's ear. "Ooh . . . *two* snaps!"

The African-English girl scowled at Lyon and Bordeaux. "If you two skinny gorms say 'snap' one more time," she said, "I'll *snap* you like a crisp."

Lyon glared at the dark fuzz nesting atop the girl's lip. "And *who are you,* Miss Mustache?"

"The name's Jordie," the girl replied, squaring her jaw like a sawed-off shotgun. "And you *don't* want to brass me off."

Marlo rushed over to the Grabbit. "What is that wonderful place . . . up above?" she asked, staring up at its unreadably jolly facade. The half rabbit, half robot—*rabbot*—quivered back to pseudo-life.

"You feed on my patience,
just like a piranha.
In trade for your silence,
that place? It's Mallvana."

"*Mallvana?*" Lyon spat, the corner of her lip tugged up to her nose as if by an invisible pulley. "You've *got* to be kidding me."

"See for yourself," Marlo said, pointing back to the warm golden sheen of the ceiling grate.

Lyon popped her pink bubble gum with explosive disdain. "It's probably some dumb trick," she sneered, "like the one fate played on your face."

Bordeaux giggled like an asthmatic shih tzu. "Three snaps, you're out!"

Jordie stood up, nostrils flared. "I warned you, ya saft bint!"

Lyon rose to her feet, still exuding haughty runway perfection despite her GRANDMA'S MY NAME AND SPOIL-ING'S MY GAME sweatshirt. She trained her cornflower-blue eyes on Jordie. "Zip it, hair lip," she hissed between wet chomps of gum. "No one here speaks fish and chips, anyway."

Jordie glared at Lyon with dark, simmering, seen-it-all-before-and-didn't-like-it-the-first-time eyes. Her jaw shifted from side to side, as if she were carefully considering which part of Lyon to hurt first.

The imposing girl tightened her red silk head scarf, preparing for battle. Marlo could see an ugly scar peeking out from beneath her headdress. She had a feeling that, however Jordie got down here to Heck, it wasn't peacefully in her sleep.

But just as things were about to get hair-pullingly, face-scratchingly fun, the Grabbit nipped the fight-to-be in the bud.

"Now, now, mesdemoiselles,
let's not be so crass.
Let's trade our farewells,
then shuffle off to class."

With a slicing sound, like two keen knives sharpening one another, a golden gate opened into a grand hallway. Unlike the dark, unsettling tunnels through which Marlo and the other girls had traveled, this passage was as gaudy and extravagant as the Grabbit's warren. Two demons wearing green vests, brass spats, and—unfortunately—nothing else, stood in the doorway, beckoning the girls with impatient waves of their pitchsporks.

Bordeaux, the Japanese girl, and the drab stubby

girl with the unfortunate haircut, rose to their feet, joining Marlo, Lyon, and Jordie. The girls—each swaddled in sweatshirts adorned with hideous appliqués—hesitated. Marlo felt as if there was some invisible force field surrounding the Grabbit, some magical glue that made it hard to leave. She looked at the other girls, and they, too, seemed like struggling, freaked-out flies stuck fast to supernatural flypaper.

Marlo took a labored step toward the demons. She felt twitchy and uncomfortable, like she had fire ants in her pants. She strained to break free of the Grabbit's magnetic grip, though each hard-earned stride made the feeling grow worse. The ants started to bite, the pants were now made of burlap, and her heart became so hungry it hurt.

Prodded painfully by the demons, the girls around her reluctantly shuffled away, each fighting the Grabbit's eerie pull.

Marlo made it to the hallway, where the feeling of anxiety dulled into a gnawing sense of longing. She looked back at the Grabbit's sneering puzzle of a face. She hated it. She loved it. She hated loving it and loved hating it.

The golden gate shut, and in that instant, Marlo felt like a newborn baby whose umbilical cord had been abruptly snipped. That confusing swirl of electricity was replaced by an excruciating emptiness.

"No!" she shouted as she ran for the door. She pounded it with her fists until a demon grabbed her by the shoulders and heaved her down the hall.

The elegant hallway featured two fading paintings: Van Gogh's *Starry Night* and Picasso's *Boy with Lobster* (the only way Marlo knew the names was because of the huge brass plates underneath). The paintings weren't fading in the traditional "timeworn, sun-damaged" sense but were actually disappearing before her very eyes. She inched close to the Van Gogh and pressed her finger through the blobby golden moon until her chewed nail touched the wall. The entire place was in a constant state of ghostly redecoration.

"So sad," the Japanese girl said.

Marlo jumped. The girl's sudden presence startled her but distracted her from the emptiness she felt inside.

"Pretty painting is going away," the girl continued with a comic look of confusion. The mousy girl with the rat's-nest hair*don't* was at her side.

Marlo turned and attempted a smile. "Jujitsu," she said.

The girl covered her mouth and giggled. "That's *ka-jitsu*," she replied. "Good day to you, too. My name is Takara."

Takara was cool, Marlo thought. She was one of those Harajuku girls in Japan (or used to be, anyway)—the ones who dressed up in all the crazy costumes like living, breathing pieces of art. Of course, now she was wearing a bulky beige sweatshirt with QUEEN OF THE QUILTING BEE written on it in sequins, but she still had her cotton-candy hair and matching lipstick. *You can take the girl out of her style,* Marlo thought with a smirk, *but you can't take the style out of the girl.*

"Marlo," the elder Fauster sibling replied with a lop-sided grin.

"I'm Norm," the other girl mumbled.

"Norm?" Marlo replied. "As in *Norma?*"

"Actually, it's short for Normal," the girl replied. "My mom was so happy that I was born normal, un-like my brothers and sisters—extra toes, fingers, even nipples—that she named me 'Normal,' which pretty much condemned me to a less-than-normal life."

Marlo laughed. Nothing like a fellow misfit to make you feel like you fit in.

Takara squinted at the Picasso. "Why does the boy with the lobster sit on the table without pants?"

Marlo sidled up beside Takara to scrutinize the strange, disappearing painting.

"One of life's great mysteries," Marlo mused.

The "boy," or whatever, had a face like a Mr. Mashed Potato Head. Maybe everyone back in Picasso's time just felt sorry for him and acted like his paintings were really good so he wouldn't cut off his ear like Van Gogh.

"Hurry!" one of the demons shouted back at them, herding the rest of the group ahead.

"Yeah, yeah, keep your spats on," Marlo grumbled, rubbing her sore pitchsporked bottom.

"Me too," Norm said, noticing Marlo's pain in the butt. "Those stagecoach drivers are a bunch of prod-happy poets, apparently."

"Mine was a pretty bird," Takara chirped. "Said his name was Keats. I thought he meant parakeet, and he got really mad."

"I got tenderized by Lord Byron," Marlo added.

"Keats hates Byron!" Takara said with wide eyes. "He squawked about how he was a meatheaded melancholic!"

Marlo shuddered. "He's more than just meat*headed* now," she said.

"Mine was a homely lady named George," Norm offered.

Marlo shook her head as she turned to walk away. "A regular dead poets society," she said before taking one last look at the painting.

There was something about the boy's overly trusting eyes. And the dorky hair, like his mother had spit on a comb and scraped it straight for a family portrait. The boy reminded her of Milton—her brother, whom she had tricked into shoplifting, sending him straight to Heck after the marshmallow bear blew up. He had managed to escape, but to who knows where? All she knew for certain was that she missed him, dorky hair and all.

Takara stared at the painting as it finally vanished into thin air.

"Lobster boy is gone," she said in her sweet, doll-like voice. "Like he was never here in the first place."

Marlo sniffed back a tear as her eyes bored through the green wall to a place lifetimes away.

"Yeah," she said weakly. "Like he was never here at all."

3 · BUTTER OFF DEAD

"DAMIAN'S ALIVE?!" cried Milton Fauster, a haunted, bedraggled boy who had seen more than his eleven years could comfortably contain. Milton stood by the flagpole of Generica Middle School as Hans Jovonovic fidgeted, staring down at his way-too-white Keds.

"Well, in a coma, anyway," Milton's once-close friend replied in the same distant, nervous manner that everyone had adopted since Milton's return from the dead. "Maybe he'll come back to life like . . . like you did."

"Hopefully not, though," interjected Humberto Stiles, a tall, pimply beanpole in a NEXT STOP: M.I.T. sweatshirt. "Considering what a colossal, menacing jerk he was . . . is . . . *whatever.*"

"We're glad *you* came back, though," Hans added with haste. "Of course."

Hans shot Humberto a furtive glance before staring glumly at the flagpole, now at half-mast to commemorate the death of Milton's sister, Marlo.

Hans, Milton, and Humberto were the founders of the Generica Middle School Model Chessetry Club, a club that had held woefully underattended matches using model rockets shaped like chess pieces. Before that, they had been the Middle Earthlings, Warp Factor Three, and even Monty Cylon's Flying Circuits (which had won *Modern Outcast* magazine's Geekiest School Club Name of the Year award). But despite all they had been through together, it was obvious that Milton was now a third wheel, and they were all far too old for tricycles.

Strangely, though, Milton didn't feel all that bad about how awkward things had gotten between him and his friends. Since his "death," what had once seemed so interesting to him now joined the ranks of Hot Wheels and Lincoln Logs in the landfill of his heart.

Even Milton wasn't completely sure if what had happened had *really* happened. Had he actually died and gone down to Heck—where the souls of the darned toil for all eternity or until they turn eighteen, whichever comes first—or had it all been nothing but a near-death delusion?

His faithful ferret, Lucky, had thrown up bits of what Milton believed to be the contract for his everlasting soul. But considering the things that his voracious pet ate on a daily basis, he couldn't be 100 percent sure. For all Milton knew, his "contract" could have merely been the result of a day's newspaper nibbling.

So that left Damian: Milton's brutish earthly nemesis turned slick, savvy, and exponentially more dangerous after having descended to the Netherworld. Although in a coma, he was still—at least legally—*alive!* Damian was Milton's only connection between this world and the next. And maybe, if Heck was real, there was some way Milton could use Damian to make contact with Marlo.

"Where is he?" Milton asked. Hans and Humberto stared mutely at Milton, as they had been doing for the past minute while Milton had been engaged in a private wrestling match with his own thoughts.

"Who?" Humberto asked with fearful caution, as if talking to an armed gunman or a cheerleader.

"Damian!" Milton shot back.

"Why is it so important for you to see him?" Hans asked.

Returning to the land of the living moments after his own death, Milton had somehow arrived before Damian's departure. It was as if he had stepped off a metaphysical merry-go-round at the very point he had boarded. The only explanation that made any sense to

Milton was that—having been sentenced to Limbo where time didn't pass—he had escaped back to the Stage, or Earth, *whatever*, as if nothing had ever happened.

"I just need some . . . *closure*," Milton lied. "Because"— he stared up at the blue Kansas state flag fluttering halfway up the pole—"because of Marlo."

Hans sighed. He had harbored a secret crush on Marlo since fourth grade. Marlo, like most every girl in his life, had made fun of Hans because of his woolly or- ange hair. But Marlo had always taken the time to come up with unique ways of insulting him, like when she pretended she could talk to God through his flaming bush of red curls. It was those thoughtful little touches that he had found so endearing.

"He's at Generica General," Hans replied sadly.

Milton turned to leave.

"But they won't let you in," Hans continued. "Not unless you're part of his awful, messed-up family, that is."

Milton froze. Although he had spent much of his life ducking down hallways and hiding behind drinking fountains to avoid the sadistic scrutiny of Damian, Mil- ton had to see him now more than anything.

"Do you guys want to come and help me?" Milton asked, turning back toward his once-friends. "You know . . . to pay your *lack of* respects?" Even though

Milton felt he was on a solitary mission, he could use some company.

Hans and Humberto glanced at each other uneasily for guidance.

"Um, we've got a . . . *social obligation,*" Hans said with a stunning lack of conviction.

Milton glared at the less-than-dynamic duo.

"Fine," he sighed bitterly. "Then consider this my official resignation from the Model Chessetry Club."

He walked away.

"Social obligation my once-dead butt," Milton, the outcast of the outcasts, grumbled with disgust as he crossed Rubicon Street toward the hospital, on a mission he didn't fully understand. Whether Milton had truly been reborn or had simply lost his marbles while hovering at death's door, one thing was for sure: he was irrevocably changed, and nothing would ever be the same again.

Generica General Hospital resembled a huge concrete Rubik's cube too boring to solve. A pair of chuckling security guards strode into the hospital through its automatic sliding-door entrance.

Milton, some twenty feet away, froze in his tracks. He needed to find some way to get inside the hospital, some way to slide past security, like a pig greased in . . .

Butter.

Something caught Milton's eye in the visitors parking lot. A large stick of butter with wheels was double-parked beside two Land Ravagers and a Ford Cilantro. Painted on the side of the automotive depiction of fatty, churned cream was the following: GOT A FRIEND WHO'S SICK? GIVE 'EM A STICK! THE SYMPATHY EXPRESS GET BUTTER MOBILE.

The driver was chatting with a bored teenage girl working a coffee cart outside the hospital.

Opportunity is where you find it, thought Milton as he crept behind the Butter Mobile, *sometimes even in a big stick of butter.*

He stealthily opened the side door, and there, on the seat, was just what he'd suspected: a fiberglass butter costume with a matching cream-yellow leotard.

Milton peered nervously over the stubby hood of the vehicle. There was no way he'd be able to make it across the parking lot dressed as a stick of butter without the driver noticing.

He looked down the driveway leading to the hospital's back entrance. At the end of the slope was an empty delivery area. Milton snatched the costume and a sympathy balloon, sucked in a deep breath, and wrapped his sweaty palm around the vehicle's parking brake.

Maybe I'm not such a goody-goody after all, Milton

reflected, releasing the brake and backing away from the Sympathy Express vehicle as it crept backward down the incline.

He stole toward a patch of nearby hydrangea bushes for cover. The Butter Mobile slowly gained momentum as it rolled down to the delivery entrance.

"My Butter Mobile!" the driver yelped. He dropped his coffee and ran down the parking lot.

Just then, a bread delivery truck entered the rear parking lot.

"Look out!" the Sympathy Express driver shrieked as his wobbling vehicle slammed into the approaching Your Daily Bread van.

The fiberglass butter pierced the van's side with a horrid, grating squeal. The driver leapt out of the van just as it burst into flames.

"Are you okay?" gasped the Sympathy Express driver as he grabbed the frazzled bread driver by the shoulders and pulled him away from the wreckage.

"I . . . I think so . . . ," the man huffed. "Do you think my van will be okay?"

Flames licked the side of the van. Painted depictions of freshly baked loaves bubbled and dripped down the vehicle's side in molten clumps.

"I think it's toast," the Sympathy Express driver sympathized.

The great cube of charred, fiberglass butter melted, ultimately collapsing upon itself.

"Is that real?" the Your Daily Bread driver asked, wiping oily soot away from his eyes.

"The butter?" the Sympathy Express driver replied. "No . . . it's fiberglass."

"Wow. I can't *believe* that's not butter," the man replied in awe.

Meanwhile, Milton climbed into the costume, which was several pats too large for him. Taking advantage of the diversion, he trotted into the hospital. He pulled up the saggy yellow fabric bunching down around his knees and approached the reception desk.

"H-hello," Milton managed from inside the costume.

The middle-aged nurse smirked. "You're not the usual guy. What are you, some kind of butter substitute?"

"Um . . . y-yes," Milton stammered. "He . . . he's having a vehicle malfunction. I'm kind of his apprentice."

"Oh," she replied absentmindedly while systematically checking off a stack of forms on her desk. "That's cute . . . and a little sad."

"I'm here to see Damian Ruffino."

"Hmm," the nurse murmured while scanning a stack of admissions records. "He's in *ICU*, so you *can't see him*." She looked up over the horn-rimmed glasses teetering on the tip of her long nose and eyed the bobbing GET BUTTER SOON balloon.

"Aren't you supposed to have a gift or something? I mean, the balloon on its own is just kind of . . . well, *pathetic*. Even to a kid in a coma."

Milton gulped and, after a moment's hesitation, set the backpack he had been clutching in his left hand onto the counter. He rummaged through it, stopping with surprise, pulling out a small, gift-wrapped package.

"Uh, yes, here it is," he said, "ready for poor little . . . *Damian*."

The nurse glanced uneasily from side to side.

"Okay, I shouldn't really do this. But go on up. Just be quick . . . and take the stairs, to be on the safe side."

Milton shuffled off. "Thanks," he said with a wave just as the nurse's phone rang.

"Hello, Generica General. What? In the parking lot?"

Milton rushed into the "Staff Only" stairwell. He was panting so hard he sounded like Darth Vader having an asthma attack. The suffocating costume smelled like that Udderly Unbelievably Nothing to Do with Dairy! spread that his mom bought to save money after the family had been hit with a larger-than-expected bill for Marlo's funeral. Mom and Dad had gone all out, going for the Deluxe Simu-Marble Cryptoleum, even springing for the Gothic lettering and Take-It-for-Granite trim. Marlo would have loved it. *Marlo . . .*

Milton's legs wobbled, and his head started to spin and lurch like a dryer with sneakers in it.

"Oh no," he murmured as he leaned against the wall, holding the rail with trembling hands. "Not another spell."

The stairs, the NO SMOKING sign, the metal handrail, the buzzing fluorescent light, they all seemed to reel in wavering arcs across his field of vision. It felt like full-body vertigo, like every part of his body wanted to puke but couldn't.

Milton had some dream or memory—he wasn't quite sure—that when he had died, he'd lost his sentient body, the energy "glue" that held him together, to something called the Transdimensional Power Grid. And ever since his return to the living, he had been experiencing these weird, sudden "skips" in himself at odd moments, usually when he was stressed out about something, which was practically all the time. From the murk of either memory or madness, he could hear a dead pirate talking about physical and etheric bodies, shifting out of phase. . . .

Finally, the nauseating carnival ride slowed to a stop, and Milton's reality—if you could call it that—settled into place. He gulped, drew in a deep, stale buttery breath, and stared at the present in his hand, the one that had, inexplicably, been in his backpack. It was so light it was no wonder he hadn't noticed it in his bag.

It was wrapped in shiny silver paper that warped his reflection. There was a small rocket ship–shaped tag that read simply: *To Milton, From Mom.*

She must have put it in my backpack before school, thought Milton. *She's been so strange, ever since . . .*

Milton heard voices from above. He had to hurry before someone kicked his butter back out into the street. He passed by two nurses as he entered the children's ward on the fourth floor.

"You know they say that wearing a butter costume is actually better for you than wearing a margarine costume," deadpanned the curly-haired nurse to her friend.

Milton walked down the hall, touching the smooth, cool wall with his fingertips to steady himself. He poked his head into a room. Through the eye slits in his costume, Milton could see a dark lump surrounded by blinking boxes. A symphony of dull beeps, staccato chirps, and labored wheezes swarmed about this claustrophobic, pine-scented tomb. In the middle of it all, conducting this high-tech orchestra, was Damian.

A plastic tube snaked out of his mouth, winding its way to a mechanical bellows that sucked and puffed in a slow, steady rhythm.

Milton gently closed the door and knelt beside Damian. An IV tube was spliced into his wrist, while a heart monitor blipped and blinked like a first-generation

Atari game. He looked so peaceful. But Milton knew better. Damian was a nuclear bomb swaddled in blankets. Beside him, on the nightstand, were cartons of popped popcorn, in various flavors. Actually, boxes and bags of popcorn were piled all over the room. *Damian must have really liked popcorn,* Milton thought. *Who knew?*

"Damian," Milton whispered nervously. Even though Damian was, for all appearances, dead to the world—*this* world, anyway—cold sweat trickled down Milton's back out of sheer habit.

Milton shook Damian's sturdy, lifeless arm. "It's me . . . Milton. C'mon. Don't you want to beat me up?" he said.

The comatose bully's eyes darted about beneath his eyelids.

Ignoring the old adage "Let sleeping thugs lie," Milton tried shoving Damian awake, but he wouldn't budge.

Footsteps echoed down the hall. Hard patent-leather shoes slapped against the linoleum floors, getting closer with each step. Milton slammed his fiberglass shoulder against Damian's side.

"Heck," he whispered. *"Is there a Heck?"*

Damian's eyes fluttered open. He registered Milton's presence with flat, dilated pupils.

"B-butter?" he gasped.

Damian's eyes closed and he fell back into unconsciousness.

The footsteps in the hall drew closer. Milton didn't have much time. If he wanted proof that he wasn't crazy, he had to get it now.

With all his might, Milton slammed into Damian's side. Little did he estimate that his slight build could be amplified by pounds of fiberglass. Damian rolled violently to the wall, then—like a human pendulum—barreled back with such force that he lurched off the bed in a tangle of cords.

The life-support machines came crashing down, yanking out plugs and wires.

Milton gasped. Panic wrapped its fingers around his heart as his mind was dragged back to Heck, to the time that Damian had first entered Limbo.

"Well, after the . . . incident," Damian said while absentmindedly twirling one of the soiled bandages unraveling from his head, "I was taken to the hospital and hooked up to a machine. Some idiot tripped on the cord and unplugged me, though. It's all a little hazy. I think I saw a gigantic stick of butter holding a balloon that said 'Get Butter Soon'!"

Milton looked up at the bobbing balloon he held clenched in his trembling fist. A bad taste formed in the back of his mouth before slowly trickling down his throat. *Milton* was the butter. *He* was the one who had, inadvertently, sent Damian down to Heck, unleashing upon the woebegone children of the Netherworld a demonic force that made the torments before seem like a library puppet show. It was all true: *Heck was real!*

Alarms and buzzers sounded. An unwavering tone sliced through the din, the unmistakable sound of a patient flatlining. Milton bolted down the hallway. To his right was a gaggle of nurses and candy stripers.

"Stop that stick of butter!" one of the nurses shrieked.

Milton scrambled toward the stairwell like a frightened animal. Another bout of vertigo spun his internal compass, and he fell down a flight of stairs, a rolling pin of squealing fiberglass and tights. Shaken but unhurt, Milton slammed through the emergency exit and out into the parking lot.

He dove into a thatch of nearby shrubs and wriggled out of the costume like a big sweaty larva abandoning its egg. As he stepped out of his tights, Milton was struck by the feeling that he had forgotten something. Then, as he kicked the gnarled ball of hose away, it hit him: his backpack was still in Damian's hospital room.

He reviewed the contents of the bag—books, mostly—and relaxed a little. There was nothing in it that connected directly back to Milton, nothing that could possibly identify him. . . .

Milton's stomach sank down into his sneakers. The "To Milton, From Mom" gift.

Several security guards emerged from the hospital. Milton would have to postpone feeling sorry for himself until he got home. He crouched down and darted through the maze of dense shrubs, hoping that there was something—*anything*—that could make him "feel butter" about his desperate situation.

4 · DEAD GiRL'S BLUFF

A HIGH-PITCHED peal of piercing whines echoed down the hallway. The squeaky-wheel-of-a-broken-shopping-cart sound burrowed under Marlo's skin like a sonic porcupine in the throes of death.

"Wait," one of the demon guards said to the other as they herded Marlo, Norm, and Takara to their first class. "She's doing it again. It's a hoot!"

The demons followed the shrill sounds to a pair of green metal doors labeled GIMME. Snickering, they set their pitchsporks against the wall and pressed their snouts against the doors' inset windows.

Marlo elbowed her way to one of the smudgy panes of glass. It was reinforced by embedded chicken wire. *Probably so it won't shatter due to the screeches,* Marlo thought. She peered inside.

The room was lined with elevated shelves stuffed

with shiny new toys and candy. At the center was a human pyramid of raging toddlers mewling with want, their faces slick with a mixture of tears, drool, and snot. One little boy with a look of righteous entitlement teetered at the top with his trembling hand outstretched toward a glass jar brimming with fresh-baked cookies. The delicious odor was so powerfully enticing that Marlo could smell it even through the thick metal door.

Just as the furious boy was about to touch the jar, it was yanked away, suspended by fishing line. Marlo followed the translucent cord up to the ceiling, where it coiled through a pulley, then stretched across the room to a long pole manipulated by a chuckling demoness wearing a tiara. The creature reeled the line in with the teasing, expert hand of an old Greek fisherman, until the pyramid of whining children collapsed.

As the bruised, undeterred children clambered over one another to start their futile efforts anew, a herd of deep voices and clomping footfalls thundered from an intersecting hallway.

"I ken not wait to show you boys ze expensive, state-of-ze-art arcade we have just sealed up," a snooty Frenchman sneered, tugging his flowing red velvet robe along the floor. The man was followed by ten miserable-looking teenage boys who shambled along behind their teacher, staring at their shabby penny loafers.

"Yes, Cardinal Richelieu," they chanted dejectedly.

Norm stared at the group and blushed. "Boys," she

mumbled while attempting to fix her hair, despite it being past the point of repair.

Hmm . . . Rapacia for boys, Marlo reasoned. *Girls and boys pried apart, then locked away in their own gender-specific torment. Just like in Limbo and European boarding schools. Brutal.*

One of the boys gave Marlo a quick once-over from the corner of his deep brown eyes. He shuffled down the hall with cool charisma, his hands thrust deep inside his pants pockets, giving him a permanent shrug.

Marlo smirked to herself. *A fellow klepto, no doubt,* she thought as she watched the intriguing, pale— almost translucent—boy disappear down the hall. *He even has to steal a* look.

The bell rang. The demon guards grumbled as they grabbed their pitchsporks.

"Looks like you girls are already tardy," one of the guards said while picking its snout. "On your first day, no less."

"That's not fair!" Norm complained.

The other demon guard jabbed Norm in the bottom. "Neither is having corns on your toes the size of . . . *corn* . . . and sentenced to spend eternity on your feet," it spat. "So just deal with it!"

The girls were prodded, poked, and nudged down the hall toward their first class.

★   ★   ★

The smoke in the classroom was thick and acrid. It curled Marlo's nose so much she felt like her nose hair was getting a perm.

At the eye of this stinky, swirling cloud was a glowing orange ember—the tip of a foul cigar that flared and cooled in tireless rhythm. As Marlo groped for her seat in the carcinogenic fog, her movement fanned the smoke clear. At the desk was a wrinkled, jowly old woman puffing away at a small tobacco-filled log. She wore a man's work shirt, a khaki skirt, a frayed straw hat, and an expression like a rusty bear trap. The woman's desk was covered in green felt with a deck of cards fanned out before her. Marlo's breeze had caused the cigar to burn like a fuse, rapidly turning half of it to ash.

The woman leveled her cold eyes at Marlo. "Do you know how hard it is to get a Cohiba down here?" the woman rasped.

Marlo sat down at the only unoccupied desk, which was, unfortunately, right up front.

"I can't say that I do," she replied flatly.

Behind her, Bordeaux coughed. It was like the thin wheeze of a balloon animal.

"Aren't there, like . . . laws against . . . smoking in a . . . classroom or . . . something?" Bordeaux managed between petite hacks.

The woman smiled around her cigar. "That must be

why it tastes so dern good," she said, her voice rippling like liquid tar paper.

"Don't worry," Lyon whispered to Bordeaux. "Second-hand smoke is a totally awesome appetite suppressant. Plus, coughing is great for the abs."

A display screen lowered behind the teacher. The lights in the room automatically dimmed, and the old woman rested her head on her desk, using her swollen hands as a pillow.

THIS CLASS IS BROUGHT TO YOU BY HALO/GOOD BUY, LOCATED ON THE FOURTH TIER OF BEAUTIFUL, EVERLASTING MALLVANA.

A confused old woman nervously approaches the Pearly Gates. St. Peter is there behind a stately lectern, furiously scribbling away with a quill on a long sheet of parchment.

"Am I on your list?" the woman asks meekly.

St. Peter looks up, startled. "What? My list . . ."

He laughs uproariously. "No, of course not!"

The woman skulks away sadly while St. Peter returns to his writing.

"This is my shopping list for Halo/Good Buy," he chirps happily to himself, "where divine deals and beatific bargains flow like milk and honey!"

The old woman sneaks past St. Peter and tries to push open the gate.

"Can't . . . budge it," she gasps breathlessly.

"Can't budget?" St. Peter replies to the camera. "No problem! With bins overflowing with irregular sizes and damaged returns, you can always leave Halo/Good Buy with a heavenly harvest, even if in debt you did part!"

The old woman nudges open the gates and tries to tiptoe inside. St. Peter rolls his eyes and pulls a massive lever. A trapdoor opens beneath the old woman. She falls into the flaming pit, screaming.

HALO/GOOD BUY. IF OUR PRICES WERE ANY LOWER THEY'D BE, WELL . . . DOWN THERE. HALO/GOOD BUY: ONLY IN MALLVANA.

The lights came up, and the screen slid back into the ceiling. Marlo trembled. It didn't matter that the store itself seemed kind of lame, she thought as she bit her nails. The hypnotic commercial had stoked the flames of desire burning within her to such a degree that beads of sweat formed on her greedy brow. She took a deep breath, clutched the sides of her desk, and looked around her. Norm, Lyon, Bordeaux—all of the girls— were gazing imploringly at one another with the pained look of QVC addicts who hadn't paid their phone bills.

What was it the Grabbit said? Marlo reflected. *"So*

much for you to long for; the rub is you can't have it"? That must be the whole point of this place. Rubbing our faces, day and night, in things we don't have or need but somehow need to have.

The teacher yawned deeply. From Marlo's unfortunate vantage point, she could see that the inside of the teacher's mouth was coated pitch-black. The old woman chomped back down on her cigar, pushed back from her desk, and lumbered toward the chalkboard. She wrote her name in quick squeaks and scrapes: "Ms. Tubbs: Consumer Math."

The teacher turned to face the group of choking girls, all of whom were rubbing their bloodshot eyes.

"But y'all can call me Poker Alice," she said, scooping up the deck of cards on her table and absentmindedly shuffling them in her wrinkled hands. "Welcome to Consumer Math. Here you'll be learnin' the essential skills necess'ry to fueling a capitalistic society: establishin' credit, abusing credit, and vital debt accrual strategies. . . ."

Bordeaux's bony, bronzed arm shot into the air.

Poker Alice gazed down at her seating chart. "Yes, Miss . . . *Radisson?*"

"Well, like, what's there to know?" Bordeaux said. "I mean, like, all you need is to make sure Daddy gives you several major credit cards, in case the magnetic stripey thingy gets all worn on one. And also maybe, like, to have his assistant give you some of that paper stuff in case you're in a trendy boutique in a weird part of town that doesn't take cards."

The teacher took a long drag of her cigar and flicked the ash away with a weary wave.

"Well, Miss Radisson, firstly, you can put your arm down."

Bordeaux looked up at her slender hand and giggled. "I, like, *so* forgot!"

"Secondly," Poker Alice continued, "not all of us are lucky enough to be havin' yer assets."

Bordeaux smiled smugly. "I work out a lot."

The teacher chomped down on her cigar irritably. "The important thing is that there are many roads to financial ruin. After all, it's not what yer economy can do fer you, but what you can do fer yer economy."

Marlo had had enough. She waved her hand in the air. "What has this got to do with anything?" she said impatiently. "This just in: *We're all dead.* What's the point of money here? I thought you *couldn't* take it with you?"

Lyon and Bordeaux tittered. Poker Alice scowled at Marlo, glanced down at her seating chart, and exhaled a puff of stinky smoke. "Yes, Miss Fauster. Did you have a question?"

Marlo sighed. "I just don't understand why we're wasting our time in a classroom when the coolest mall to end all malls is right above us, taunting us, just crying out to be exploited."

Norm mumbled from her seat in the back row. "It *is* kind of mean," she said in a voice that seemed incongruously deep for her body. "Considering why we're here, and all."

Lyon leaned into Bordeaux and whispered just softly enough for her voice to still, technically, be a whisper. "She probably wants to see if there's a sale on wigs."

The teacher smiled despite herself and took off her straw hat, revealing a ratty nest of matted gray hair. "Though the currency is diff'rent down here," the teacher continued, "the concept is 'sentially the same. The value is in the exchange: an intricate series of bets 'n' bluffs. The money itself is worthless. But what it represents is priceless."

Poker Alice shifted her timeworn bulk on her chair with a screaming creak. "Let me put it to you this way, girls."

She shuffled her deck of cards with uncanny skill. The cards rippled together like twin waterfalls cascading into one. "The Netherworld Soul Exchange, or NSE, is the afterlife-blood of the postmortem economy. It circulates, it feeds, it courses through everythin' to the persistent throb of its own pulse."

She dealt a hand before her, and another, facedown, at the front of her desk. "Miss Fauster, play the cards you've been dealt."

Marlo gulped. She was an accomplished bluffer, to

be sure, but as far as cards went, her Go Fish floundered, her Crazy Eights were only somewhat mentally unstable, and her War was positively Swiss. But Marlo could tell by her teacher's dull glare that she would just have to gin and bear it.

She scooched her desk forward.

"The keys to winnin' any fortune are discipline, observation, unpredictability, and money management," the teacher said coolly. "Discipline to wait fer the right opportunity and to keep yer emotions under yer hat at all times."

Sighing, Marlo gathered her five cards: a King Henry the Eighth, a Jack the Ripper, and three sixes. Even Marlo knew that this was a pretty decent hand. She glanced over her cards at her opponent. Poker Alice was expressionless. It was as if she had Botox injections all over her face.

"Observation," the grizzled old woman continued. "Most of each game isn't spent playin' yer hand, but playin' yer opponent. Study 'em. Watch 'em. Listen. And use that information against 'em."

Her eyes bore through Marlo. It was like sitting across from a saggy old X-ray machine. Marlo looked at her hand again. Three sixes: the hand of the beast. The corner of her lips twitched up slightly in satisfaction. Marlo looked up and saw Poker Alice drinking in her face with her creepy eyes. *Great,* she fumed. *I get a decent hand, then smile like an amateur.*

"Unpredictability," Poker Alice continued. "Changin' gears, smoothly and without detection. If yer opponent is nervous, be calm—and vice versa. Draw?"

"No, I'd like to keep playing," Marlo said. Lyon and Bordeaux laughed.

"I kid," Marlo lied. "Two cards, *por favor*."

Poker Alice shook her head and grumbled. She slid two cards across the green felt tabletop and scooped up Marlo's discard.

Marlo had, naturally, traded her King Henry the Eighth and Jack the Ripper. But she had no idea she'd pull two queens: Catherine de Medici and Marie Antoinette. Marlo could scarcely believe her luck: she had a *Facts of Life*, or a *Growing Pains*—some terrible old TV show—oh yes, a *Full House*!

She fought to restrain her facial muscles. Marlo felt Poker Alice's stare graze her cheeks.

"I'll hold," the teacher said. "That means *I don't want any more cards*."

Marlo knew she held a winning hand, but poker wasn't about how much your cards were actually worth but how much everyone *thought* they were worth. So to win, Marlo thought, she had to play the player, not the game.

"Phew," Marlo muttered. "I'm glad we're not playing for anything."

Poker Alice glared at her. "What was that?"

"I mean"—Marlo cleared her throat—"I was saying

I . . . uh . . . wish we could play for something, but since we're not, I guess I'll just fold and go back to my . . ."

The teacher smiled, causing her stogie to flare in shared amusement. Poker Alice looked like a bored cat wanting to extend her playdate with a hapless mouse. "To better understand losses and personal bankruptcy, we should be makin' this interesting." The teacher grinned with yellow-brown teeth. "In the event that ya beat me, what would you like as yer winnings?"

Marlo trembled to contain her glee at baiting her trap so expertly. "Well," she mumbled. "If I were to, um, to win, I'd like to . . . to teach the class one day, *any way I'd like.*"

Poker Alice couldn't help but laugh. "High stakes, indeed," she mocked. "If I lose, I get a vacation. Tarnation! Well, I *never!*"

Poker Alice grinned wickedly. "And when—*if*—you lose," she continued, "my good fiend Principal Bubb and I could arrange a little student exchange. She could use an assistant, I reckon, after all the trouble your brother stirred up."

Marlo shivered, though she was clad in several ugly sweatshirts and thermal stirrup pants. *Bea "Elsa" Bubb, Principal of Darkness.* Just the thought of her turned Marlo's blood into a Type O negative Slurpee. She was in over her thirteen-year-old head, but there was no going back now.

"Lastly, money management," Poker Alice said smugly. "Only play in games you can afford. You must have a bankroll large enough to weather shifts in the undulatin' liquid of luck."

Poker Alice laid her cards out on the table. Each was blood-red, like five fresh gashes. She smiled smugly. "Miss Fauster, here, bet more than she could comfortably lose," the teacher said. "So, naturally, that leaves her broke, and me looking like a—"

"Full—" Marlo began.

"Fool?!" Poker Alice cut in, aghast.

"No, *full*, you fool, as in *full house*," Marlo said triumphantly while spreading her cards out on the table.

Poker Alice's face practically slid off the front of her head. She stared at Marlo's winning hand in disbelief— the wicked queens, the three ghastly sixes. Jordie, Norm, and Takara whooped with delight, while Lyon and Bordeaux's mouths dropped open in shock.

Poker Alice chewed on her cigar as the class bell tolled. She huffed and puffed and practically blew Marlo down with a look so dirty no soap known to man could ever hope to clean it off. Her teacher belched out one final, noxious cloud of cigar exhaust.

"Get out of my class—NOW!" Poker Alice roared while fumbling at her waist for a .38 pistol she had left up on the Stage years ago.

And though Marlo knew jack about poker, she *did* know when to walk away and when to run.

5 · THUNDER FROM DOWN UNDER

BEA "ELSA" BUBB dusted her armpit with a can of Secrete Industrial Strength Odorant until the aerosol propellant rattled empty.

She tossed the spent can onto the floor, then clacked hurriedly toward a dangling skeleton that currently functioned as a clothes hanger. Beneath it was a three-headed Pekingese with three wet little noses sniffing the air.

"Snookems," she cooed down to Cerberus, "would you be Mommy's whiffle fluff bottom and fetch me my favorite truss? *He's* going to be here in—"

Bea "Elsa" Bubb looked up at the motionless clock on the wall, which—being as her lair was in Limbo—

never ticked nor tocked. Still, her clock was at least right twice a day, and the object of her supreme affection—the Big Guy Downstairs himself—was due here at any moment.

Her back hair still in curlers, the principal yanked a purple taffeta dress with bile-green bows from her dressing skeleton.

Cerberus dragged behind him a beige truss and hernia belt, and deposited it at Bea "Elsa" Bubb's shiny black hooves. She clapped her hands together with appreciation.

"What a good boy, my tri-headed prince of puppy-wuppies!"

A pair of claws scraped outside the entrance to Principal Bubb's lair.

"Forgive me, O glorious Son of Perdition, I'm running a little late," the principal twittered girlishly as she cinched her truss and reached for the door latch. "I cleared my schedule so the two of us could spend the afternoon together over a pot of animossy-tea and devil's food . . ."

She flung the door open, hoping to feast her yellow goat eyes upon her nightmare in shining armor. Instead, there was a tall, willowy blond creature with cold green eyes and a toothy, predatory grin.

". . . cheese cake?"

Bea "Elsa" Bubb drooped with disappointment.

Cerberus poked from between her hairy legs and snarled.

"Sounds lovely," the woman said with a smile as bright and cold as a full moon in January. She extended her slender hand, a gesture that was less "Hello, nice to meet you" and more *"En garde!"*

Principal Bubb was at a rare loss for words, which was probably fortunate, considering the words that she was likely to use.

"Lilith Couture," the comely stranger said with obvious pride. "Devil's advocate, Satan's secretary, Lucifer's lieutenant, the Archfiend's aide-de-camp—"

"I get the idea," Bea "Elsa" Bubb replied.

"And you must be Principal Blob."

"Bubb. B-U-B—"

"Of course," Lilith said, strutting past the principal and into the office as if, in midstride, the room had suddenly changed owners. Bea "Elsa" Bubb stared at the lithe creature's trendy fashion accessory: an Italian-leather tail cap (made from *real* Italians) with inlaid flint accents that created a mesmerizing trail of sparks as her posterior appendage swayed from side to side.

As Lilith sat in the chair normally reserved for the Principal of Darkness, a wave of anger swept the cobwebs away from Bea "Elsa" Bubb's brain. "And why are you here, exactly?" she asked.

Lilith put her feet up on the desk. Her hooves were blood-red, lacquered to a brilliant gloss. "To clean up your mess, dearie." She grinned, this time with *genuine* pleasure. "An escape? From Heck? If it weren't shockingly true, it would be almost laughable. And that's a big *almost*. The Big Guy Downstairs did many things when he heard the terrible news, and I can assure you that 'laughing' wasn't one of them."

Lilith regarded the look of disappointment draped across the principal's face. "You didn't seriously expect that *he* would come . . . *here*?"

Lilith snorted demurely. Her near-skeletal frame trembled with mirth. "Oh, you poor deluded thing." She smirked, lifting her long legs from the desk and straightening her dress. "As if Lucifer would have the time to drop by your little Netherworld nursery to change soiled, procedural diapers."

Bea "Elsa" Bubb was furious. Her nostrils flared. The veins on her neck bulged. She even *smelled* angry (an odor akin to musky black pepper). But she fought to restrain herself. Lilith was not one of her charges who could be easily bullied. She held a power and status, at least by association, that the principal desperately wanted. Bea "Elsa" Bubb was *not* going to be sold down the River Styx.

That four-eyed runt Milton Fauster had made her the laughingstock of the underworld. His unprecedented escape had turned an otherwise smooth-running machine into a flaming bureaucratic wreck. So both she and Heck were under "review," and the principal would just have to suck it up and *deal*. She should, in fact, consider herself lucky. While the Fauster Incident was something of an embarrassment (okay, make that a *career-crippling humiliation to end all humiliations*), it had diverted attention from the fact that some glitch, some wrinkle, some heretofore unthinkable boo-boo had sent Milton Fauster down to Heck in the first place. Judging from the size of his file—a Post-it for a misdemeanor crime he didn't even know he had committed—and the inarguable purity of his soul, Milton Fauster was a do-gooding goody-goody who should be tuning his harp on some cloud, not taking up bunk space in her joyless juvie.

In any case, she would have to humor the flawless, infuriating she-demon who was now, currently, warming *her* chair (not to mention ruining the wide trench in the cushion she had worked so hard to create).

"Penny for your thoughts," Lilith purred. "Keep the change."

Bea "Elsa" Bubb smirked. If Miss Couture wanted to play hardball, then she would bring her bat and mitt.

"How droll," the principal said dismissively. "I was just thinking that it must be as busy as, well, h-e-double-hockey-sticks down there for His Unholiness to send someone so unimportant to help deal with our recent . . . *unpleasantness*."

Lilith's sneer evaporated. She sat up, hackles literally raised. "I'm practically his right claw," she hissed.

"Now, I don't expect us to be Ya-Ya sisters or anything, but it is in *both* of our interests to shovel some cat litter on your doo-doo—and quickly—so I can go back to helping rule the bottomless pit of eternal perdition, and *you* can get back to wiping runny noses and confiscating slingshots."

The principal's eyes constricted into a pair of angry yellow slits. This scrawny, rancorous stick of a woman wasn't going to stand between her and the love of her afterlife. Nor was she going to impede a successful career that had been steadily going down, down, down for time immemorial.

"Of course, Miss Couture," Bea "Elsa" Bubb replied calmly. "We can start by going through my files."

Lilith sighed, looking the principal up and down. "I only wish that dirty work wasn't so . . . *dirty.*"

Principal Bubb looked down at Cerberus, who was faithfully at her hooves, snarling at the bony intruder in their midst.

"Don't worry, my wittle wuzzle woo," she murmured as she went to exhume her first crate of files to be scrutinized. "We shall overcome."

The principal brushed aside the collection of porcelain kitten figurines on her desk to make room for her first stack of files.

Overcome, indeed, she stewed before absentmindedly sending one cat crashing to the floor. She hovered over the fractured feline.

"Chairman Meow," she whimpered before flushing crimson with rage.

I'd like to overcome, overpower, and overwhelm one Milton Fauster, Bea "Elsa" Bubb fumed. *And where exactly is that no-bad scab of a boy at the heart of all this aggravation?*

6 · SOUL SURVIVOR

"HELLO, MRS. HILDEBRAND," Milton said as he entered the library.

The redheaded woman behind the desk flashed a quick, nervous smile before turning to answer a phone that hadn't rung.

For years, Mrs. Hildebrand and Milton had been partners in numerous antiquarian book searches and heated literary discussions. But now she was treating Milton like everybody else was: like a freak, a zombie, a boy who shouldn't have come back.

Milton sighed and shambled toward a table that was, unsurprisingly, empty by the time he got there. He sat down, sick to his stomach.

He had only meant to visit Damian, not pull out his plug. Actually, to be precise, Damian had pulled out his own plug when he toppled over onto the floor, but there was no way Milton could rationalize his way to innocence. He *had* been responsible for dispatching Damian—technically, anyway. Somehow worse, in Milton's mind, was that he had set Damian's sadistic soul loose on his sister, his best friend, Virgil, and even *himself* down below.

Damian in a coma had been perfect. In that cocoon of unconsciousness, he couldn't cause harm to either the living or the dead. But Milton's curiosity had killed the catatonic. At least he had proved to himself that Heck was a real place—a real *bad* place that needed to be shut down for good.

Milton knew he should have stayed at Generica General and faced the music, even if that music was the sound of snare drums accompanying a firing squad. But what good could he do Marlo and Virgil locked up in a jail cell? Not only that, but his spells would only get worse. Unless he found a cure—and fast—he could be permanently out of phase.

Milton grabbed a collection of newspapers and splayed them out across the table. For the past week, he had scoured periodicals from all over the world for peculiar phenomena, bits of seemingly unrelated weirdness that could, perhaps, be attributed to Milton's breakout from eternal darnation.

When his balloon of bad-boy's clothing had burst somewhere over Des Moines, Iowa, the buoyant, agitated souls that had provided Milton's lift had scattered in each and every direction. That meant a dozen or so freed souls desperately looking to move back into their former homes, regardless of their current, dismal conditions.

Perhaps this is what Annubis, the dog god that had plucked out Milton's soul to be weighed in the Assessment Chamber back in Limbo, had meant about breaking the Prime Defective. Souls weren't supposed to come back, not like this. It was supernaturally unnatural. And, judging from the series of freakish accounts culled from across the globe, this new twist on "soul searching" was some sticky business indeed.

There was a Viktor Farkas from Budapest who had reunited with his body much like Milton. The only problem was that little Viktor had passed away in the seventeenth century from the plague, and his body wasn't exactly roadworthy.

Izabella and Zofia Kaczynsk, a pair of twins from Warsaw who'd died in the mid-1930s from choking on the same kielbasa, were currently on a posthumous tour of Polish eateries.

Lastly, there was the case of Penny Selsby, an Australian girl killed by her own boomerang, who had been cremated and placed upon the family's mantel. According to an article in the *Gold Coast Bulletin* titled "A Penny Saved Is a Penny Urned," Miss Selsby's bronze vase was now menacing her family with its vibrating tirades.

Milton stopped reading. He could feel the prickle of being stared at. He peered over his stack of clippings, and sure enough, there she was: Necia Alvarado, probing Milton with her dark, shining eyes. She had just entered the library, set down her overstuffed bag, and smiled at Milton's return gaze, waggling her tiny, rodent-like fingers in greeting.

So this is what it feels like to be stalked, thought Milton as he barely-smiled in polite reciprocation. Necia had always been one of those peripheral people in Milton's life, sort of like an extra in his ongoing movie, a grade below him. But ever since his return, Necia had gone from supporting player to aspiring lead: In fact, she was in every other scene. It would be one thing if she just came up and talked with him, but she seemed content to simply gawk from afar. *Oh well,* Milton mused, *that's the price you pay for being a living, breathing, one-boy sideshow.*

Necia's smile beamed bright and cold, like the headlights of an oncoming car with some dark secret locked away in the trunk.

Milton looked down at his calculator watch: his "counseling session" was almost over. His parents had insisted he get therapy after his return, so, to humor them, he would take their money and pretend to see his imaginary counselor, Dr. Cerebro (it was the first thing that came out of Milton's mouth, but luckily his parents weren't too sharp lately). Lying, taking money, accidental mercy killing . . . you could take the boy out of Heck, it seemed, but you couldn't take the Heck out of the boy. But Milton needed the unsupervised time and monetary resources for his research. Every day, he'd hobble over to the library and scour the Legal Reference section for some way of shutting down Heck for good. But just when he picked up the scent of a new trail—a stray thread to possibly unraveling the supernatural mess down below—he'd succumb to one of his "spells," shaking his mind blank and forcing him to start from scratch the next day.

Speaking of which, Milton could feel another one coming on, stirring deep in his stomach.

He scooted close to the table, clutching the side until his knuckles were white. A small ad on the border of the *Pitch*, Kansas City's weekly newspaper, caught his eye:

GRAND OPENING: THE PARANOR MALL!

The Last Stop on Your Metaphysical Mystery Tour! Want the 411 on UFOs and ESP, ASAP? Then come to Lester Lobe's Paranor Mall, in beautiful downtown Topeka. It's a museum filled with answers to mankind's most baffling questions! Get to the bottom of:

- Life after death
- Telepathy
- Déjà vu

- Time travel
- Astral projection
- Voodoo economics
- Extraterrestrials
- Cryptozoology
- Déjà vu
- and the subtle energies that hold us together!

IT'S ALL HERE . . . AND LES! COME TO THE PARA-
NOR MALL IN TOPEKA TO PIQUE YOUR CURIOSITY!
4400 Avenue 51, at the corner of Fact and Fiction.

Sure, the ad was on the back of one of those kooky alternative newspapers, the kind hipsters read while waiting for their pizza or for their new piercing to stop throbbing, but still: It was *something*. Milton had always considered himself a skeptic. But as time went by, he had grown so skeptical that now he even questioned skepticism. Plus, after what he had seen . . . *down there* . . . his eyes had been pried open to all sorts of unbelievable things, and there was no way that they could ever shut again.

The subtle energies that hold us together . . .

Milton read the sentence again . . . and again . . . and . . .

The library began to reel and rock. Milton felt his physical and etheric energies gradually part company as the swirl in his stomach grew thicker and faster, causing a "spiritual" seizure that knocked him out of whack like a scratch on a CD. But this time, the queasy, spinning flops weren't strictly due to a shift in "subtle" energies. They gnawed deeper than that. It was guilt that was eating away at him. He closed his eyes and laid his feverish forehead on the cool marble of the desk. Images of his sister and his best friend, Virgil—the two people he had left behind and below—filled his mind. The hushed voices of those nearby cut through the static in his head. But he didn't care. Though slumped over a table in the Generica Main Library, Milton's thoughts were miles away. Miles *below*.

7 · MALL OR NOTHING

"YES," **MARLO PURRED** softly to herself as her trusty safety pin coaxed open yet another defenseless lock. She pressed her palms on the warm golden door and lifted it up, squeezing through the gap beneath and creeping cautiously across the Grabbit's warren.

She was supposed to be back in her bunk, dreaming of shiny, unattainable things like a good little greedy dead girl. Yet, instead, she padded in the darkness, unable to sleep, unable to eat, unable to think of anything but Mallvana—the Happy Shopping Grounds above her blue-haired head—and the confounding cast-iron cottontail that seemed to hold her nervous system hostage.

She was nearly there, beneath the ornate grate that revealed the spectacle above. Flashes of multicolored neon exploded in the dark like fireworks. The light illuminated the motionless Grabbit's frozen leer. It was a grin that cleaved its brightly colored rabbit-clown face in two. The eyes that never moved followed her nonetheless. Though the Grabbit was as still as a statue, the air around it crackled with invisible electricity, as if—while everyone else in Rapacia slept—it was wide . . .

"Awake are things that never sleep,
  no dreams to fill their heads.
  Why is it that you sneak and creep
  past Rapacia's selfish beds?"

Marlo swallowed the thumping lump in her throat. "I—I was looking for a little inspiration," she stammered, "for my Consumer Math class. I needed to make some observations and take . . . some notes. You see, I won a bet with Poker—Ms. Tubbs—and get to teach tomorrow's class—"

"Of course I've heard about your bet.
  Your chances were remote.
  You got your teacher quite upset,
  in fact, you got her goat."

"Right. Very good. Nice meter," Marlo replied. "It's just that, I never expected to win, so I'm not really sure what to do. I was never that good in school, but I know

I can teach the girls *something*. And I know *where* I want to teach them. I just don't know *what*."

The Grabbit was still, even for a mostly motionless object. It was odd, Marlo thought as she stood before her mute vice principal in the dark: She felt like she was in the presence of a higher power, something that obliterated her own sense of self, a towering contradiction that held Marlo tight in its unbearable electrical lasso. Finally, the Grabbit's unsettling voice broke the quietude.

"Your touch is light; your nerves are steel.
There's hustle in your flow.
They'll take your class and learn to steal.
Just teach them what you know."

The clouds parted inside Marlo's head. What she needed to do shone through like the sun she hadn't seen for weeks. She felt like she could have it all . . . like she *should* have it all. She wasn't sure if it was this new opportunity or the deeply disturbing effect of the Grabbit that made her feel this way. Marlo stared at its painted-on eyes and white smear of a grin. The Grabbit was either the least-alive living thing or the most-alive dead thing she had ever encountered. Whatever it was (or wasn't), it held her firmly in its electromagnetic clutches.

She had found a way to sate her hunger, a way to stuff herself at the ultimate buffet of raw, shameless materialism. There it was, above her, so close yet so far. Not anymore. Tomorrow she would take her class on a field trip, of sorts. An in-the-trenches test, in the ultimate classroom of consumerism: Mallvana.

"Thank you!" Marlo chirped. "I'll teach them what I know!"

The Grabbit simply grinned back at her. Marlo shifted anxiously from foot to foot. "So, um . . . looks like I have a curriculum to write. Have a good night's . . . *whatever*."

Marlo squeezed beneath the door and into the hallway. She felt good, but she had a long night ahead of her. She gamboled away to her bunk, whistling "Material Girl," yet with each progressive step, she grew heavier and hungrier. Marlo felt like she was starving, only not just in her stomach: She felt as if she were starving *everywhere*. She turned toward the Grabbit's warren, thinking—*hoping*—she heard something. Was it the Grabbit calling after her?

She tiptoed back to the golden gate and peered inside. The warren was deathly still. Then suddenly the Grabbit's voice—only now somewhat deeper and darker—broke the silence.

"The only thing I really need
is everything I want.
Every moment, green with greed,
its hunger is a taunt.

And though I cannot leave this spot,
trapped I am, in thrall,
this Grabbit's hatched the perfect plot,
and soon I'll have it all."

Marlo watched the brazen, flickering lights of the mall dance across the Grabbit's face.

"And more."

8 · GOING TO CRACKPOT

THE PARANOR MALL was less a "mall" than a crazy old man's garage sale. Except that there was no garage. And, to the best of Milton's knowledge, nothing in the countless overflowing boxes and unruly stacks of yellowing paper was actually for sale. The crazy-old-man element, however, was spot-on.

"Of course, I don't have to tell you about cattle mutilations," the mall's owner, Lester Lobe, said between coughing fits.

Milton pretended to be interested in a "life-sized" fiberglass alien statue. "Yeah, you're right," Milton replied. "You don't have to tell me."

Lester, with tufts of wild gray hair snaking out from beneath a fez, shuffled closer to Milton, who was, unsurprisingly, the only other person there. Milton noticed that, though the man was fully dressed, he wore a pair of fuzzy green *Mars Attacks!* slippers.

"Have you heard about the mysterious rash of dead 'half-cats' found in Canada?" he inquired. "Obviously a message from alien visitors."

"Maybe the half-cats were just half-curious about something," Milton quipped.

Lester Lobe stared at Milton blankly with eyes bloodshot with fatigue and quivering from too much caffeine. He suddenly erupted with laughter.

"Good one!" he guffawed, rubbing his gray goatee and nodding. "It's humor that separates us from the extraterrestrials—unless you find kidnapping and human experimentation humorous."

Milton looked glumly at the fiberglass alien's emotionless head. "Not particularly," he murmured.

Lester scrutinized Milton's face.

"You're that kid," he whispered with awe. "The one who came back. I just finished clipping out the newspaper articles."

Milton had hoped he'd stumble upon some cure for his out-of-body predicament without having to solicit the help of a crackpot. But the cure for this vexing condition clearly sat outside Milton's realm of rationality . . . though, considering the events of the last few weeks, he worried that perhaps he himself sat outside that comforting realm.

Milton sighed. "Yes, I'm the zombie kid who shouldn't be here but is," he said.

Lester smiled, revealing a mouth full of crooked, nicotine-stained teeth. "Then you've come to the right place," he said with frenetic energy. "The Paranor Mall is all about things that shouldn't be here but are. I boil down all of the urban myths, hysteria, psychobabble, and weirdness that make up our culture today and inject it straight into your eyeballs. It's a lot like watching daytime television."

Milton eyed the mall's Elvis Abduction Chamber. It was a photo booth—or something—covered with rhinestones and clippings from the *National Midnight Star Weekly,* that magazine Milton's grandmother used to pick up at the checkout counter of the supermarket, with stories about Bigfoot's secret daughter brawling at a New York club with E.T., or the Olsen Twins revealing that they were time travelers sent here to caution humanity about our warlike ways. That sort of thing.

Milton fondled the tarnished brass doorknob of the chamber and peered inside the dark opening. The Elvis Abduction Chamber was just a six-sided box lined with mirrors.

"I need some help with a . . . p-problem," Milton stammered. It had been about twenty minutes since his last spell, so he wanted to get to the point before his train of thought derailed again. "After reading your ad, I thought that I might find some answers."

"Yes," Lester said, blowing the tassel of his fez out of his eyes. "Lots of people come here, all for different reasons. Drew Barrymore was here, mainly because she was kicked out of the place across the street for smoking. She *did* buy some T-shirts, though, and some unicorn-on-the-cob holders—"

"The ad mentioned . . . subtle energies," Milton interrupted, "the ones holding us together."

The man looked Milton up and down.

"Of course," he said with a mad twinkle in his eye. "Someone in your situation is probably missing a little in that department. I could tell by your aura. Faint, but nearly spotless. So clean you could practically eat off it."

A blinking flying saucer suspended overhead seemed to blur and wobble. Milton's energy was beginning to loosen and split.

"Do you know anything about," Milton mumbled, "*etheric* energy?"

"Hmm, *etheric* . . ." Lester abruptly walked away to a leaning tower of books and expertly yanked a volume from the middle without disturbing the rest. He flipped through the book, titled *Everything You Know Is Wrong*, and walked back to Milton, skirting stacks of junk and pop-culture debris while never once taking his eyes off the pages.

"Nothing specifically about *etheric* energy," he mumbled, "but there are many accounts of missing energy at the point of death. Twenty-one grams worth, in fact."

"Grams?" said Milton weakly. "But energy is measured by watts and volts . . ."

"Yes, of course," Lester continued. "But the human body, after death, weighs exactly twenty-one grams *less* than it did when it was alive. Many philosophers theorize that this must be the approximate weight of the human soul, which—as it is invisible when leaving the body—must be a form of vaporous energy that . . . are you okay, little dude?"

Milton was swaying with full-body nausea. He wiped his beaded-sweat mustache. "I'm just not . . . the same," Milton whispered as Lester pulled a milk crate of old magazines close for the boy to sit on. "I may have lost some energy by coming back."

"Interesting," Lester replied. "You obviously still have both your body and soul, or you wouldn't be here. Plato, the ancient Greek philosopher, felt that man was composed of *three* aspects: reason, emotion, and appetite. Reason being the rational mind, hungering for wisdom and truth; the body hungering for, well, just about everything; and the emotional body, which acts as a sort of bridge, or glue . . ."

Glue, thought Milton as he fought to hold on to himself even though his world was now a spinning

Tilt-A-Whirl. Ever since his return, he had begun to feel listless and strangely hollow. Perhaps that's because his emotional, etheric energy—the spiritual glue that had been his emotional body—was now helping to power the Transdimensional Grid.

". . . could probably refill it by getting some etheric juice back into your pineal gland."

Milton shook his head. "What was that?" he managed. "Something about a gland?"

"The pineal gland," Lester repeated. "It's this cone-shaped part of the brain, and no scientist really knows what it's for. Some ancient cultures, however, felt that it regulated mysterious dynamic forces within us, perhaps even the soul. In the early 1900s, Sir Edward Tylor, Oxford professor of anthropology, electroshock therapy advocate, and founder of the Subtle Energies Commission, had a theory that if one were to harness the power of other living creatures and direct that power straight to the pineal gland, then a living person could advance to the next step in human evolution. It is speculated that this technique could even reanimate the dead."

"The dead . . . the . . ." Milton's sense of reality winked on and off like the old, run-down television in Limbo's cafeterium.

Lester kneeled close to Milton. His breath was hot, musty, and sharp with dental decay. "You don't look so good, kid," he murmured. "If you're going to die again, can you not do it here? I have enough problems with the authorities as it is. It's all an intricate government plot. Of course, you've heard of the Illuminati and how—with the Freemasons—they've established a New World Order that . . . ."

The blinking UFO, the plastic alien, the moldy towers of paper, and Lester's convoluted conspiracy theories crowded together in Milton's consciousness until they formed a big clot, like some gross, hairy clump clogging a drain.

Then, with a few sudden jerks, the Etch A Sketch of Milton's mind shook itself blank.

9 · STEALING THE SHOW

The Greedy Girl's Guide to Getting Great Goods

By Marlo "Sticky Fingers" Fauster, Your Substitute Teacher

Shoplifting is an art. Not like those boring old paintings that slowly disappear here in Rapacia. But an art you can actually <u>use.</u> By following these five rules, you will totally rule the school of Sticky Fingers.

+ Rule One: Dress Appropriately. Sure, a trench coat with pockets sewn on the inside might make for a righteous haul,

But if it's hot enough to fry an egg outside, the heat will be on <u>you</u> inside. Dress like your dorky little brother or like you have audio books on your iPod or have seen all of the <u>STRAWBERRY SHORTCAKE</u> videos fifty times each with your mom.

+ Rule Two: Carry a bag but never stash anything in it. If security gets suspicious, they'll check your bag. If it's empty, then they'll probably just let you go—with whatever you took.

+ Rule Three: Carry a fake shopping list. Amateurs usually act on impulse. Not you, girl. Look at your list from time to time instead of looking over your shoulder. Look confident, dry, and secure—like you just coated your entire body with roll-on antiperspirant specially pH-balanced for the greedy girl you are.

+ Rule Four: Never pocket or conceal items near their shelf location. Major Duh, reporting for duty! Take your goods to an aisle full of crap like paper towels and toilet paper, stuff that's too big and worthless for security to hang around and protect. No guard is looking

FOR their next Bounty By A stack of
Bounty.

+ Rule Five: If you get caught, Lie! Lie
through your teeth! Lie Like A Rug! Lie as
if your presidency depended on it! Don't
act tough or talk Back. cry. Beg.
Whatever. Getting caught can ruin your
Life, even if you're dead.

So c'mon, girls: Let's make some Art,
or at Least make off with some cool
stuff!

The girls read Marlo's blotchy handout as they followed Poker Alice through a long, coiling corridor. The
empty hallway sloped upward at such a steep incline
that it gave Marlo shin splints.

Even though she had stayed up all night writing her
shoplifting ground rules, Marlo was kind of buzzed.
She had a dopey grin smeared across her face (along
with some blue ink from her leaky pen) and her fingers ached. But despite her fatigue and discomfort,
Marlo was oddly proud. She had, as the Grabbit had
suggested in its creepy, rhymey way, taught what she
knew.

The corridor's gleaming floors reflected the fluorescent lights above so that it seemed like you were walking on the ceiling, which is exactly how Marlo felt.

Her gravity-defying mood irritated Poker Alice to no end. *"Miss Fauster,"* the weathered hag groaned. "Exactly what is this . . . *paper?"*

Marlo smiled with bleary energy. "It's a list of ground rules," she replied, "for our class field trip."

Poker Alice shifted her cigar from one corner of her mouth to the other and grumbled.

Marlo's bloodshot eyes sparkled. "You know, the *field trip*," Marlo repeated, rotating the words slowly like a knife in her teacher's abdomen. "The one that the Grabbit said I could lead, taking the class on a learning expedition, up to . . ."

The teacher's eyes bulged out from behind their droopy folds. "I know what the Grabbit said!" the teacher barked, her cigar slipping out and falling onto the ground below. Poker Alice stared at the smoldering, now-broken cigar and trembled with rage. Slowly, the teacher raised her head, her neck creaking like that of a library gargoyle brought to sudden uncomfortable life, and locked eyes with Marlo. "What I would like to know is what the blazes shoplifting has to do with Consumer Math?" Poker Alice seethed.

"Well," Marlo said nervously, noting that Poker Alice without a cigar was like a monstrous baby without its pacifier, "since we don't have cash or credit down here, we're forced to put up something else of value, in our case, risk of capture. So the very act of trying to steal something is, to us, like racking up debt. Think of it as . . ."

Marlo followed the lines and crinkles of her teacher's face, hoping they would lead her to some conclusion that Poker Alice would, if not quite buy, at least rent for the day.

". . . a gamble. An *educational* one."

"What's that?" Norm asked, pointing ahead.

The girls stopped. Before them, just around the final coil of the ascending corridor, was a collapsible steel gate, barring a pitch-black metal hatch, with a sign above reading DO NOT DARKEN DOOR. DOOR DARK ENOUGH ALREADY. Poker Alice yanked a wad of keys from a keychain attached to her belt, unfurling the line as she held a stubby bronze key to the dangling padlock. With a twist, she opened the lock and pulled open the rusted gates. She leaned on the hatch and plucked a cigar from the back of her petticoat. The teacher struck a match on the sole of her well-worn granny boot.

"Jess because the bunny says ye can all have a field trip," Poker Alice said with a steely calm, "doesn't mean you lot can spend the whole day makin' mischief. A class lasts an hour . . . a long hour, granted, but an hour nonetheless. And takin' into account the walk here and back, as I see it, that leaves 'bout fifteen minutes for yer little learnin' expedition."

"Fifteen minutes?!" the girls carped as one gape-mouthed school of fish.

"That's barely enough time to get my credit card warm," Lyon whined.

Marlo chewed her lower lip in contemplation. "What if we were to make this a little . . . *wager?*" she proposed to her teacher. "In exchange for a full hour, that is."

The butt of Poker Alice's stogie flared in contemplation.

"What kind of *wager?*" she replied suspiciously.

Marlo eyed the hatch with extreme longing.

"We . . . we could," she faltered, before her dark eyes grew round with inspiration. "Divide the class into teams. *Yes!* Make it a shoplifting bee. Whoever's team lifts the most, passes. The other fails."

Poker Alice smirked despite herself.

"Interesting," she rasped between puffs. "You certainly know your antes."

"Actually, I hardly knew them," Marlo said. "They lived halfway across the country."

Poker Alice hacked indelicately, coughing up a glob of something so thick and gross she had to chew it a few times before she could swallow it down.

"Fine, then," the old woman rasped. *"A half hour."*

"Deal!" chirped Marlo.

Poker Alice clutched the sides of the hatch's rusty metal wheel, turned it with a squeak, then kicked it open with her boot as the girls cheered with unhinged glee. "Mallvana!! Mallvana!!"

YOU HAVE DIED AND GONE TO MALLVANA:
A LITTLE SLICE OF HEAVEN WHERE
YOU'RE NEVER MORE THAN A FEW
SANDAL FLOPS FROM THE OBJECT OF YOUR
ONCE-BEATING HEART'S DESIRE.

Poker Alice led Marlo's class beneath the white marble sign inlaid with gleaming brass letters and through a long tunnel of multicolored neon scaffolding. The class emerged into Mallvana's concourse level, bustling with herds of little old women, grinning and chattering with one another.

If Marlo had still possessed a lungful of breath, it would have been taken away the moment she entered Mallvana. It was like wandering into the palace of an ancient god. Mallvana was a cathedral of consumerism with massive, intricately carved marble columns propping up lavish level after lavish level, capped off by the dazzling prism of colors that danced at its domed, stained-glass ceiling. At the center of the colossal mall were twin spiraling escalators that coiled like massive strands of DNA.

The air itself had an invigorating, citrus sweetness about it. Every breath lifted Marlo's spirits higher, as if she were sucking in helium and her lungs were twin balloons soaring aloft.

Countless rows of stores edged with marble balustrades stretched out in great sweeps, girding the cavernous concourse. Each store radiated its own peculiar power, twinkling and dazzling like glittering lures, row after row meticulously designed to catch their own unique fish. Music spilled out over the crowd, a soothing wash of smooth jazz agitated by a constant throb gurgling beneath, the pulse slightly faster than a heartbeat, forcing one's nervous system to frantically catch up.

Overstimulation didn't even begin to explain what Marlo was feeling. It was as if she had grown several new senses to overwhelm, since five couldn't possibly digest this much sensory information.

"Who are all these people?" Marlo asked her cigar-chomping teacher, who was also clearly under Mallvana's spell.

"What?" Poker Alice asked with her mouth hanging open yet still somehow supporting her ever-present stogie.

Marlo waved away an especially noxious cloud of burning dung-scented smoke. "These people," she repeated. "They don't seem like tormented souls undergoing eternal punishment—unless the prices are ridiculously high, or there's a lousy return policy."

"Oh, them," the teacher replied as she stared, entranced by the mesmerizing helix of escalators upholstered in black velvet. "Mallvana is one of the lesser heavens, strictly Cloud One material. That Grabbit's got a lot of pull—"

"Heaven?!" Marlo stopped abruptly in her tracks. "You mean I'm in Heaven??!!"

Poker Alice laughed like a bagpipe full of soot. "Oh mercy, no! For graspin' gals like us, this is still Heck."

"That makes no sense at all."

The teacher's face wrinkled up into a bitter accordion of creases and folds. "Teenagers," she muttered with disdain. "They read one page and think they know the whole book."

The girls filed by an opulent, heart-shaped fountain of cascading champagne, dancing laser lights, and golden koi fish with little scuba tanks on their backs—probably filled with water, Marlo thought—so that they could breathe.

"Contextual surreal estate," the teacher continued. "One place that serves as many. Punishment for some, reward for others. The difference is circumstance . . . and credit limit."

Several grinning old women tottered by carrying spacious leather shopping bags. Marlo noticed that they had wings sprouting from their backs, not majestic like an angel's but small and trembling like a parakeet's. Jordie, keeping up the rear of Marlo's class, leapt out of ranks and growled at the old women. The women clutched their chests, then flopped away in their sensible orthopedic sandals. Jordie laughed uproariously.

"Miss Fauster," said Poker Alice, leaning into Marlo with a smirk. "Keep your class in line."

Marlo looked back at Jordie and sighed. "Hey, Jordie," she called back halfheartedly, "let's try to be cool, okay?"

Jordie glared at her. "I'm always cool," she said in a low rumble. "Like a morgue on Christmas."

Marlo gulped. "Right. Of course. Good job. Thanks."

Lyon and Bordeaux laughed in derisive unison.

The girls neared a trio of long-legged women whose bodies managed to be curvaceous without an ounce of body fat. It was as if they had been designed by a college fraternity.

"Oh my *gawd!*" squealed Bordeaux. "It's Faith, Hope, and Charity! Those three supermodels that died on that humanitarian aid mission to Africanastan!"

The three flawless creatures sprayed the girls with perfume as they stepped onto the escalator. Normally, Marlo would have doused them with pepper spray—as the staff of Scents and Sensibility back home knew all too well. But the particular fragrance that the three dead-yet-still-super supermodels spritzed upon her was . . . *amazing . . . delicious . . .* like an aromatic rainbow.

"Chanel Number Six!" Lyon gasped. "It's, like, supposed to be made from a patented blend of supermodel pheromones and puppy breath!"

Giggling drunk from Mallvana's intoxicating cologne, the girls stepped onto the escalator. Marlo gripped the plush, vibrating handrail. It felt cool and calming to the touch, like petting a sleek Persian kitten, and sent waves of relaxation throughout her body, until she could barely keep her eyes . . .

Marlo let go. She fought to stay focused amidst all the heady distractions. She concentrated on her surroundings, casing out this burglar's buffet of retail riches.

The first floor of the main rotunda housed a Heaven on Ice rink and Seven Deadly Cinemas Complex. The second floor, from what she could make out, was home to an Om Depot, Epiphany's Jewelers, and a store called Cleanliness, right next to another store called Godliness.

The girls alighted off the escalator and onto the gleaming, diamond-encrusted floor. To their left was a massive plasma-screen display—at least forty feet tall. On it was a gyrating, computer-generated teenage girl, dancing and singing into a sparkling headset.

"I'm so cool. I'm so hot.
I am everything you're not!
I'm as fresh as raw sashimi.
All the girls, they wanna be me."

The shimmering girl, her face lined with gold-glitter makeup, danced with an athleticism that mocked the laws of physics. Her voice hit notes so high that it probably sent dogs into seizures. Her silver spandex hot pants looked as if they had been applied with a spray can. Her poreless complexion was so fine that she not only reflected light but also exuded it.

"My body language never stutters,
moves as smooth as melted butter.
I'm as steamy as a sauna.
You know my name: Yojuanna!"

Marlo crossed her arms and scanned the screen, a display so large it hurt her neck to take it all in. Norm ambled next to Marlo and gaped at the pixilated pop-music tart on the screen.

"I wish I was that sure of myself," Norm muttered. "At least I think I do."

Takara skipped up to the two girls, clapping her hands.

"Yojuanna B. Covetta!" she yelped. "I can't believe she here!"

"I've never heard of her," Marlo said.

"That's because she was made in Tokyo," Takara replied. "She was just about to make the big time before the accident."

Norm squinted at the display. Yojuanna now had a small keyboard strapped across her perfect abs, her fingers dancing across the keys like nectar-crazed hummingbirds.

"She doesn't *look* Japanese," Norm commented slowly. "She looks . . . *everything*-ese."

Marlo turned to Takara.

"Made?" she asked. "Accident?"

Takara brushed pink bangs from her twinkling eyes.

"She was made in Tokyo laboratory," she replied.

"You mean like Frankenstein?" Norm asked.

Takara held her small hand to her mouth and giggled.

"No, not like a monster, like a *video game*. Digital. Perfect pop star that can be downloaded anywhere, always ready to sing and dance, never grow old, never have scandal—unless it's a really cool scandal."

"So what happened to her . . . *it?*" Marlo asked.

"She started taking up too much space on Sosumi computers," Takara continued. "Too demanding. Difficult to contain. Bad influence on other computers. Made other programs lazy, so they only worked after noon. So scientists took a big magnet and erased her."

"Then why is that bit o' computerized crumpet here?" asked Jordie, who had been listening in from behind.

"I guess even *fake* greedy people come here when they die," Marlo declared as Yojuanna dove off the stage. "Isn't that right, Lyon?"

Lyon glared at Marlo with a disgust one might reserve for a dissected frog in biology class. "You're just bitter in the presence of things so cool that everybody likes them," she sneered.

"Yeah," added Bordeaux, her scrawny arm pressed into the place her hip should be. "And since no one likes you, you pretend that you don't *want* to be liked!"

"Wow," Marlo deadpanned. "You can read me like a book—which is weird, because you two peroxide morons couldn't read the large-type edition of *Pat the Bunny*."

"Snap!" said Norm with a shy smirk as Bordeaux shivered.

"*Daddy's scratchy beard*," Bordeaux murmured, disturbed.

Marlo smiled, though her eyes were frowning. Bordeaux was, definitely, a few MP3s short of a playlist, but even in her dumb-as-a-box-of-hair way, she had managed to strike a nerve.

For some reason, the face of the sullen boy that she'd seen checking her out in Rapacia popped into her thoughts like a sly, smirking jack-in-the-box. There was something about him, a kindred spirit who seemed completely familiar, even though he was a stranger.

And despite her fierce independence, the boy's attention made Marlo feel better about herself somehow.

Poker Alice leaned her smoke-ravaged face into Marlo. It looked as though her bulbous nose had been sculpted hastily out of red clay.

"Now, remember, *substitute*," Poker Alice seethed

between stained clenched teeth. *"THIRTY MINUTES* or else I sic the guards on you, got me?"

"Fine," Marlo said, squaring her jaw in defiance. "I can do a lot of damage in thirty minutes."

Poker Alice clapped her callused hands. "Okay, girls, here are your teams," she barked. "Miss Sussex, Miss Kitayama, and Miss Sheraton, you take Salvation Armani. Miss Radisson, Miss Fauster, and Miss . . . um . . ." The teacher stared at Norm, hoping to recall the visually unremarkable girl's name.

"Rickett," Norm said with the calm resignation that comes when a specific humiliation is continually repeated.

"Right," Poker Alice continued. *"Miss Rickett.* You three take Halo/Good Buy."

"Halo/Good Buy?" complained Marlo. "That's a bargain bunker! I'll have to lift twice as much as them!"

"That is your playing field." Poker Alice shrugged. "But if you want to forfeit the game . . ."

"No, no, no," Marlo interjected. "We'll still win. I just wanted to go on record as saying that the playing field was uneven."

"Agreed," Poker Alice acknowledged, "and disregarded."

Lyon swaggered up to Marlo, looking down her surgically perfected nose.

"I've made grown shopgirls wet themselves with fear," she relayed with a malicious grin. "I can make an assistant manager's hairline noticeably recede with just one transaction."

Marlo stood on her tiptoes to look Lyon in the eye. "Bring it on, Barbie."

Poker Alice pulled out an antique watch on a chain, attached to her worn vest by a tarnished fob.

"Oooh, two dead little girls squaring off at one another, enough to soil my bloomers—if I were wearin' any." She smirked, staring at the small clock's dusty face. "On your mark, get set . . ."

The six girls ran off, the group breaking in two as each team rushed toward its assigned destination.

"Go," Poker Alice muttered, deepening her permanent scowl with a fresh grimace.

Marlo looked back over her shoulder, watching her teacher shove her cigar back between her thin, creased lips and plod toward the Angel Food Court.

Thirty minutes to fill up my pockets with out-of-fashion markdowns, Marlo thought. But she had to get—and get a lot—while the getting was good.

10 · LOOK WHO'S STALKiNG

MILTON AWOKE ON an olive-drab army cot in Lester Lobe's office. Crowded with stacks of old newspapers, the room looked more like a nest built by some obsessive-compulsive bird than an office.

"Welcome back, earthling," Lester joked while rolling a cigarette.

Milton's mouth was as dry as a ball of cotton in a bottle of aspirin. "Water," he rasped.

Lester put down his cigarette and handed Milton a dented canteen. "This should wet your whistle," he said.

Milton gulped down the liquid and, despite his thirst, nearly spit it out across the room. "Ugh," he gurgled. "What is this junk?"

Lester smiled a mouthful of brown teeth. "It's my own special blend," he explained. "You can't trust the water. The government puts all sorts of stuff in it to keep the public passive and easily controlled. So I make my own Turbo Juice. It's a power drink, with Kombucha mushroom tea, blue-green alga, and NoDoz pills, all mixed up. Keeps me on my toes . . . and in the head a lot," he added, gesturing to the toilet in the corner.

Out of his head, more like, thought Milton as he tried to wipe the terrible taste off his tongue. He desperately wanted to tell Lester Lobe all about his descent to Heck. He knew that, unlike all the other people he had encountered upon his return, Lester wouldn't just gaze at him with that pitying blank stare after hearing his tale. And that was part of the problem. For as much as Milton needed to talk to someone about his ordeal before it faded into a half-remembered dream, he was worried that Heck would become just another crackpot myth in Lester's mad museum. Sandwiched between the miniature crop-circle garden and the fossilized Bigfoot droppings, Heck would become a big joke—and Milton a candidate for a padded cell.

He looked up at the IF YOU AREN'T PARANOID, YOU AREN'T PAYING ATTENTION clock above Lester's door-on-cinder-blocks desk.

"Five o'clock?!" Milton yelped, getting up a bit too fast. He sat back down on the side of the cot, waiting for the wooziness to pass. This was getting ridiculous, he thought. At first it was just dizzy spells. But blackouts? He must be getting more and more out of phase.

If he didn't pull himself together soon, his next phase might be his last. He had to do something quick.

"What's the rush?" Lester asked.

Milton staggered to his feet. "I've got to get back home. My parents think I'm at my therapist's."

"Well," Lester replied, "maybe you are."

He handed Milton a piece of binder paper with sloppy scribbles and doodles all over it. Milton squinted down at it through his Coke-bottle glasses.

"What's this?"

"It's a shopping list and some notes I had about how you might get that energy boost you've been looking for," he replied with a lopsided grin.

Milton studied the list more closely. Jumper cables, meat thermometer, power drill . . . it was like supplies for one of his old science-fair experiments. *Science fairs,* Milton reflected. So much had happened since those carefree days where the most important thing in the world to him was a blue ribbon and a good grade. The stakes were so much higher now.

"Thanks," Milton said as he thrust the list into his pocket and made his way back through the Paranor Mall. He hesitated at the Elvis Abduction Chamber. There was something strangely compelling about the dark booth. Milton picked at a peeling, yellowing picture of Lisa Marie Presley, Michael Jackson, and a chimpanzee dressed as a cowboy lacquered to the booth's side.

"I'm not surprised you're drawn to the Psychomanthium," Lester Lobe said as he followed Milton into the museum.

"Why?" Milton said defensively. "Because I'm a psycho?"

"No," Lester countered. "I'm the last person to be calling anyone a psycho. A Psychomanthium is a chamber used to communicate with dead spirits."

Milton's mind cracked. This freaky box was a connection to the beyond. It was his opportunity to contact the world below, the one that held his thoughts in its frosty grip.

"Supposedly, the spirits can be seen in the reflection of the mirrors," Lester continued. "You're supposed to say a fancy little spell and—presto changeo—there the spirits are, trapped in the mirror like the evil dudes in that second *Superman* flick. Not that I've ever tried it. The Psychomanthium is one of the few things here that gives even *me* the creeps. It sounded cool on eBay, but, boy, when I cracked open the box, I got a first-degree case of the willies and gave it the full-on Elvis makeover."

Milton had a sharp yet mercifully fleeting bout of vertigo. His thoughts were slipping on broken ice and fighting for balance. He held on to the fiberglass extraterrestrial and shook his head clear.

"I've g-gotta g-go," Milton stammered. "I have a feeling I'll be back, though."

Lester Lobe followed him to the door. "My doors are always open," he said. "Seriously, I can't get this darned lock fixed. Be sure to tell me how your experiments in subtle energies turn out. I know how lonely the quest for truth can be. No one wants to follow you, and when you come back, no one wants to hear about it."

Milton looked over his shoulder and gave the man a nervous smile as he opened the door to the street. "I gotta go. Thanks again."

Milton walked down the sidewalk toward the bus stop. He stopped by a telephone pole, plastered with a dozen copies of the same flyer:

Before Stepping Into a Court of Law . . .
. . . Get Yourself a Quart of Cole's Law!

I'm Algernon Cole. While I am, technically, not a lawyer—yet—I have the most popular law blog on the Internet.

I've helped countless people, just like yourself, tell the difference between a tort and a torte, a civil suit and a leisure suit, and a subpoena and a submarine. If no one will touch your case with a ten-foot affidavit (a written statement made under oath . . . see?), I'm your man. Did I mention I'm cheap?

Call me today at 1-800-COLELAW for your
FREE consultation: your place, not mine (I'm in
between offices . . . don't ask!)

A lawyer! Exactly what I need! thought Milton, someone to help crack his confounding contract with the
Principal of Darkness. If a lawyer could find some contractual loophole, some ambiguity to render Milton's
contract null and void, perhaps he could find a way to
unravel EVERY dead kid's contract, or at least free his
sister and Virgil from eternal darnation.

Milton pulled off the number, printed on perforated
tabs beneath the flyer.

The price is definitely right, thought Milton, *and Algernon Cole seems open to entertaining . . .* unusual *cases. But
where could I set up a meeting?*

"Happy trails, zombie boy," Lester Lobe yelled from
down the block.

Milton turned and saw Lester in his doorway, waving, squinting at the setting sun. An idea struck him on
and about his tired brain.

"Is it okay if I stop by tomorrow?" Milton called back.

Lester shrugged and rattled his doorknob. "Like I
said," he shouted. "Always open."

The Topeka/Generica Express pulled up to the
curb. Milton waved at Lester and hobbled on. As the
bus drove away, Milton saw a girl dart behind a cluster
of lilac bushes across the street.

"Necia Alvarado?" Milton mumbled as the bus lurched from the curb, sending him tumbling into a fat man's newspaper.

"Sorry," Milton apologized as he fought his way against the g-force of the accelerating bus to find an empty seat. He looked out the back window, but between the bus's jerks and the dizziness of an oncoming spell, Milton couldn't make out the figure behind the bush. Maybe he was seeing things, he thought as he scooted into a vacant seat. He seemed to be seeing a *lot* of things recently. But the girl had that same bony, nervous weirdness of Necia. The ghost image of the girl burned into the back of his retinas. She had been dressed like a peppermint candy, all in stripes, and was holding what looked like a small gift-wrapped package.

11 · NERVES OF STEAL

MARLO STEPPED THROUGH the automatic doors and onto the sensible, off-white vinyl floor of Halo/Good Buy.

"Ah," she said to Norm as they surveyed the unspectacular labyrinth of cut-rate merchandise, "looks like we're flying coach."

Norm shrugged. "I don't know," she said in her slow, vague way. "It's kind of comforting. Reminds me of shopping with my mom. I used to hate her dragging me to these places—all quantity, no quality, ya know? She'd always force me to try on things that just made it screamingly obvious what a dumpy lump I was. But I'd give anything to be complaining to her right now."

Norm sniffed and wiped her nose on her sleeve.

Marlo patted her on the back. "I know what you mean," she said with a faraway voice. "All the stuff that seemed so awful doesn't seem so bad anymore. It's probably just another way for them to torture us, from the inside, with memories."

Bordeaux rolled her eyes as she joined the two girls. "Oh, *boo hoo,*" she said mockingly before scanning the store. "Ugh. This place is, like, *so* gross. I had to go to one of these once with our cleaning lady the first time my father was indicted. It was so depressing . . . there wasn't even a concierge!"

Marlo rolled her eyes at Norm and walked up to a small trash receptacle and stuck her arm in. "Ah," she said after a moment's fishing. "Here we go." Marlo exhumed a receipt. "That's the ticket," she said. "Always nice to have a little security in case of—"

Marlo scanned the store and stopped at a middle-aged man with aviator glasses who was pretending to be interested in skeins of multicolored yarn and a selection of knitting needles.

"—security. Five-oh at five o'clock."

Norm scratched her head, which was exposed in patches thanks to her really bad haircut.

"That guy," Marlo continued. "*Totally* a security guard. He's got 'the look,' like some dork who couldn't make the police academy and settled as a department store rent-a-cop. But, despite Guardilocks over there, it's nice to be back in 'the maze.' C'mon . . . let's get our unfair share."

Bordeaux pointed to a large red and white sign on a

nearby wall: ALL SHOPLIFTERS WILL BE PROSECUTED TO THE FULL EXTENT OF THE LAW . . . AND THEN SOME.

"Don't get your Underoos in a knot," Marlo replied. "That's just to put off amateurs."

Bordeaux shrugged, and the three girls walked down the Beauty, Bedpans, and Bermuda Shorts aisle. After browsing through an assortment of lip liners and glosses, Bordeaux found a tube of Kiss Off! lip glaze in bright Tickled Pink.

"Ooh!" she said enthusiastically. "This is the stuff that has actual bee venom in it so your lips, like, get totally swollen!"

She found a wall-mounted mirror at the end of the aisle, unscrewed the tube of lipstick, and smeared it on her already collagen-enhanced lips.

"Filching fun fact," Marlo chimed in. "Normal mirrors are sheets of glass with silver stuff on the back. Two-way mirrors—the kind that let security sit back and snoop on you—have the silver reflector stuff on the front, so they can see you but not vice versa."

Marlo took a mascara wand (Suburban Dismay's "Lash Out") and held it to the mirror.

"See?" she commented. "There's no gap between the tip and its reflection. That means it's time to smile your prettiest smile and do your dirty work elsewhere."

The girls walked down the next aisle, which featured

bins of discounted polyester jogging suits in odd sizes.

"So, are they on to us?" Norm whispered. "I mean, with the mirrors?"

Marlo smiled knowingly. She hadn't been this happy since she was alive. "Yes," she said through the side of her mouth. "But we have the upper hand since we *know* they're watching us. Get it?"

Norm nodded, though she was far from *getting it.*

"Hey, Frosted Flake," Marlo called to Bordeaux, "it's time to make yourself useful."

Bordeaux strutted over. "Well, there's certainly nothing worth buying here," she replied, still not fully understanding that none of the girls could indeed buy anything. "What do you want me to do?"

"You've been ID'd already," Marlo said, "so walk around the store acting suspicious, so the lame-o guard follows you while Norm and I make like bandits."

"Great," Bordeaux replied, "then I won't have to hang out with you freaks and get your dork stink all over me."

Bordeaux skipped away, singing to herself.

"My body language never stutters,
moves as smooth as melted butter."

The security guard touched his finger to a receiver in his ear, dropped a handful of crochet hooks, and followed Bordeaux down the Polydent, Pooper Scoopers, and Porcelain Figurines aisle.

Marlo tugged the sleeve of Norm's sweatshirt. "Okay, we're going to use the buddy system," she whispered. "Your job is to build the nest."

Norm stared at Marlo with a look of utter incomprehension.

"*The nest*," Marlo repeated louder and slower, the way some people do when they try talking to people who speak a foreign language. "You take some stuff to a low-traffic spot, like the maternity section. I mean, we're all dead, so who's going to be pumping out little bundles of joy? *Anyway*, you store it for Magpie Number Two, yours truly, whose job is to pocket the goods and flutter out the door with *our* little bundle of joy. Got it?"

Norm smiled. This time she got it perfectly. "Birds of a feather steal together," the large, shapeless girl said as she set out, with a spring in her step and a sparkle in her eyes, toward the Plastic Wrap, Plates, and Plumbing aisle.

Marlo brushed away the blue bangs from her face and walked confidently toward the Ziplocs, Zithers, and Zucchini aisle. But there was something—someone—in the corner of her eye. A dark blob matching her gait footfall for footfall. A shadow, only this "shadow" was obviously, by his feigned interest in a tube of Gee, Your Hands Smell Terrific! lotion, a security guard.

"Excuse me," she called out to the barrel-chested man with the mirrored sunglasses (*please*). The man jumped and tried desperately to will himself invisible by reading the ingredients on the back of a jar of Papaya Smear face mask. "Sir?" Marlo persisted, skipping up next to him. "You obviously work here . . . could you direct me to the feminine hygiene section?"

The man's face flushed deep fuchsia. His mustache wilted over his thin lips. "Um, n-no, I . . . ," he stammered before sighing with resignation. "Aisle seventeen. Hobbies, Horseradish, and Hygiene."

Marlo grinned. "Thank you, sir!" She giggled as she skipped away, stopping at the end of the aisle and calling back over her shoulder. "Oh, and by the way, I'll be at Macaroons, Megaphones, and Moist Towelettes, if you need me. See ya there!"

Marlo could practically hear him deflate, like a weather balloon over a javelin throw. Yet just as she was about to make her final approach toward Norm's nest, an announcement squawked over the store's public-address system.

"Attention Halo/Good Buy shoppers," croaked an ancient, tremulous voice over the speakers. "For those of you *mature* enough to remember the Victorian era firsthand, you're in for a treat! In Fan Belts, Fanny Packs, and Fashion, we have a sale on antique skirts and petticoats, vintage corsets, and assorted mourning wear. Take a walk or wheelchair ride down memory lane!"

Marlo stopped dead—or *more* dead—in her tracks. *Well*, she thought, *maybe I could afford a brief little detour. I mean, how often does one get to try on authentic Victorian clothes with authentic Victorians?*

12 · *SPREE DE CORPSE*

SURE, MARLO REFLECTED as she shuffled toward the Halo/Good Buy foyer, *I got a little greedy . . . okay, a lot greedy, but it's what this place does to you.*

Marlo's prelift anxiety had been off the charts. Usually a few outfits were enough to calm her down, but she was still so famished for fashion that she had actual *hanger* pangs. Just when she thought she might have actually taken enough to sate her greed, she'd think of the Grabbit. She'd feel a slow constriction, like a snake tightening itself around her—until she felt empty again. Hollow. And wanting to prove herself to the source of her torment, that maddening metal hare, more than anything.

Without warning, the foyer in front of her teemed with security guards. They chewed the lips off their Styrofoam coffee cups with agitation, scanning the aisles for trouble. *My bad,* Marlo thought. Perhaps exposing the undercover cop and gloating in his lameness hadn't been the smartest play. Well, live and learn . . . and since Marlo wasn't alive, she'd go easy on herself. What she needed now more than anything was an alternate escape route.

Unfortunately, she could barely move—partly because her path back to the mall concourse was now blocked, but also because of the silk mourning gown, wool chintz wrapper, black button-up bodice, embroidered cream-colored shirtwaist, and several petticoats she was wearing underneath her horrid Rapacia sweat suit. Marlo turned and waddled away toward the emergency exit at the back of the store. She wobbled like a Victorian penguin with an underactive thyroid up the Pimentos, Pine-Scented Cleansers, and Pom-Poms aisle, the bright green EMERGENCY EXIT sign in sight.

"They're at it again," said a bored shopgirl buffing her nails a few yards away, peering through the large stained-glass window inset in the emergency exit door.

Another girl, wearing a white laboratory coat and a great deal of makeup, joined her. "They are so gross," the girl said, wrinkling her orange, artificially tanned nose. "They're like roaches with shopping carts."

The shopgirls turned toward Marlo.

"May I help you?" they said as one, their request to serve coming off more as an offer to "help" Marlo right out of their immediate future.

"Um, no thanks," Marlo managed through her suffocating heat prostration. "I was just . . . wondering if there was something wrong, like . . . an emergency."

The shopgirls locked eyes briefly before glancing out the window.

"Oh, *that,*" said the one with the nail file. "It's just the PODs again, going through the Dumpsters down in the alley. I'm sure security will shoo them away soon enough, once they get around to it."

"PODs?" asked Marlo.

The girls glared at Marlo as she swayed slightly from side to side in her personal, one-girl oven.

"I'm new to . . . Cloud One," she added hastily. "My wings haven't even broken through."

The girl in the lab coat smiled weakly. "Yeah." She nodded. "That can hurt like . . . well, like *you know what.*"

"Well, speaking of *you know what,* that's where those PODs should go," the other girl said while examining her manicure. "The *Phantoms of the Dispossessed.* They come and raid the bins every so often, taking whatever they can before wandering off to the next realm. Thank goodness they can't get in here."

Marlo peeked through the stained-glass window, getting a warped view of an alley through the clear, crystal wings of an angel. The alley was several flights below, at the end of a gleaming fire escalator. In the alley were beautiful titanium Dumpsters loaded with all the excess that Mallvana produced regularly. Milling about the crowded bins were dozens of haggard spirits pushing shopping carts overflowing with castaway trinkets. They worked diligently in silence, performing specific roles like a kind of roaming insect colony. A tattooed man with long, stringy black hair pored through castaway containers with the intensity of a prospector panning for gold. A bearded man with a grubby Elysian Fields cap flattened cans with his work boot, kicking them toward an old woman who nimbly crammed as many in her cart as possible.

"Where do they come from?" Marlo asked dimly.

"Who knows?" Lab-coat girl shrugged. "Who cares? They just wander from place to place. They never stay anywhere, because they don't *belong* anywhere."

"Gratuitous displays of mercy at two o'clock," the other shopgirl said, pressed against Marlo by the window. Faith, Hope, and Charity wriggled their way down the alley to the PODs in their fashionably impractical shoes and dresses.

Marlo could see a POD with a thick, Civil War–era mustache holding up an intricate, handblown decanter containing a few drops of a strange, silver liquid that glittered coldly like a melted mirror. He tried pouring the drops into an old two-liter jug half-full of the liquid, but Charity fell into the man while trying to crush cans in her high heels.

He bellowed angrily as he spilled some of the liquid.

Once free of the bottle, the liquid hit the ground and darted away into the shadows.

Suddenly, a blast of walkie-talkie static detonated behind Marlo. She looked back with a start. The group of security guards had abandoned the foyer and were now storming down the aisle *straight toward Marlo.* She swallowed, which was difficult considering how many vintage lace and velvet collars clutched her throat.

"Finally," the shopgirl next to Marlo muttered sarcastically between gum smacks. "Security guards to the rescue. *My heroes.*"

Grim and purposeful, the guards marched closer.

This is it, Marlo thought. *At least I'll be forced into shoplifting retirement at the top of my game.*

The security guards reached Marlo, shooting her suspicious sideways glances, then proceeded to file past her through the emergency exit and down the fire escalator. Soon the alley was filled with guards strutting about like ruffled, uniformed roosters, squawking into walkie-talkies.

The phantoms—in a flurry of precision activity—fell into a long, snaking line and wheeled their squeaky carts toward the horizon.

"Are you okay?" the lab-coat girl asked, staring at Marlo. "You're sweating . . . which is weird, because it's always seventy-two degrees here. *Always.*"

"Yes, I'm . . . fine," Marlo replied with sluggish relief. "I'm . . . on an herbal cleanse. I ate some devil's food cake before I died, and it didn't agree with me. Excuse me, but I think my ginger colonic is calling, if you know what I mean."

Marlo turned on her heel and rustled away. As she searched for an *alternate* alternate escape route, she passed the Marshmallow Peeps, Mason Jars, and Maternity Wear aisle. Stuffed behind piles of large bright-orange dresses with GESTATING, NOT JUST EATING written across them were stacks of clown plates, creepy hobo figurines, and pewter Noah's ark gravy boats. *Norm's nest.* Marlo stared, mesmerized by the figurines' ugliness, and contemplated escape: from the store, from Poker Alice, from Rapacia. There was no reason she *had* to return to her class, waiting outside. She could be a free agent, living off her wits (she could almost hear Milton snicker at that thought). But something made her feet heavy, besides the multiple pairs of vintage hose.

The Grabbit. Marlo absentmindedly clutched her throat as if she were wearing an electric eel for a collar. She couldn't let . . . *it* . . . down. Marlo wanted to prove that she had what it took to take . . . anything. *Everything.*

She sighed and wiped a salty trickle of sweat from her stinging eyes. She knew what she had to do.

She peered around the corner of the aisle at the foyer. It was wonderfully guard-free. *Finally,* the path was clear.

Marlo casually glanced over her shoulder, then stuffed clown plates in her pants, tucked gravy boats underneath her sweat-stained sweatshirt, and slid a porcelain hobo in each sock. She wouldn't let the Grabbit down.

Having a conscience sucks, she moaned to herself as she rattled down the aisle and out of the store.

13 · CAUGHT SHORT

"MARLO!" NORM CRIED as she saw her friend emerge from Halo/Good Buy. Marlo smiled weakly as she shuffled closer with muffled clatters before collapsing in a heap.

Takara and Norm helped Marlo to a bench where the girls were assessing their collection of amassed booty.

"Thanks," Marlo replied feverishly. "Uh-oh . . . I think one of my Bungling Brothers Circus plates cracked," she added as she shifted uncomfortably on the bench.

"Wow-wee," Takara said as she took off Marlo's sopping-wet sweatshirt, "you swiped out. You like walking garage sale. How you make off with all this with no getting caught?"

"The guards must've had bigger fish to fry," Marlo replied groggily, "probably all the phantoms . . ."

Lyon stepped up to Marlo and folded her arms in judgment. She was so padded with concealed stolen underwear that she almost resembled a regularly shaped girl. Her smug face was like smelling salts to Marlo, clearing the fog from her head.

"Okay, then," Marlo said, straightening up. "Put your price tags where your collagen is."

Lyon, Jordie, and Takara ripped and peeled off price tags and set them down on the bench.

"Takara," Lyon ordered. "Add them up."

"Why me?" Takara replied.

"Well," Lyon said, "you're Japanese, right? Good with numbers?"

Jordie sighed and scooped up the price tags. "Yeh racist toffee-nosed git," she snarled. "Let me add 'em up. I'm smashing at maths."

Jordie pushed aside her stack of pilfered British hip-hop CDs, screwed up her eyes, and within a minute (she was indeed smashing at math), she added the dozen or so price tags in her head.

"Two thousand, one hundred forty dollars," she said. "One thousand, five hundred fifty-three euros, or one thousand fifty-five British pounds, depending on today's currency rates."

Bordeaux rolled her protuberant orbs. "Who cares how much they *weigh*?" she said.

"Okay, Blue Tag Special," Lyon said, settling her

own negligible weight on one hip, "show us what you've got."

"Here," Marlo said, handing Jordie a fistful of yanked tags.

Jordie thumbed through the stack quickly yet thoughtfully. She crinkled her nose briefly in thought, before announcing the sum.

"Eighteen hundred dollars," she said. "One thousand, three hundred seven euros, or eight hundred eighty-seven British . . ."

"What?!" Marlo yelped, bolting up. "That can't be right."

Jordie stiffened, becoming larger and more intimidating. "Are yeh saying I miscounted?" she asked in a smooth rumble that matched the flat darkness of her pupils. "Or that I'm on the fiddle?"

"No," Marlo replied. "Of course not. It's just . . ."

"Would you like me to wrap your latest humiliating experience?" Lyon said in her most annoying, please-hit-me-smack-dab-in-the-nose-job voice possible. "And don't forget your receipt."

Receipt, thought Marlo. *Of course!*

"How much time do we have left?" Marlo asked.

Takara looked at one of three different watches she had dangling off her wrists. "Four minutes left," she replied.

"I'll be right back," Marlo said, peeling off her

sweatshirt and stepping out of her sweltering silk mourning gown.

"Are you kidding me?!" Lyon snorted. "There's no way . . ."

Marlo fished into the pocket of her sweatpants and reeled in the receipt she had gotten from the garbage can earlier.

One Yellow Canoe: $349

Marlo smiled slyly. This was going to be good.

"Okay, then, Blandie," she said. "How about this: I come out of that store in four minutes with a canoe, making me the queen of thieves. If I don't, you are the personal, undisputed ruler of *me* for all eternity. I'll even draft an official document saying as much."

Lyon's eyes narrowed. After a moment's scrutiny, she shrugged her shoulders and smirked. "Whatever," Lyon said, eyeing her gold Rolex. "You've got about two hundred seconds until Poker Alice supersizes your humiliation, anyhow. Go for it."

Marlo skipped back into Halo/Good Buy, straight toward the Sponges, Spoons, and Sporting Goods aisle.

One hundred and ninety seconds later, a series of alarms went off throughout the mall. The girls looked around the now-even-noisier mall with apprehension.

"Look!" said Norm, pointing at the Halo/Good Buy entrance.

The automatic doors slid open with a pneumatic whoosh. Out shuffled Marlo. Trailing behind her were two burly security guards, with a large red canoe perched atop their shoulders.

"Uh-oh," muttered Jordie. "Looks like the bird was nicked by the plod."

Lyon glowered at Jordie. "Does anything you say *ever* make sense?"

Marlo walked cautiously to the marble bench, with the guards in close pursuit. "I think my grandfather will be *much* happier with red," she said sweetly.

The guards put the canoe down and glared at Marlo.

"Will that be all?" asked one guard, chewing gum in military time.

"Yes, thank you," Marlo replied with a girlish titter. "You've both been absolute angels!"

The guards shared the briefest of sideways glances before leaving with a sharp, synchronized bow.

"Thank you for shopping at Halo/Good Buy," they said in unison before making an abrupt about-face and marching back into the store. Tiny white parakeet wings poked through their starched khaki uniforms.

The girls stared at Marlo with a blend of shock and reverence. Even Lyon's admiration grudgingly shone through, like a zit through concealer.

Norm rushed up to Marlo and grabbed her hands, beaming. "How did you do it?!"

Marlo grinned back. "Trade secret."

Marlo peered over her shoulder at Lyon, her grin becoming something just short of a sneer.

Anxious shoppers filed by the girls toward the atrium. Marlo unclasped hands with Norm and took in the commotion around them.

"What's with all the alarms?" she asked.

"We thought it was because of you," Takara said with a dainty shrug.

Then, on another giant plasma screen in the commons, Yojuanna appeared. The computer-generated creation appeared to be munching a digital carrot. She tossed the carrot top over her shoulder and sang into her gleaming headset.

"To the SkyDeck, on the double.
An old lady, she's in trouble.
She went down, all Humpty Dumpty,
so be careful: she's way grumpy."

A group of security guards trotted by, their ears pressed against their squawking walkie-talkies.

Marlo grabbed one of the guards by the sleeve. "Hey, what's going on?" she asked. The security guard glared at Marlo. "I mean, is there some kind of emergency?" she added. "Something that could result in a lawsuit if me and my friends were to be hurt in any way?"

The security guard gulped. "Um, no, uh . . . *ma'am,*"

he replied. "Just some crazy old woman up on the SkyBridge, chomping on an Adam's Rib; apparently she saw her reflection below and went crazy, jumping off, trying to get the 'other rib.' "

"Is she okay?" Norm asked.

"Well, she busted more than just her rib, I hear. But it could've been worse, if she hadn't had all those aces stuffed in her blouse. Now, if you'll excuse me . . ."

The guard trotted away. Marlo and Norm traded looks of excitement.

"Poker Alice!" they squealed together before high-fiving.

Marlo hopped up and down like a terrier after slurping up an espresso.

"*Girls,*" Marlo said with her hands on her hips, "any moment, some nasty dead teacher or demon guard is going to come and round us up, so let's make the most of our day out. The clock is tickin', and there's stuff to be pickin'."

Yojuanna smirked, her slightly bucked teeth grazing her bubblegum lips. She rapped in her trade-marked (literally) helium voice to the accompaniment of what sounded like kettledrums and dueling band saws:

"*Bad at good, so good at bad,*
   those girls could be the best we've had.
   Perfect for the plan we've hatched,
   to make sure everything is snatched."

After brushing back dazzling strands of translucent hair away from her face, Yojuanna scratched her diamond-studded ear—an ear that seemed longer and pointier than it had been only moments before. With a shrill giggle like the backfire of a clown car full of laughing gas, the digital diva kicked her feet into the air and resumed her manic hopping.

"C'mon!" Marlo said, beaming, feeling as if she were doing the backstroke in an Olympic-sized bowl of Lucky Charms. For the moment, she was a prisoner in a pretty awesome cage. *Perhaps the only difference between incarceration and vacation is perspective,* Marlo thought as she skipped down the mall, certain that she was soon to become the preferred "pet" of a ginormous jack rabbot with a highly electric personality.

14 · ENERGY CRISIS

"I THOPE THITH workth," Milton said to himself as he held the poultry thermometer underneath his tongue.

After his parents had gone to sleep, Milton had snuck into the garage to conduct his late-night experiments with subtle energy.

Lester Lobe had given him a printout listing the "secret" experiments of Sir Edward Tylor and his Subtle Energies Commission.

Sir Edward's experiments with complex patterns of electric shock had led him to believe that there was indeed an after-realm, as he put it, a "spirit world crowded with countless detached essences removed from their respective material bodies. These insubstantial images, vapors, films, and shadows are, I believe, the very cause of life and thought, independently possessing the personal consciousness and volition of their corporeal owner."

Easy for him to say, thought Milton as he bit down on the thermometer and straightened the jumper cables leading from his mouth to the industrial-strength bug zapper (the Insecticide 3000) suspended from the basketball hoop outside. Sir Edward made the "after-realm" seem like a noble place full of freedom and possibility, unlike the vexing bureaucratic freak show Milton had encountered.

Lester Lobe had written some notes—cribbed from various electricians' manuals, alongside Sir Edward Tylor's observations—that detailed how to make an etheric energy "trap." Of course, due to practical considerations such as "where would an eleven-year-old possibly get a two-thousand-volt transformer," Milton had to make some compromises, the biggest being that under no circumstances was he going to drill a hole to the center of his brain in order to hot-wire his pineal gland.

Sir Edward had used extensive animal testing to achieve his aims. There was even an unconfirmed account that he was able to reanimate a dead man using the life force of a convict facing execution. And while Milton may have accidentally killed his archenemy, he wasn't going to cause harm to others simply to be "whole," energy-wise.

Lucky, his faithful ferret, undulated into the garage, sniffed Milton's sneakers, and looked up at his master with an expression that said, "Now I've seen everything."

Milton scratched Lucky in that prime spot at the top of his neck, and the ferret billowed away out into the night. He had performed some rough calculations and deduced that, if a human conducted an average electrical current of three hundred kiloamperes, then—based on body weight—he would need either several large dogs, a dozen cats, or a hundred mice to get enough captured etheric energy to fuse his physical and sentient bodies together.

Milton could never bring himself to sacrifice an animal. He did, however, have no great love for insects. And, on a late summer night in Kansas, he was pretty sure he could harvest the death energy of countless moths and mosquitoes. He would need a lot, but Milton thought that by sleeping out in the garage with an electrified meat thermometer in his mouth, he should wake up with at least a little more spring in his step.

He plugged in the Insecticide 3000, slipped into his sleeping bag, and waited.

Zzzz.

Milton tingled at his first, albeit paltry, pulse of etheric energy. He turned and looked out the half-open garage door. A bright star twinkled low on the horizon. He made a wish.

Please make everything be okay.

Milton's "star" moved slowly over downtown Generica as it made its descent into Buffalo Bill International Airport. Milton sighed and closed his eyes.

Zzzz.

As he drifted off to sleep, Milton imagined his soul as a translucent, rainbow-speckled glob (which was easy for him to picture, having actually *seen* his soul) piloting a craft, his body—a plane of existence flying through the night sky—flapping its arms as his soul gently nudged it into playful barrel rolls.

Outside, Lucky had been tracking a leathery flapping noise that made him twitch with frustration. Every so often, he could hear a high-pitched whine bouncing off a tree branch or garden shed, which only drove him crazier. He looked up, and there, streaking across the full moon, swooping jaggedly behind a living cloud, he saw it—a weird, shiny black bird-rat thing.

With his head held high in the air, Lucky followed the creature as it chased a swarm of bugs toward his very home. Such luck!

He had no time to lose. The flapping creature was herding the buzzing cloud to that strange humming lantern his master had hung above the garage. Lucky galloped toward the garage at full speed, then—with all of his keen senses tingling—leapt into the air to seize the odd leather bird just as it flapped into the lantern.

Zzzzz . . . zzzzz . . . zzzzzz . . . zzzzz . . . zlot . . . BAP . . . BAP . . . kapow . . . z-zwap . . . swizz-a-swizz-a-ZAP . . . zokazlott . . . sizza . . . ZORP!!!

15 · HOPELESSLY DEVOTED

BEA "ELSA" BUBB did *not* like people going through her things. She arranged her office as a reflection of herself—inscrutable, challenging, and possessing a beauty of form so perfect as to be nearly imperceptible to the untrained eye.

And here she was, forced to stand idly by while Lilith Couture—*ugh, the name itself made one's tongue contort grotesquely,* Principal Bubb fumed—riffled through her files.

A music-video program played on the plasma screen behind them.

"Welcome to *Total Request Dead!* I'm your host, Carson Nightly with the latest video from Yojuanna B. Covetta, 'I'm L8 'n' Gr8, Gonna Make U Saliv8.'"

"Ugh," Lilith said as she punched the MUTE button of the remote.

As Yojuanna danced on the crest of a shimmering tidal wave, Lilith resumed fingering her way through a stack of bulging folders.

"The only words I can think of to describe this travesty of a filing system aren't suitable for a children's facility."

"You don't know what it takes to run an institution such as Heck," Bea "Elsa" Bubb said haughtily.

"And neither do you," Lilith replied with a voice like a snooty sorority girl with a head cold. "This isn't just about your sloppy management skills, Ms. Blob."

"*Principal* Blobb . . . er . . . *Bubb*," corrected Bea "Elsa" Bubb.

"Do you follow the Netherworld Soul Exchange?" Lilith inquired. "It's an organization that issues, trades, and redeems souls, with each transaction—"

"Yes, of course I am familiar with it," Principal Bubb replied defensively. "I've only got my retirement tied up in the thing. Did you notice that I happen to have a stock ticker on the wall?"

Lilith looked over at the pulsing stream of letters and numbers on the wall and smiled weakly to herself. "Well, then," she said, "you may want to rethink your retirement plan. There's been considerable volatility recently. And the embarrassment of you allowing a little boy to escape Heck, the first such escape ever recorded, was just more kerosene on the brimstone."

Lilith put her dainty feet up on an Ottoman, a mummified Turkish sultan preserved on all fours.

"While the Powers That Be and the Powers That Be Evil grapple with the deeper issues vexing the soul market," Lilith went on, "it is up to me—us—to work with Chairman Mammon to stave off an after-realm recession . . . *or worse.*"

Chairman Mammon, the principal contemplated. *The legendary entrepreneur . . . the cunning, merciless lone wolf responsible for the Netherworld Soul Exchange and—in turn—the entire underworld economy!*

"So, dear heartless, you and I have a lot of work ahead of us," Lilith said, rising and strutting across the lair to the desk, each step sounding like another nail in the coffin of Bea "Elsa" Bubb's career. "We start by renovating your little babysitting operation, showing that we are reacting swiftly and decisively to your bungle with the Fauster child."

Principal Bubb cringed. The mere mention of that once-again-living brat's name caused her skin to prickle, as if a frostbitten Eskimo were giving her a back massage.

"And, to instill faith within our infernal investors," Lilith continued, "Heck is going to play host to the most precious gems in the underworld: the Hopeless Diamonds."

"The Hopeless Diamonds?" the principal gasped. "Here?!"

On the plasma screen, Yojuanna—the glamorous eye of a hurricane comprised of twirling male dancers—stopped dancing in mid-gyration. She tiptoed closer to the screen and pressed her ear against the glass.

Lilith smirked as she straightened up a pile of folders and dusted off her hands. "The ultimate act of faith in Heck security," she said. "The value of human souls may fluctuate, but the safe money is always on commodities you can trust, such as rare, useless minerals."

"W-wow," Principal Bubb stammered. "I suppose they could go in my private safe, along with the rest of my precious things."

Cerberus nudged his way between Bea "Elsa" Bubb's ankles. Principal Bubb smiled down at him. "*Most* of my precious things," she cooed, scratching the beast on the back of its middle neck (her personal favorite).

Lilith looked on with distaste. "The Hopeless Diamonds will be kept in the last place here that anyone would want to go, much less be able to access."

"The teachers' lounge?" Principal Bubb offered.

"SADIA!" shouted Lilith. She composed herself, smoothing a lock of shiny blond hair behind her ear.

"Mammon and Luci . . . *Lucifer* are still working out the details below," Lilith said. "As soon as the particulars of the transfer are ironed out, you'll know exactly what you need to know, perhaps less."

Lilith's hand beeped. In her palm was one of those

new ClawCommander organizers, the ones that are surgically attached to your hand, paw, or mitt, depending.

"Speaking of the market," Lilith said while staring into the small blinking readout in her hand, "it's time for *Laughing Stock.*"

Lilith picked up the remote control on the desk and waved it at the plasma screens lining the walls of Principal Bubb's lair. Yojuanna, grinning from ear to ear, kicked up her heels in manic delight as the channel switched to a bald, apoplectic demon with smaller-than-usual horns bouncing around a studio set. The set looked like a more masculine version of Principal Bubb's lair, with blinking screens and a ceaseless parade of stock information, only—instead of velvet wallpaper and brimstone—the room was decorated with wood paneling and hunting trophies.

"Okay, caller," the demon said, "I'll make you a deal: if your stock actually earns a profit, I'll personally polish the Pearly Gates. How about that? Boo-ya!"

Bea "Elsa" Bubb scrunched up her already scrunched-up face. "Who is this whack-job?" she asked.

Lilith stared at the screen, entranced, her green eyes drinking in every pixel. "Follow the stocks, you say?" she grunted. "How can you say that if you've never heard of Otto Seight and *Laughing Stock*?"

The host leaned close to the screen and arched his eyebrows. "Sorry about that last outburst," he apologized to the camera. "The NSE has me in debt up to my keister, and some bad, bad demons want to collect. Hear my cries, believe my lies! Boo-ya!!"

Lilith snorted girlishly. "What a card!" she commented.

Yeah, a joker, thought Bea "Elsa" Bubb as she grimaced at the screen. *And that's exactly what Milton Fauster has made of me. If I ever see that boy again, it will be too soon for me, and too late for him.*

16 · FERRET OUT

A BAND OF early-morning sunlight slashed across Milton's face. He blinked his eyes open and, to his surprise, found that he had wriggled out of his sleeping bag and was curled up in a ball.

His tongue felt very strange, as if he had eaten a bowl of scalding hot soup and chased it with a heaping spoon of Vick's VapoRub. He also experienced a series of uncontrollable nose twitches.

The poultry thermometer lay a foot away from his barely used pillow.

I must have spat it out, or it was yanked, he thought as he followed the jumper cables leading out of the garage and into the driveway.

The Insecticide 3000 was shattered underneath the basketball hoop, outlined with the ashes of thousands of small insects. Beside the wreckage of blackened wire grids and smoldering transformers was a charred black bat, and—wrapped around it—the twitching paws of a smoking white ferret.

"Lucky!" Milton yelped as he rushed to his pet's side.

Flecks of foam covered the ferret's slack mouth, and his eyes were rolled back in his head.

Milton scooped Lucky up and placed him on his lap. He stroked his smoldering fur and checked to see if he was breathing. Milton opened his pet's pointy mouth. Out came a gush of anchovy breath. The ferret's fuzzy white belly gently swelled.

Alive, thought Milton as he held his pet close. *Barely.*

Lucky's eyes rolled back into their proper place and a peculiar sensation overtook Milton. A nervous energy cascaded throughout his body. He felt whole again, but . . . *different.* Antsy. Restless. Kind of like—

Lucky's pupils came into focus. Milton blinked. In that blink, he saw a picture of himself as viewed from his own lap.

—*a ferret.*

Milton's experiment in subtle energies had been a mixed blessing, like the *Star Wars* prequels. He had regained etheric energy, gluing his physical and sentient selves back together, but it wasn't *his* etheric energy . . . or even human energy, for that matter. So while he was held "in phase," it was through the skittish energy of gnats, mosquitoes, a bat, and—apparently—part of a little ferret.

Milton took Lucky into the garage and gave him a sip of water from his thermos.

Milton's *own* mouth felt cooler and damper somehow. When he blinked, he still had those weird intermittent images of himself as seen from a ferret's eyes. It was as if two different takes of the same scene had been spliced together in one movie, one from his perspective and another from Lucky's.

"Honey?" Milton's mom called from inside the house. "Is everything okay?"

Hardly, thought Milton. He had been avoiding his mom ever since he had left the present behind at the hospital. He had no idea what the gift was and couldn't spill the beans—not only to save his own skin, but also to spare his parents yet another child-inflicted trauma.

"Everything's fine, Mom," he lied. "Just cleaning up my science experiment for school."

"Okay, hon. Do you need a ride to school?"

"Nope, I'm good," Milton replied. "I'm going to go in early and . . . hit the books."

"All right, then. Have a good day. Did you have a chance to . . ."

"Gotta hustle," Milton interrupted. "Love you."

"Love you, too, sweetie."

That should buy me some time, Milton thought. *But I can't keep putting her off forever.*

Lucky shook himself fully awake and hopped off Milton's lap. The weird ferrety energy seemed to get more intense as Lucky became more alert. Milton looked down at his watch, fighting for focus among a storm of convulsive fidgets.

He really *did* have to hustle. Milton had made an appointment to see Algernon Cole, the lawyer, at the Paranor Mall before school. It was a bit out of the way—he had a sneaking feeling he'd be a little late for Mr. Castaneda's Spanish quiz—but *que sera, sera*. Milton had a plan that could result in both free legal counsel and its direct delivery to the place where it was needed most.

17 · A SiDE OF COLE'S LAW

"I'D LiKE TO say I've had consultations in weirder places than this," Algernon Cole said when entering the Paranor Mall, "but I can't. This is the icing on the fruitcake."

Lester Lobe's mellow was officially harshed. "It's a museum," he said tersely.

"Whoa, chill, Wavy Gravy," Algernon Cole said, palms out. "You definitely have an interesting place. I meant no disrespect. I *dig your scene.*"

Milton came rushing through the door. "Sorry I'm late," he said, panting. "I woke up not feeling quite myself."

Algernon Cole cocked his eyebrow and simpered. "Wait," he said while slapping his hands together. "You're the kid who was in the paper the other week!" He thrust his hand out to Milton. "Algernon Cole," he said while pumping Milton's hand vigorously. "Practically-lawyer, at your service."

He dropped Milton's hand.

"Ooh, sweaty," he said while wiping his palm on his dark, ill-fitting suit. "So, you want to sue the medics who revived you or something? Unnecessarily rough intubation? Allergic to the stuff they used to wash your hospital sheets?"

"What?" Milton replied with a twitch. "No, no. Nothing like that. I wanted to talk to you about . . . a book I'm writing."

"A book?" Algernon Cole replied, swiping his hand through his thinning, ponytailed hair. "So you want to talk representation, right?"

"Not exactly," Milton replied. "Let's talk . . . in here. I get an hour, right?"

Milton fidgeted. He couldn't help it—he had a squadron of restless gnat energy swarming inside him.

"Sure, right," Algernon Cole said warily.

Milton had worked on his story during the bus ride. He thought he had a good chance of pulling this off, if only he could keep his newly acquired bug-bat-ferret constitution in check. He motioned toward the Elvis Abduction Chamber, otherwise known as a Psychomanthium.

"For privacy," Milton said after a pause. "The book isn't finished, and, you know, I'm just a little superstitious, that's all."

Algernon Cole snickered.

"I understand completely," he said. "I'm sure we can keep you safe from those publishing sharks." He tapped the side of the chamber. "Knock on wood."

Lester Lobe turned away.

"Don't mind me," he said as he walked toward a box in the corner. "I just got a haunted ballot box in the mail today. From Florida. An old lady said it bit her as she cast her vote."

Lester flipped on a classic-rock radio station and unpacked the latest addition to his museum.

Milton and Algernon Cole entered the Psychomanthium and sat across from each other on Fat Elvis beanbag chairs. Milton reached up and yanked on the cord to an electric bulb. The soft red light came on with a rattle and click.

"Cozy," Algernon Cole commented, squatting down with a one-two pop of his knees. "So, what's your story, morning glory?"

Milton laced his fingers together fitfully.

"As you may have read," he relayed, reading from the teleprompter of his mind, "I was . . . *dead* . . . for a while."

"What I wouldn't give for a vacation," Algernon Cole interjected. "Sorry, go on."

"And that's when I got the . . . the idea. For my book." Milton drew in a deep breath.

"It's called . . . *Heck*."

"*Heck,*" repeated Algernon Cole, shifting uncomfortably in the beanbag.

"Yeah, *Heck.* See, I had these, um, *images* I guess you could call them, and I thought they would make a great book."

"I'm something of an author myself," Algernon Cole said.

"Great." Milton nodded. "So it's about what happens when—"

"Would you like to hear my idea for a book?"

Milton squirmed. He needed to stay on track if he was going to get through this.

"Maybe later," he offered.

Algernon Cole folded his arms together. "Right. Your hour," he huffed. "Continue."

"So, the book—*Heck*—it's about what happens when kids die. Bad kids."

"Sounds dark," Algernon Cole said dismissively. "Who's your audience?"

"Look, I don't really want to talk about any of that," Milton said as a glaze of perspiration formed on his forehead. "I need legal advice for this . . . character of mine."

"The protagonist?"

"Yes. See, he was sent to Heck by mistake. He's a good kid. Never did anything bad in his life. Well, at least his first one."

"Oh, I get it," Algernon Cole said, nodding. "Heck, it's like an allegory for—"

"Yes," Milton continued. "My character—the protagonist—signed a contract with the Principal of Darkness."

Algernon Cole chuckled. "That's not half bad."

"But the contract is bogus—it just has to be," Milton said desperately. "I've got to find some loophole in the contract, or a way that I can prove that the whole place is just a big sham and shouldn't exist at all. If I don't, my sister and my best friend will be there . . . for . . ."

Milton put his head in his twitchy hands. Algernon Cole rolled his eyes and leaned over to pat Milton on the back.

"Wow," he said, "you've certainly got a lot invested in your characters. That's good. They'll be more believable that way, especially since the story you're writing is so . . . *far-fetched*."

Lester Lobe's radio music drifted into the chamber—a spooky song about a white rabbit.

Milton sniffled and wiped his nose on his sleeve. "So you think . . . Do you think you can help me?"

Algernon Cole pulled up his mismatched socks and sat up straight to the sound of dried, settling beans.

"Always willing to help out another struggling writer." He looked at his Mickey Mouse watch. "We've got fifteen minutes. Enough to give you a taste of your options. If you find my advice helpful, then you can put me on a retainer and call me anytime."

Milton had a feeling that Algernon Cole's retainer would cost about as much as, well, *Milton's* retainer had cost. So it was now or never. All Milton had to do was activate the Psychomanthium—*somehow*—and give Marlo some supernatural legal counsel, something that she could use to build a case against the Powers That Be Evil from the inside.

"Firstly," Algernon Cole said, "your protagonist is a minor. Under eighteen years of age. Without a *Guardian Ad Litem* to represent the minor, I'd think that it would be hard to uphold the legality of a contract such as yours in a court of law."

Milton nodded and looked down at his hand. In his palm, he had written a summoning spell that he had seen last night on a *Taliswoman* rerun. The problem was that his palms were sweaty, and he had smudged the spell when shaking hands with Algernon Cole. He squinted in the low, red light to read the smears in his hand.

"Spirits, hear my cry," Milton murmured. "I . . . cinnamon? *Summon* you from the other side. Come to me and cross the Greek decline."

"What was that?" asked Algernon Cole.

"Oh, um, nothing," replied Milton. "I'm just trying to memorize what you're saying."

Algernon Cole shrugged and shook his head. "It's

your time. You paid for it. Or didn't, technically. So, as I was saying, being a minor, it's doubtful your protagonist could be bound by such a contract. At least by the laws of the living. However, the rules in your 'Heck' may be different, being that it's a place overrun by minors."

"Great divide!" Milton said. "Cross the *great divide!*" He looked around at the six mirrors surrounding him. Despite the spell, he could still see only six of himself and a half dozen of Algernon Cole.

The pseudo-lawyer stared at Milton, troubled and irritated.

"Do you want to do this another time, kid?"

Milton shook his head. "No," he said urgently. "Please, go on. I'm just . . . This is all really good stuff. I'm excited, that's all."

Algernon Cole glared at Milton suspiciously.

"Well, I hope you include me in your acknowledgments. Or think of me when you start licensing Heck toys."

Outside, Lester Lobe turned up his radio.

"I haven't heard this song in years!" he cried enthusiastically.

Heavy guitars and loping drums filled the chamber.

"I really *must* get an office," Algernon Cole complained.

"Please," Milton begged, "go on."

Algernon Cole sighed.

"Fine," he said. "There is also the possibility of duress."

"A dress?" Milton asked above the noise.

"No, *duress*," Algernon Cole clarified. "Though a boy forced to wear a dress would definitely be a form of duress. Was your protagonist coerced into signing this contract?"

"Yes!" Milton replied. "I can still feel the bite marks from the snake pens."

Algernon Cole rubbed the back of his neck.

"Okay, then. Well, being threatened with a dangerous animal would definitely count as duress."

The music throbbed through the Psychomanthium.

"Your love is groovy like a disco light.
You're so far out, you're out of sight!"

"This contract, though, could contain a subclause where the signee expressly agrees that the contract was not entered into under duress. I've read of cases like that before."

Milton looked down at the ink streak smeared across his clammy palm.

"Guardians of the spirit gum . . . *realm*," he murmured.

The hippie music droned outside.

Algernon Cole plugged his ears.

"Then there's fraud," he continued. "But, I would think that by the Principal of Darkness's very nature, he—"

"*She,*" interrupted Milton.

"It's nice to know that there's equal opportunity in the afterlife," Algernon Cole quipped. "*She* would be prevented from engaging in fraud or deceit."

"Hear and guide my pee . . . *plea,*" Milton chanted.

"Either that," Algernon Cole said, "or just the opposite: the legal assumption that every transaction she oversaw was fraudulent, thus rendering the notion of fraud obsolete."

"Out of sight! Out of sight!
So far out you're out of sight!"

Suddenly, a gust of cold wind filled the chamber. The mirrors seemed to warp and ripple like the surface of a disturbed pond. Milton could see a faint image joining that of Algernon Cole and his own in each of the six mirrors. It was a figure. A bald little . . . *creature* . . . with nubby horns. It was bouncing around, yelling, in what appeared to be a television studio.

"Good vibrations every night.
You're groovy, baby. Out of sight!"

"Otto Seight," the bald creature hollered. "Back at ya here with more *Laughing Stock* . . ."

Milton trembled as the horned-man's image gelled in the mirror. He had actually made contact with the underworld!

"What the . . . ?" The little creature snorted, glaring at Milton.

18 · WE iNTERRUPT
THiS PROGRAM . . .

LILITH COUTURE HANDED Principal Bubb a large empty milk crate.

"Try to fit in as many files as possible," she said. "Organize them by infraction, *not* by judgment. I'll go through them myself when you're done."

Bea "Elsa" Bubb groaned as she took the crate in her quaking claws.

Lilith snickered as she walked away.

"I'll be in the little demoness's room. I've got to powder my snout."

Bea "Elsa" Bubb set the crate on her desk and frowned at the bottomless stacks of folders strewn about her lair.

"Ugh!" Lilith yelped from Principal Bubb's facilities.

"This is a pit of despair if ever I've seen one. Remind me to get up-to-date on all my shots when I get back to uncivilization."

Principal Bubb made a rude gesture with her claw in Lilith's general direction and sat down in her chair.

"I'm going to reach right through this TV screen, caller, and choke the death right out of you if you don't sell that stock now!" barked Otto Seight from Principal Bubb's plasma screen.

Bea "Elsa" Bubb grimaced. "Where is that remote?" she mumbled, searching beneath the layers of reports on her desk.

The image on the screen winked and wrinkled. Now, instead of the host of *Laughing Stock* jumping up and down like a jack-in-the box, there was a man and a boy in a dark, red chamber.

Algernon Cole stood up and brushed smooth his slacks. "I don't have time to watch TV," he said snappishly.

"Wait!" Milton yelped. "Don't leave. Please. Just one more minute."

Algernon Cole smirked knowingly. "We writers are all the same," he said. "Always wanting to know what each other is working on. Fine. You dragged it out of me. Here's my book idea. . . ."

Algernon Cole grinned widely at Milton, his face a blank screen anticipating the feature presentation to come. "It's called . . . *Chicken Pants,*" he said finally, positively brimming with pride. He paused to let his words sink in.

"*Chicken Pants,*" repeated Milton flatly, unable to think of any other way to respond.

"*Chicken Pants!*" said Algernon Cole triumphantly. "It's about a boy who finds a magic pair of . . . guess."

"Um . . . chicken pants?" Milton answered tentatively while looking over Algernon Cole's shoulder at the energetic demon in the mirrors.

"You got it!" cried Algernon Cole with a clap.

Meanwhile, the image of Otto Seight scowled out from the mirrors. "What's going on?" he screeched. "Who's been messing with the monitors again?"

"And when the boy puts on the pants," Algernon continued, oblivious, "it gives him all sorts of strange, *chickeny* powers. And, boy, can he ever dance!"

Bea "Elsa" Bubb gaped at the plasma screen. A balding man with a ponytail pressed his fists into his underarms and began to flap and strut to a raucous beat, pummeling a tuneless tune. In the background, sitting in a beanbag chair, was a gawky boy with glasses.

Principal Bubb's pus-yellow eyes burned with recognition and rage.

Milton Fauster.

★ ★ ★

"Marlo!" Milton called as he pressed his palms against the mirror. "Get me Marlo Fauster!"

The veins on Otto Seight's stocky neck bulged.

"Carl!" he shouted off camera. "We're getting some interference, a nerdy kid playing with a camera. And a guy who thinks he's a chicken. Must be some EwwTube video."

Milton pounded his fists on the chamber walls.

"My name is Milton. My sister . . . she's in Heck. I'm trying to get ahold of her. . . ."

Bea "Elsa" Bubb screamed.

"Lilith! Get out here! It's him!"

After a flush and some grumbling, Lilith came hobbling out of Principal Bubb's Unrestroom.

"What is it?!" she said irritably while securing her sleek Gucci belt around her waist.

Bea "Elsa" Bubb thrust her remote toward the main plasma screen. "Look!"

The screen's image billowed and shimmered until it settled on Otto Seight, grimacing at the camera.

"Oh," he said, startled. "Looks like we're back in action." He spit into his hand, then polished his horn nubs. "Can't keep a demon like me off the air! Let's hit the phones. Caller, you're on *Laughing Stock!*"

Lilith glowered at Principal Bubb. The tap-tap-tap of her shiny red hooves sounded like the ticking of a chic, designer bomb.

"It was him," Bea "Elsa" Bubb grumbled. "Milton Fauster. I saw him."

The devil's assistant flipped back her head and laughed uproariously.

"Milton Fauster! Of course! I'm sure you see him everywhere—the television, the mirror . . . you probably see his name spelled out in your afternoon bowl of alphabet soup!"

Lilith plucked her monkey-fur shrug from the back of a chair and wriggled it over her shoulders.

"This unpleasantness has upset us all," she pronounced on her way to the door. "Let's say we take a little break. Do whatever you do to relax: nibble a bone, go for a roll in some mud . . . anything. We'll meet back here in an hour. Hugs!"

Lilith sashayed out the door and into the hallway.

If Milton Fauster is trying to contact his sister, Principal Bubb thought, *I need to find out why. And who better to help me than the boy who sent them both here to begin with?*

The long, sludgy rock song that Lester had been listening to on the radio finally ended.

"They don't write 'em like that anymore," Lester said from outside the chamber.

In the mirror, Otto Seight slapped his bald pate with frustration.

"Again?! Well, then, Carl, just turn everything off and on. That usually works. Do I have to do *everything* here?"

The demon disappeared, and warmth crept back into the still chamber.

Algernon Cole lowered his imaginary tail feathers and straightened his tie.

"Well, I don't expect *everyone* to get it," he said, affronted. He looked at his watch. "Besides, I've got to boogie. I have another client—a *paying* client—who wants to sue a hospital that accidentally unplugged his stepson."

Algernon Cole stepped out of the Elvis Abduction Chamber, with Milton close behind.

"Unplugged?!" Milton shouted. "Was it Damian Ruffino?"

Algernon Cole stopped suddenly and glared at Milton.

"A lawyer can't divulge the interests of his client," he said haughtily. "But, seeing as that I'm not a real lawyer—*yet*—then, yes, Damian Ruffino. Friend of yours?"

"No," Milton said while staring at the ground. "I don't think he was a friend of anyone, actually. Damian was in the explosion . . . at the mall . . . he caused it."

Algernon Cole grabbed his briefcase by the door.

"Be that as it may, his family—and I, for that matter—still deserve *something* for the hospital screwing up like that."

"Can I come with you?" Milton asked eagerly. "Maybe I can help you find some, um, *evidence*. A clue or something."

Algernon Cole smiled sadly and knelt down to address Milton eye to eye.

"Look," he said, putting his hand on Milton's shoulder, "I know you're all hung up about almost dying and all that, but you're a kid: You'll get through it. Years from now, you'll look back on all this and laugh!"

Milton was furious. The hundreds of mosquitoes in his nervous system wanted to suck all the blood from Algernon Cole's body.

The nearly-lawyer looked at his briefcase.

"Hey, I almost forgot."

He rummaged through it and pulled out a small tub of coleslaw, with COLE'S LAW printed on it.

"Here you go! Get it? Cole's Law. *Coleslaw.*"

Milton stared at the tub and crossed his arms defiantly.

"Fine, then," Algernon Cole said as he opened the door.

Lester Lobe walked toward them. "Hey, I'll take that," he said, grabbing the coleslaw from Algernon Cole's hands.

"Sure thing, Ben and Jerry," Algernon Cole said as

he stepped onto the sidewalk. "And don't you worry, Milton. I'm sure Damian will get exactly what he deserves. Who knows? Maybe he's in Heck right now!"

He walked down the street, cackling, bobbing his head subtly, as if he were about to cock-a-doodle-do another dance.

Milton shivered and wrapped his arms around himself. "That's exactly what I'm afraid of," he murmured.

19 · A SAVING GRACE

THE CLASSROOM TOSSED from side to side, subtly, as if the room itself were a barge floating on a mildly perturbed sea. The effect was unsettling, because nothing in the class seemed to be physically moving (Marlo's somersaulting stomach notwithstanding). Though judging from the shade of queasy green cast across the other girls' faces, she wasn't the only student who hadn't developed her sea legs yet. The only person in the room who seemed unfazed by the sickening sway was the vivacious teacher at the front of the class.

The teacher took off her woolen cap, releasing an avalanche of red curls that cascaded down her shoulders like molten lava.

"There, thass mooch better," she said in a comfortable Irish brogue.

Marlo sighed with longing. The teacher's hair was like a maple tree in autumn.

If I had hair like that, Marlo pined, *I wouldn't* have *to dye it.*

But the teacher's appeal was more than hair-deep. Norm had said that their new Corporate Strategy teacher used to be a pirate queen back in the sixteenth century. How cool was that: a *pirate queen*? Though, judging from the long, slender scar slashed across the teacher's neck, not everyone shared Marlo's glowing opinion of her teacher.

In any case, she was *definitely* cooler than that nasty old hag Poker Alice, who was currently on the mend in Rapacia's infirmary.

After Poker Alice's accident, some peeved demonesses sent from Rapacia had rounded up the girls. Their booty was promptly confiscated and brought back to the Grabbit's warren.

The lights dimmed and a screen descended from the ceiling at the front of the class. The teacher shook her red hair disapprovingly.

This class is brought to you by Epiphany's Jewelers, located on the second floor of beautiful, everlasting Mallvana.

Fade in to Marilyn Monroe, looking glamorous on a bearskin rug. She is singing softly to herself while blowing on her fingernail polish.

"A kiss on the hand may be quite continental, but diamonds are a girl's best . . . oh, hello! Marilyn here . . . with a perfectly sad story for you!

"Once upon a time, outside the Spedale degli Innocenti orphanage—the world's first, built in Florence, Italy, in the fifteenth century—was a fountain where, for generations, orphans would come to weep. Boo-hoo!"

Marilyn pouts and rolls across the rug. She cradles her head in her hands, wiggling her fingers. Each is adorned with a glittering diamond ring.

"Their tears would seep into the ground, sinking through hundreds of miles of sand and gravel, where—after centuries of pressure and heat—they became something so sad, and yet . . . so beautiful . . . the Hopeless Diamonds!

"These two twinkling teardrops are nearly a hundred times more precious than any diamond known to exist on the Stage! Wowie-zowie . . .

"Though these diamonds are part of a private collection, Epiphany's Jewelers is proud to sell genuine diamelle replicas of the Hopeless Diamonds so you can have some of this glittering gloom for your very own!

"And don't think that diamonds are only a **girl's** best friend . . . you guys, be sure to visit our two-thousand-carat baseball diamond, signed by late great sluggers Joe DiMaggio, Babe Ruth, and Mickey Mantle!"

Marilyn blows a kiss for the camera before applying polish to her toes.

"Stay fabulous!"

Epiphany's Jewelers.
You Followed the Rules, Now Get Your Jewels.
Only in Mallvana.

The lights came up, and the girls shivered as the icy fingers of want strummed up and down their spines. *This is excruciating,* Marlo thought, *which is the point, I'm sure, of having all of Mallvana's spendy splendor rubbed in a greedy girl's face.* The girls chewed their lips, fidgeted in their chairs, and shivered from the cold sweat of appropriation withdrawal. It was a punishment that was cruel but hardly unusual in this underage underworld.

The teacher straightened her belt—which holstered both an antique pistol and a cutlass—and tossed a piece of chalk playfully in her hand.

"Me name is Grace O'Malley," she said while surveying the class full of girls. "And I'll be teachin' ya the finer points of corporate strategy."

Jordie raised her hand. It swayed like a bobbing brown mast.

"Aye, me ferst question," Ms. O'Malley said with a smile.

"Why is the . . . whole barmy room . . . rockin' back 'n' forth?" she asked in nauseated fits and starts. "It's makin' me so dicky, I'm near honking."

The teacher smiled. "If yer wantin' to be corporate pirates, then ya got to be learnin' to hold yer own while everythin' 'round ya is as wobbly as closin' time at the local pub."

Lyon's arm shot up like a tan cobra ready to strike. "I just want to know," she said snidely, "what an old pirate from Leprechaun Land knows about corporate strategy?"

"That's rather the point, isn't it?" Ms. O'Malley said, her eyes a pair of blazing emeralds. "To see what an old leprechaun like me knows."

The teacher paced in front of the chalkboard. Her green cape billowed behind her.

"As I see it," she pondered aloud, "thars scarce little diff'rence between bein' a pirate and runnin' yer own corporation. Fer one, there's hostile takeovers—"

Bordeaux raised her hand.

"I'm glad to see me talk is stirrin' up all sorts of questions," Ms. O'Malley said with a grin. "What's on yer wee mind, luv?"

"Do you know Johnny Depp?"

The girls giggled.

"No, lass," Ms. O'Malley replied. "Just the bonny deep . . . now, enough with the interruptions, ya bony gulls."

The teacher rubbed her chin and inspected her desk.

"Ah," she said as an idea struck her, "here's a way to explain it."

She grabbed a stapler and held it out to the class.

"Let's say this here is the S.S. *Junk Bond*. And this," Ms. O'Malley continued, holding a Scotch tape dispenser in her other hand, "is the *Raging Equity*, which gets an ambitious gust in 'er sails and decides to take over the *Junk Bond* by any means necess'ry."

Ms. O'Malley set the stapler and tape dispenser on the edge of her desk, side by side, then tied her hair back with a velvet scrunchy.

"First, she pulls alongside the *Junk Bond,* and the captain bellows, 'Attention, crew! Overthrow yer captain and end his reign of error! Join our merry, thievin' family, where ever'one gets their fair share!' "

The stapler and tape dispenser pitched and yawed in the agitated, imaginary sea.

"But the market was angry, me friends," Ms. O'Malley continued. "The captain of the *Raging Equity* has to act fast and wages a fierce raid before the *Junk Bond* loses all its perceived worth. He preys upon the other crew's vanity, greed, and weakness and wins it all without spilling a drop o' blood."

Ms. O'Malley pulled up her plaid wool trews and sat down behind her desk.

"Any questions, lasses?" she said, winded, wiping

beads of perspiration from her brow. "Or are ya gonna just stare at me like a herd of seals that've been in the sun fer too long?"

The girls traded uneasy looks. Takara raised her hand.

"Yes, lass . . . a copper for what rests on yer mind," Ms. O'Malley said.

"I like pirate story very much!" Takara gushed.

Ms. O'Malley sighed.

"Aye, yer welcome, miss. Perhaps I'll strike the colors and scuttle this particular lesson for today. Besides—"

The teacher clapped her hands together and pushed herself away from the desk.

"—it's time to play a little game!"

Ms. O'Malley stood up.

"I want ya all to shove yer desks to the sides of the room."

Marlo and Norm heaved their bulky desks to the wall in squeaky bursts. Lyon and Bordeaux tried vainly to budge their respective desks but, considering that their combined weights barely crossed the triple-digit barrier, managed only a few scrapes. Jordie, her desk the first to hit the wall, grinned as she watched the two skinny girls struggle.

Lyon blew a frosted bang out of her face. "Can someone move this for me?" she whined.

Jordie walked over to her. "I'll move it for yeh," she said, "if I can punch yeh hard in the arm for afters."

"Whatever," Lyon said with resignation.

Jordie smirked and shoved both of the girls' desks to the wall in three heaves. Then, true to her word, she walked back to Lyon and slugged her hard in the shoulder.

"Oww!" Lyon yelped. "Teacher! Jordie just hit me!"

Ms. O'Malley's green eyes twinkled with amusement.

"Ye struck a bargain, lass," she replied. "Then ye had ta make good."

Lyon rubbed her arm and fumed.

"Look!" Takara chirped while pointing down at the floor. "Class big game board!"

Marlo looked down. Sure enough, the floor was striped with electrical tape to simulate—judging by the inclusion of spaces such as Boardwalk and St. Charles Place labeled with Magic Marker—a large Monopoly board.

"Monopoly?" Lyon yawned. "How boring. My father owns half of these places for real, anyway."

"I think it's cool!" said Marlo. "I get to be the car!"

"The dog would be more appropriate," Lyon mocked with a sneer.

"I want to be that cool three-wheeled European convertible!" Bordeaux exclaimed.

The other girls passed the same look of confusion back and forth with one another.

"You mean the wheelbarrow?" asked Norm finally.

Ms. O'Malley stepped from behind her desk and out to the middle of the classroom.

"Would you girls stop yer harpin'?" she said with her hands on her hips.

None of the girls knew exactly what their teacher was asking of them but assumed it had something to do with them being quiet.

"That's better," Ms. O'Malley remarked. "A good word never broke anyone's teeth, ye know. Besides, ye lasses won't be needin' any game pieces, as you *yourselves* will be the pieces."

The teacher handed each of the girls $1,500 in funny money.

"Now, if all of ya will stand over there in tha corner that says 'Go.' "

The class congregated in the corner, lurching across the gently rolling floor. They crowded and fussed to fit in the same tape-outlined square.

"Good," Ms. O'Malley said while seating herself cross-legged. "Now, ya may be wonderin' why we're playin' a game in class. If ya hadn't already a'been told by poor dear Poker Alice—which I sincerely doubt, judgin' from her track record—yer all being trained ta join the ranks of the Netherworld Soul Exchange, when ya grubs turn ta butterflies, that is. That's basically what Rapacia is, a prep school to pump out new blood to feed the NSE."

The girls stared at their teacher with faces blanker than a hobo's bank statement.

Ms. O'Malley smirked. "There's plenty of time fer all that later on," she said, scooping up a pair of dice. "We've got ourselves a game ta play. We'll be doin' things alphabetically, so, Bordeaux, ya ken go furst."

The teacher cast the dice between her sandaled feet. "Eight! Good start, lass. Off ya go."

Bordeaux skipped to Vermont Avenue.

"So, lass," asked Ms. O'Malley. "Do ya wanna buy it?"

Bordeaux shook her head. "We already have a cabin in Vermont," she replied.

Ms. O'Malley smirked and shook her head. She scooped up the dice and rolled them again. "Five! Go fer a walk, Jordie."

Jordie stumbled over to the Reading Railroad and took two hundred-dollar bills from her stack. "Stonking!" she exclaimed, handing her money to the teacher.

"Congratulations," Ms. O'Malley said while taking Jordie's pretend money. "Smart move . . . for a Brit," she added with a sly wink.

The teacher rolled the dice.

"Four . . . ooh. Sorry, Lyon," Ms. O'Malley said.

Lyon fumed and stomped to Income Tax (Pay 10 percent or $200).

"Income tax?!" the spoiled girl snapped. "My family doesn't have to pay taxes—we're rich."

"We're playin' a *game*, luv," Ms. O'Malley said.

Lyon wadded up two hundred-dollar bills and threw it at her teacher's feet. "Keep the change," she huffed.

Ms. O'Malley sighed to herself as she rolled the dice. "Ten . . . ouch. My condolences, Miss Fauster."

Marlo frowned. She wobbled ten paces across the lurching floor to Jail.

Lyon laughed wickedly. Just then, the door opened.

"Yes?" Ms. O'Malley inquired.

A warty demoness with scraggly white hair stood in the doorway.

"I'm here for Marlo Fauster," the demoness rasped in low, husky tones.

"Wow," Bordeaux whispered. "She really *is* going to jail."

"Ha!" Lyon snorted. "I might learn to like this game after all."

"—and Lyon Sheraton," the demoness finished.

The corners of Lyon's mouth drooped slowly downward.

"And what is this all about, then?" Ms. O'Malley rumbled fiercely.

"The Grabbit." The withered demoness gulped. "It wants to see the two of them. Immediately."

"Oh," replied the teacher as the winds of ire left her sails. "Of course."

Ms. O'Malley smiled at the girls, but the concern in her eyes betrayed the reassurance of her warm grin.

"I'm sure it's nothing, girls," she said unconvincingly. "Two people shorten the road, ya know."

The two girls looked at each other and frowned.

Marlo had a sinking feeling that the road ahead, while admittedly short, was uphill all the way.

MiDDLEWORD

It may be that no man is an island, as the popular human saying goes, but every girl is an aisle. A place of opportunity, of hope, of freedom. She wanders down this aisle—herself—searching, browsing, assessing, filling her cart (or pockets) with shiny things. Does it make her feel better? Not necessarily. But it can fill her with a sense of who she is, or at least who she wants to be. But, in some cases, when you put the cart in front of the girl, she may soon wonder who— or what—exactly she is filling it for.

See, sometimes, want is a carrot dangling before your eyes. You stumble forward, blind with desire, and before you know it, you find yourself in some ghastly place with no idea of how you got there, and—worst of all—no carrot to show for your troubles.

This want—the inexorable urge to follow some-thing shiny and new, not carrots specifically—can be overwhelming, pushing all reason and perspective out of your head. It can quickly become an electric, all-consuming hunger that drives wanting wanters to do almost anything to get whatever it is that the havers have. The problem is that these wanted things, much like carrots, aren't particularly worth following (as they can only lead to salads). And sometimes, if you're not careful, that carrot of want can lead you to the feet of something terrible—something like a giant, greedy, frighteningly powerful rabbit with a cataclysmic agenda.

20 · UP AND ATOM

CLAD IN A reflective catsuit, Yojuanna B. Covetta slunk undetected across the Mallvana plasma screen. Shoppers bustled by, oblivious, blinded by the joy that, though death had prevented them from "taking it with them," in Mallvana they could buy it back, return it, or exchange it for something in their size.

Yojuanna reached the edge of the screen, which bordered the Science 'n' Séance store. She crouched down, thrust her arms in front of her, leapt from the screen—breaking up into billions of little ones and zeros—and reassembled on a computer terminal inside the store.

She wiped beads of digital sweat from her brow and hid behind an open document on the screen—the very one she had come to get.

FOOLISH FRENCH PHYSICIST
FUTZES WITH FATE
By Wolf Larkin, Global News Account Totality
(GNAT)

SKROOZ-TOULOUSE, FRANCE—Last week, the French Organization for Outlandish Learning and Investigation of Scientific Hazards (FOOLISH) conducted a series of experiments at the organization's facility in the town of Skrooz-Toulouse, on the Franco-Swiss border. By taking materials of extreme density and placing them in their Radial Intensity Super Kinetic Yielder (RISKY), the FOOLISH scientists were able to create a small, yet intensely powerful, black hole.

Conventional black holes are infinitely dense relics of dead stars: bottomless pits in space exhibiting gravitational appetites so voracious that not even light can escape.

FOOLISH's RISKY is an unusual machine due to its patented spiral design, allowing atomic particles to whip about at great speeds. Then they are slammed into each other so hard that they create energy of an intensity rivaled only by that released at the creation of the universe.

But do these scientists worry about creating

a black hole powerful enough to absorb all matter, growing exponentially until it erodes the entire universe? Professor Jacques de Manqué maintains that these FOOLISH efforts pose no threat to the world as we know it, explaining that to do catastrophic harm, scientists would need atoms from an unfathomably dense source. Locating a substance of that density, he assures, is practically *hopeless*.

Yojuanna smiled as she tucked the digital document down the front of her catsuit.

"Come right this way, ma'am," said the Science 'n' Séance cashier as he approached the register. Yojuanna grabbed several folders on the desktop and hid behind them.

The balding cashier, with tufts of wild gray hair on the sides of his head, set a large box down on the counter. "Phew!" he gasped to an old woman with a pair of spectacles balanced on the tip of her nose. "Your grandson will love this Smash 'n' Flash Atom Cannon. When is he due to arrive?"

The woman fumbled with the catch on her purse. "He has a terminal disease," she said with a trace of excitement. "So I should be seeing him any day now! And, without his mother around, I can spoil him all I want!"

"This kit is a great start," said the man with a grin. "In fact, I was just reading about some experiments in particle collision they're conducting up on the Stage. I'll print you out a copy for you to give to your . . ."

He stared, puzzled, at the computer screen.

"That's odd," the cashier said. "I just had it up. And what are all these folders doing here?"

The man tried to click on the folders, but Yojuanna grabbed the cursor and threw it across the screen with all her virtual might. The cashier dragged it back, then he—and unbeknownst to him, Yojuanna—struggled for control of his computer.

"What the . . . ?" he muttered, cursing his cursor.

The old woman sighed.

"I don't think I brought enough money," she relayed with frustration. "I'd forget my head if it wasn't attached to my shoulders. And it almost *wasn't,* after that terrible accident. . . ."

The cashier scowled at his computer.

"Maybe if I just turn it off and on," he mumbled. "That usually seems to—"

Yojuanna gulped and let go of the cursor.

The man exhaled with relief.

"There," he said. "That always seems to scare these infernal boxes."

He looked at the woman and smiled kindly.

"Don't worry about the money, ma'am. I'll just put it on your tab. It's not like you're going anywhere!"

"Thank you so much," the woman said, her face crinkled with bouquets of lines blossoming around her eyes and mouth. "Could you deliver it? I'm afraid it's a little heavy for me."

"Of course," he replied. "Cloud One, I assume?"

The old woman's forehead scrunched up with indignation.

"Cloud *Two*," she said, stretching out the "two" like a rubber band just before the point of snapping. "In the right light, you can almost see my halo."

The man looked back at her dubiously.

"I'm sorry, ma'am," he said with the even tone of someone who has worked retail for years and wishes to avoid unnecessary conflict. "Cloud Two, then. I'll send it HCW—Heaven Can't Wait—Express, so you should get it before your return."

The cashier popped up a new screen on his computer and typed in delivery instructions. Yojuanna crept from folder to folder until she reached the window. She carefully scaled the window's edge like a digital cat burglar.

"Name, please, ma'am?" the cashier asked, tapping away at his keyboard. "For the delivery."

"Thera Grandit," the woman replied.

The man typed in the name and prepared to send the order off to be delivered. Yojuanna, however, kept kicking the cursor away from the SEND button with her camouflaged boot.

"Blast it!" the cashier cursed.

Just then, a miniature cruise missile shot up from

the model rocketry aisle and dive-bombed the cashier on its race for the entrance. The old woman screamed as the missile's flaming exhaust singed her blue-white hair.

A dotty old man peered over the smoke-filled aisle. "Sorry," he called out, his face as red as a beet. "These newfangled ignition systems are touchier than a blind man reading a Braille comic book."

The cashier grabbed a small fire extinguisher from beneath the counter and trotted over to douse a series of blazes burning from the Whee! Gee! Ouija Board section.

With the cashier away, Yojuanna crawled atop the delivery form, stopping above the "To" field, and rappelled down. She hovered over the address and changed it from "Thera Grandit at Cloud Two, Heaven" to "The Grabbit at Circle Two, Rapacia," then modified the quantity, increasing it from one "Smash 'n' Flash Atom Cannon" to two.

Yojuanna tucked a strand of silver hair back into the cinched hood of her reflective bodysuit and kicked the SUBMIT button with her toe. A new window replaced the form.

Order Complete.

Smiling, she climbed off the new window and arranged the folders on the computer's desktop in a clean, even, horizontal line. Yojuanna stood on top of a folder on the screen's edge, crouched low, then ran for all she was worth. Leaping from folder to folder, she dove spectacularly off the screen and into the air—again breaking up into a misty cloud of data bits—until collecting her discombobulated self on Mallvana's towering plasma display.

Yojuanna uncinched her glossy hoodie and shook out her sleek silver hair. She clapped, summoning a throbbing dance beat, and tugged above her ear, pulling out her telescoping microphone headset.

"I do what's bad so well, so well,
  takin' it all, to sell, to sell.
  If you want it, then I got it, but you gotta get it right.
  Like a bunny—what's so funny?—I can hop it outta
    sight!"

21 · HARE-BRAINED SCHEME

MARLO, LYON, AND the carbuncled demoness guard hovered outside the Grabbit's warren. From inside came a dreadful, grating rhapsody: not the Grabbit's usual monotone soliloquy, but something that bordered on rhythmic. Almost . . . *rapping*.

> *"If you want it, then I got it, but you gotta get it*
>   *right.*
> *Like a bunny—what's so funny?—I can hop it*
>   *outta . . ."*

"Excuse me, *Grabbit*," the demoness interrupted after a dry cough. "I brought the two burgling bobby-soxers you requested."

The Grabbit grinned its cold metal grin. Marlo noticed that the dingy white paint of its teeth was beginning to peel.

"Thank you, guard, you've done your bit
and brought me back these girls so quick.
They're like a gift without the bow.
In any case, you're free to go."

The demoness gave a creaky curtsy and backed out of the metal rabbit's warren.

"Is this about our little extracurricular shopping excursion?" Marlo asked. "Because if it is, we never thought that Poker Alice would—"

"It's all Marlo's fault," accused Lyon. "It was her dumb idea, then she tried to escape, and—"

"You lying bleach-blond toilet brush!" screeched Marlo.

The Grabbit's spooky voice boomed through the burrow.

"Okay, girls, that's quite enough.
You're here because you stole.
But it seems to me you have the stuff
to help me with my goal."

"Your goal?" Lyon replied.

"I've heard there's something very dear
that's soon to be transported,
and I think that with you two girls here
this mission can be thwarted."

Marlo bit her lower lip in concentration. With its permanent grin and flat, soulless eyes, the Grabbit's true intentions were impossible to discern.

"So you want us to steal something for you—" Marlo asked with a quaver.

"—and expect us to believe that we're going to be all hippity-hoppity ever after?" Lyon interrupted with a sneer. The Grabbit oscillated, essentially motionless to the naked eye, but the distressing reverberations it sent out were some bad vibes indeed.

"Two precious gems are on their way
to someplace very grim.
I'd like to cause some disarray,
tho' chances, they are slim.
Heck's in trouble, yes indeed,
these gems are meant to stop it.
So if you both can sate my greed,
this place is in our pockets."

Marlo and Lyon studied one another out of the corners of their eyes, each looking—without *looking* as if they were looking—at the other for guidance.

What does any of this mean? Marlo wondered. *Is the Grabbit really some kind of ally, cutting us in on a heist that will sign the pink slip to this place over to us?*

Lyon held her head up haughtily and stepped forward.

"We need to, like, discuss the chain of command here, first," she said, her jaw squared, yet her lower lip trembling. "There's no way I'm trusting . . . *her*," she snarled, extending her finger toward Marlo without actually setting eyes on her. "And if you expect me to take orders from someone with more roots than a big outdoor place with trees and plants—"

"A *forest*," seethed Marlo.

"A *forest*," continued Lyon, "then you can take your plan and stick it in one of your way-too-long-to-suit-your-build ears!"

Marlo stormed forward, brushing past Lyon in angry strides. She didn't want to work with Lyon any more than Lyon did with her, but the Grabbit's proposition was too intriguing to screw up.

"Forgive Lyon," Marlo said. "She actually ate today and her brain is all muddled, trying to sort the calories. What she meant to say is that wouldn't it be more efficient if we used our skills . . . *independently* . . . so that neither of our personal snatching styles cramps the others?"

"That isn't what I—" Lyon blurted before Marlo stopped her with a sharp jab to the ribs. Another round of bickering was cut short by the Grabbit's hollow, booming voice.

"Two coaches take our treasure,
led by Byron and by Keats,
to a place devoid of pleasure
save two precious, priceless treats.
But time is short, work must be swift.
So, as part of my grand scheme,
each of you shall use your gift,
while leading your own team."

Smiles of satisfaction spread across Lyon's and Marlo's faces. "You're on," they said in unison before spinning around to openly fume at each other.

"I'm glad it seems you're both aboard,
and now we plan our blitz.
The stakes are high for this reward . . .
So—"

"Sign for both your kits?" interrupted a voice from the doorway.

The girls turned. A deliveryman, wearing immaculate white shorts and a cap with little wings on the side, stood with two large boxes on a dolly.

"HCW Express," he continued. "I have a delivery for"—he scowled at his clipboard—"the Grabbit?"

Though it was impossible, Marlo swore that the Grabbit's tin grin grew wider, brighter, and creepier.

"If one of you could sign for these,
it would help me out immensely.
Then leave and hone your expertise,
for we'll need it most intensely."

Marlo took the deliveryman's clipboard, signed for the packages, then shuffled out of the Grabbit's warren with Lyon, leaving the deliveryman to help the freak-ish, immobile machine to assemble its new toys.

Marlo's brain flickered with flashes of warning, like faraway lightning muffled by brooding storm clouds. But the rest of her—her arms, her legs, her heart, and the lattice of nerve endings that held them all together in its high-voltage web—coursed with excruciating ex-citement. She tried to ignore the warning in her head. After all, what did her brain know, anyway?

Maybe the Grabbit's plot to steal these important jewels really will shake things up down here, Marlo considered. *Wait . . . two jewels? They must be the Hopeless Dia-monds . . . the most precious gems ever produced! And I would be the girl—the Grabbit's favorite—to make it happen, pulling off the biggest jewel heist in history! Milton would be proud . . . Milton.*

She bit her lower lip with her fang, pushing the sad-ness that her brother's name inspired aside with sharp pain. Marlo would hatch the perfect plan and execute it flawlessly. She'd show Lyon, Poker Alice, Bea "Elsa"

Bubb—*everyone*—that you should never, ever underestimate a greedy girl with loads of nerve and precious little common sense. When Marlo set her mind to something, there was no limit to the amount of mischief she could stir up. And, as Marlo knew firsthand, where there was chaos, there was often opportunity.

22 · HUNG UP AND ON THE LiNE

"IT'S THE OPPORTUNITY we've been looking for," Bea "Elsa" Bubb whispered into her new No-Fee Hi-Fi Faux Phone, basically two tarnished thimbles—one each on the thumb and pinky of her claw—that she held to her ear and mouth.

The congested, snooty voice of Lilith Couture echoed down the hall.

"Of course, Luci," she giggled sharply into her own No-Fee Hi-Fi Faux Phone (a far more stylish model built into her beautifully manicured nails). "I miss you, too. But you're the one that sent me to this nauseating nursery school in the first place, silly."

Bea "Elsa" Bubb could feel an itchy rash creeping up her neck and around her ears like an invasive vine.

"I know you're still there, because I can hear you breathing," Damian said flatly over the phone. "Either that, or a donkey is trying to inhale your phone with a rusty tuba."

"Shh . . . ," Bea "Elsa" Bubb admonished as she ducked around the corner, down the hallway from her not-so-secret lair.

Lilith clopped languidly down the hallway on her imported hooves. Her erratic steps brought to mind a horse happily under the influence of a tranquilizer.

"Oh, Luci. You are terrible!" she cooed. "But don't you dare stop!" Lilith rested her sharp, protruding shoulder blades against the wall and wilted girlishly, pouting with her whole body. "Fine, I suppose we *must* mix a little business with our pleasure," she scolded playfully. "So, I just received the itinerary for the transfer of the Hopeless Diamonds to Sadia. Two diamonds, two stagecoaches. Brilliant, as always."

Bea "Elsa" Bubb thrust her curled claw around the corner so that Damian could better hear the conversation.

"And the timing is impeccable," Lilith continued. "The Grabbit suddenly announcing some big ceremony in Mallvana on the very same day. How did that freaky bunny thing get the Powers That Be to allow it to use Mallvana as a venue? Well, I guess it doesn't matter as long as it diverts attention from the main event in Sadia . . . *oh, that's brilliant:* the chairman of the Netherworld

Soul Exchange himself, using the ceremony as a platform to announce the successful transfer of the diamonds, thus stabilizing the underworld economy in one fell swoop!"

Principal Bubb crab-walked away from the corner and whispered into the phone. "Did you get all that?" she wheezed.

"Yeah. I heard her," Damian replied. "She sounds like a babe."

The principal scowled and gritted her fangs.

"Something about two stagecoaches to Sadia," Damian continued, "and the Grabbit hosting a big ceremony the same day. Got it. Now what does all this have to do with me?"

Principal Bubb rubbed her throbbing temples. Good help was so hard to come by down here.

"What it means is that I made a call to a friend of mine in Rapacia—Poker Alice," the principal explained in hushed tones. "She was more than willing to work with us if it meant the undoing of Marlo Fauster and her brother. You'll be Rapacia's newest teacher's aide, keeping one eye on Ms. Fauster and the other on this strange ceremony of the Grabbit's. Its behavior has been erratic as of late, and—like everyone in the underworld—it *must* have some kind of agenda. You got all that?"

"All except the part where anyone who isn't legally blind believes that I'm a little girl, much less a helpful one," Damian replied.

Principal Bubb grinned, exposing yellow fangs that had never felt the bristles of a toothbrush.

"Considering that nearly every cosmetic surgeon who has ever lived is down here, I think we'll have no problem drawing out your feminine side."

An intoxicating cloud of Lilith's perfume wafted by. The mist of clove, vanilla, exotic spice, and musk tickled Bea "Elsa" Bubb's snout.

"Okay, I get it," Lilith said. "I'll be seeing you tonight, then. Hugs."

Lilith grinned a sleepy grin, as if she were a kitten that just woke up from a nice nap. Then, with a brusque tug on her dress, her soft and peaceful expression evaporated, leaving behind the usual pattern of severe angles and sharp features that made up Lilith's "work" face.

"Principal Blob!" she barked. Her voice ricocheted down the hallway like a sniper's bullet searching for its target. Bea "Elsa" Bubb recoiled as Damian laughed heartily on the other end of the line.

"*Blob!*" he chortled. "That's priceless!"

The principal seethed. Her thumb thimble beeped, alerting her to another call. "Excuse me, Mr. Ruffino, but while I *so* enjoy the sound of Heck's poster bully laughing at me, I have another call to take."

"I'm sure if they're calling *you,* then it's a wrong numb—"

Bea "Elsa" Bubb hung up on Damian with a flick of her claw. She answered the other line.

"Hell—"

She glanced down at the caller ID on her pinky thimble and started: 1-666-666-DEVL.

"—oh!"

"Principal Bubb," the voice—as smooth and dangerous as an electric eel—crooned on the other end. "This is—"

"I know who this is, Luci—" Though no actual rebuff was uttered through the receiver, Bea "Elsa" Bubb could sense one nonetheless. "—fer," she stumbled. "Lucifer. And might I say what a pleasure it is to talk with you. . . ."

"You might," the Big Guy Downstairs replied coolly. "And you just did."

Bea "Elsa" Bubb laughed with more gusto than the devil's bon mot deserved.

"Principal Bubb," the Big Guy Downstairs continued, "let's cut to the chase."

Bea "Elsa" Bubb nodded, though, of course, there was no way for the devil to know that. "Firstly," he said calmly, "your job is very much on the line. This should come as no surprise to you. What may come as a surprise is that I have faith in your ability to turn this around."

Bea "Elsa" Bubb blushed inside, outside, and everywhere in between.

"Why, thank you, sir," she stammered.

"Your bungled handling of the Milton Fauster Incident has heaped a lot of attention upon Heck. But when the afterlife serves you lemons, you make something, something . . ."

"Lemony?" Principal Bubb suggested.

"Don't interrupt me," the Big Guy Downstairs snapped, his voice cracking like a whip. "The transfer of the Hopeless Diamonds to a circle of Heck is the first major event to occur down here since . . . since the *last* major event to occur down here. Only this time, all will go according to plan. Heck will be held up as a symbol of sinister security, a sweet beacon of hopelessness. And nothing is going to interfere with this. *Capiche?*"

"Bless you."

"Do you understand?!" the devil roared.

"Yes . . . of course," the principal replied, flustered.

"Good," the Big Guy Downstairs continued. "So you'll need to step back and let Lilith handle the dual shipments to Sadia." He paused, and Bea "Elsa" Bubb could hear his face crack into a leer. "It takes one treasure to handle another, I suppose."

Bea "Elsa" Bubb's face cracked as well, splintering into a jagged grimace.

"I need you, Bubb, to keep tabs on one of your vice principals," Lucifer continued, "who I fear may be turning madder than a March hare, if you catch my drift."

"Drift caught," Principal Bubb murmured. "Already on it like an Easter bonnet."

There was a sharp pause.

"Really?" the Big Guy Downstairs said with admiration. "Excellent. You may turn this around yet, Principal."

Bea "Elsa" Bubb nearly swooned.

"The Grabbit has always been eccentric," Lucifer added. "But now it's positively erratic. I guess that's what we get for putting a cursed object that we never fully understood to begin with in a management position. But, still, that bunny just keeps going and going. . . . Tremendous work ethic. Its recent predilection for rhyme and limericks, though. Quite disturbing. Just keep an eye on it during its little to-do."

"You can count on me, Master of the Flies, Father of Lies and Deceit, Old Scratch—"

"Yes, yes," Lucifer said wearily, "a devil by any other name still smells of heat. Now, don't trip over yourself getting up off the ground. Got me?"

"I wish," the principal whispered dreamily.

"What was that?"

Bea "Elsa" Bubb cleared her throat demurely. "I said, 'I wish you'd stop worrying and trust that I will do thy bidding,'" she replied.

"Hmm," the devil said dubiously. "It seemed so much shorter the first time. Oh well. I guess the devil's due for a hearing test. You'll lead an assembly in Rapacia to assure that everything goes down as smoothly as Courvoisier. I'll make the arrangements. Goodbye, Bubb. Mark well my words."

The Big Guy Downstairs hung up the phone.

Bea "Elsa" Bubb leaned against the wall as if she were about to faint.

Though her chat with the Big Guy Downstairs was meant to be a dressing-down of sorts, it only served to prop up the principal's resolve. She was determined to get in his good-for-nothing graces, but she realized that she would need to take an alternate route. Bea "Elsa" Bubb wouldn't earn his respect through fawning, prostrating, or kowtowing. She had to prove her mettle, and meddle she would.

23 · UP THE RIVER

MILTON FELT LIKE a salmon swimming upstream, thrashing against a strong current in hopes of returning to—against all odds—the creek in which he was born. Only instead of a desperate run to his ancestral spawning grounds, Milton was just trying to make it to his locker before shop class with Mr. Nelson "Nine Fingers" Cosgrove.

The hallway was teeming with children, each seemingly going in the opposite direction from Milton. But it wasn't just the physical flow that was wrong. It was everything. Milton's life seemed to be coursing conversely to everyone around him.

Then, with a sudden slam to the shoulder, Milton and his handful of textbooks tumbled to the concrete floor. As he scooped up his books, a boot stomped hard on his copy of *Calculus: Early Transcendentals*. Milton's eyes traveled up a thick denim-clad leg, across an untucked flannel shirt, and settled on the peach-fuzz-topped snarl of Tristan Parker.

"Aren't you supposed to be asleep in your crypt, freak?" Tristan rumbled.

Milton tried to tug his book free. Just as he nearly had it, Tristan abruptly lifted his foot, sending Milton tumbling backward. He fell onto his back, with his backpack both easing his fall and holding him fast to the cold concrete floor. Tristan laughed, high-fiving several of his fellow ruffians as he walked away down the hall.

Milton felt like a tortoise that had been flipped over onto its shell, left struggling and prone as predator birds crowded around it.

This scene—the aftermath of a humiliating bully episode—was not uncommon to him. Neither was the fact that nobody had tried to help. But the looks in the eyes of the children gawking down on him weren't filled with the usual detached amusement and relief that it wasn't *them* on the cold floor of the hallway. Their eyes were full of fear. The kids looked down at him as if he had a deadly, highly contagious disease, which terrified them.

As Milton struggled to right himself, a dark, bony arm thrust from the crowd and reached out to him. Not having a lot of rescue options at this point, Milton took the hand, which hoisted him up with surprising strength.

"Thank you," he said as he stood and stared into the grinning, just-shy-of-crazy face of Necia Alvarado.

She kept smiling at him, expectantly. It freaked Milton out. It made him think that they were having a conversation that he wasn't aware of.

"Well," Milton said to end the near-painful awkwardness, "I've got to get to class. Thanks again."

He turned toward his locker, which had been only a few yards away all along. It was like someone drowning while a life preserver floated, unnoticed, just out of reach. Milton's locker was hard to miss, though, considering it was the only one that had the words ZOMBIE BOY spray-painted on it.

The hairs on the back of Milton's neck stood on end. He turned. There Necia Alvarado stood, still smiling, still staring, still wanting . . . *something*.

"What?" Milton asked.

Necia was wearing her usual black wool overcoat, white stockings, and white leather flats. It was her uniform, though no school uniform policy had ever been instituted at Generica Middle School. Her plain, consistent dress had something to do with her weird religion. But Milton noticed a bright splash of color peeking out from the collar of her drab coat. A jumper with red and white stripes. And the glint of a name badge pinned to her breast: N. ALVARADO. Necia was a candy striper, a volunteer for the local hospital. The realization gave

Milton an uncomfortable sense of déjà vu. Finally, her thin lips stopped their empty grinning.

"I don't want anything," she said with her ruffled, mousy squeak. "But I *do* happen to have something you want."

Milton's stomach rolled around like an old dog attempting a new trick. He wasn't sure what Necia had in mind, but there was a dark confidence about her that he found unsettling. It was as if they were playing a game that she knew she had already won.

"Look," Milton replied cautiously as he dialed the combination to his locker. "I appreciate you helping me and not being an evil dork like everybody else here, but if this has anything to do with your religion—you know, like, 'I've got something you want: peace, faith, and eternal happiness . . . blah blah blah'—I'm not interested. I respect your beliefs and all, whatever they are, but I just—"

"I've got the package you left at the hospital," she interjected. "The gift from your mother."

Milton stopped cold. He suddenly forgot how to breathe. The old dog that was his stomach had been put down.

Necia resumed her grinning. "Want to keep playing?" she continued. "*Fine.* The package you left in Damian's room at the very moment he passed away. Does that ring any bells?"

Milton traded his scuffed textbooks for some others

in his locker. He tried to act nonchalant but couldn't stop shaking.

"Cat got your tongue?" Necia teased. "Well, if curiosity gets the best of your cat, come by my 'weird church'—the Knights of the Omniversalist Order Kinship. In the basement of the Barry M. Deepe Funeral Parlor on Jordan Avenue. I'll be there tonight, at eight o'clock, after my shift at the hospital."

She turned and walked away, whistling. Milton stared at her scrawny, sharply outlined form as the throng of chattering children slowly absorbed her.

Milton leaned against his locker, slamming the door shut with his back before sliding slowly to the ground. His head throbbed. His fate was indeed in Necia's bony hands. Getting himself arrested wouldn't help his sister or best friend, Virgil, down in Heck.

The warning bell rang.

Great, Milton thought, *and I'll be tardy to boot.*

Just then, Milton was seized by a wave of nervous, crackling sensory overload. The hallway was slick with sharp smells and noises. *Lucky must be awake,* Milton thought. When he was asleep—which was about eighteen hours a day—Milton's eerie, psychic connection with his pet was severed. But when Lucky was alert, Milton experienced temporary bouts of keen animal consciousness.

His nostrils flared, and he could sense dark, twisting fumes that became a taste in the back of his mouth. His freaky hearing could discern a complex path winding through the crowd of kids rushing through the hallway to their next class. Echolocation: navigation through sound waves.

Milton bolted up and dashed through the pathway that only he could sense, snaking through the sea of students like a greased eel.

He plopped himself in his seat at the back of Mr. Nelson "Nine Fingers" Cosgrove's shop class just as the final bell rang. Students and teacher alike gawked as Milton made it to his seat with an athletic grace the likes of which they had never seen.

At least Milton had managed to dodge another in a seemingly endless string of personal humiliations. His stomach growled loudly. What he wouldn't give for a live mouse right about now, he thought as he coughed up an imaginary hairball.

24 · iN MARM'S WAY

MARLO CRINKLED IN her plastic-coated chair. It was as if her butt were waged in a crackling, ever-shifting war of discomfort against her seat.

It doesn't just smell like chicken soup, she thought as she wrinkled her nose. *It smells like years and years of chicken soup . . . every chicken soup . . . chicken soup starring some long-extinct, prehistoric chicken, boiled along with mothballs.*

The class was Necroeconomics, a curriculum heavy on burglary and safecracking, with the promise of elective classes in blackmail and confidence games for advanced students. Normally, this would have fascinated Marlo. But her teacher, Ms. Mandelbaum—an old, two-hundred-fifty-pounds-and-counting teacher who seemed intent on being referred to as "Marm"—sucked all the life out of her potentially interesting lessons. Perhaps it was because she, like everything else in the room, was encased in the same stinky see-through rubber that was underneath Marlo's disgruntled derriere.

It was as if Ms. Mandelbaum were a piece of exceptionally ugly dry cleaning, sealed inside of a tight, zippered garment bag for all eternity. Or a fatty cut of animated meat testing the strength of its cling wrap.

The rows of desks were surrounded by a jumble of decor more fitting for a lavish drawing room than a classroom. Perhaps Ms. Mandelbaum saw herself as the hostess of an elegant soiree rather than a daisy-pushing "deaducator" of young kleptos.

A large screen descended from the ceiling, announcing yet another taunting advertisement for the supreme spoils of Mallvana.

THIS CLASS IS BROUGHT TO YOU BY JESÚS CHRIST SUPERSTORE, LOCATED ON THE SECOND TIER OF BEAUTIFUL, EVERLASTING MALLVANA.

A throng of rapturous young people with long hair, flowing robes, and sandals dance together against a stark white background. Hands entwined, they spin, laughing, around a tall, bearded Hispanic man.

"Hola!" the man calls out, waving the camera closer. "Jesús here! And welcome to Jesús Christ Superstore!"

The crowd of young people sing together in perfect harmony.

"Jesús Christ Superstore. Prices so low you'll come back for more!"

Jesús looks around at his disciples and laughs.

"Sure, I often get confused with that other guy." He grins. "No biggie. But even though I can't save your eternal soul, I can sure save you *mucho dinero*!"

The throng of giggling acolytes collapses at the man's feet.

"Whatever you need, whatever you want . . . it's all here," Jesús says. "Everything from Abyssinian cats and accordions to zebra-skin rugs and zoot suits. And if you find a better deal"—Jesús points to the glowing aura over his head—"I'll eat my halo!"

The crowd of young people wave a rainbow of varied currency in the air.

"And, unlike some places, I accept all denominations! Adios!"

JESÚS CHRIST SUPERSTORE. JESÚS SAVES . . . YOU A WHOLE LOT OF MONEY. ONLY IN MALLVANA.

The girls trembled as one agitated body, twitching for silky, shiny, forbidden things kept out of reach.

"All right, you *farblondzhet* little women," Ms. Mandelbaum said, unzipping the zipper covering her mouth as the lights flickered back on. "Maybe if I told you something about myself, you'd stop looking at me like yesterday's lox!"

Norm discreetly tossed a note on Marlo's desk.

M—
So what went down with the Grabbit?
                                        —N

Marlo scribbled underneath her friend's message.

N—
The Big BAD BuNNy LiKeD OuR
ShopLifting SKiLLz. WANtS me AND
the peRoxiDe pRiNCess to puLL OFF A
ROBBeRy thAt wiLL ReALLy mess up
thiNGs DowN here. InteRESteD in
BeiNG oN my teAm?
                                        —M

Marlo surreptitiously handed the note back to Norm.

"For over twenty years I oversaw the transport of nearly ten million dollars' worth of stolen property," the teacher said, puffing out her swollen, plastic-wrapped cheeks like a shiny blowfish chomping chewing gum. "Back then, dat vuz a lot of *gelt!*"

The note returned to Marlo's desk.

M—
Count me in! I'm sure Takara would want to,
too. Maybe even Jordie, though she seems
more like a free agent. But I wouldn't put it
past Lyon and Bordeaux to make her an
offer she couldn't refuse.
—N

"The newspapers called me 'the most successful fence in the history of New York,' among other things," the teacher snorted, her beady black eyes flickering with the career highlight reel that played in her head. "I vuz a felonious feminist zat helped many a young woman to get her criminal career off the ground . . . not that you girls care, staring at your *pupiks!*"

N—
COOL! GLAD to hAve you ABOARD.
The joB involves steALing—
I'm pRACtiCALLy positive—the
HopeLess DiAmonds! I've ALReADy
Been fooLing ARound with
some scenARios And tActics.
With you And TAKARA, we'LL
totALLy "ROCK" this jeweL thing,
"stone" COLD!
—M

Marlo tossed the note back and began doodling in the margins of her binder paper, creating criminal equations with little x's and diamonds.

The note was plopped quickly back onto her paper. She unfolded it.

Look up.

There was Ms. Mandelbaum, glowering down at Marlo beneath painted brows that held her high sloping forehead back like two pencil-greased dams. She slapped Marlo hard across the face. The Saran-Wrapped smack echoed through the sudden hush of the room.

"I've seen your type many times before," the teacher seethed, fogging up the inside of her plastic coating. "You think you're all that and a side of matzo. *But you're bupkes . . . BUPKES.* Do you understand?"

Marlo rubbed her stinging cheek. Though it hurt, it helped her to focus on what needed to be done: proving everyone wrong, in a big, bad, bunny way.

"Yes, *Marm,*" Marlo said, staring her teacher dead in the eyes. "I'm bupkes. And you can *kiss* my *bup.*"

A rap at the door stopped the teacher's plastic palm from striking Marlo's cheeky cheek a second time.

"Who is it?" the teacher barked.

The door creaked open. In rolled Poker Alice in her wheelchair. With just the lower part of her body encased in ribbons of white plaster, she resembled a mummy on Casual Friday. Her neck brace restricting the movement of her head, she wheeled herself into Ms. Mandelbaum's eye-line.

"Hello, Marm," Poker Alice said. "I wanted to come by and personally introduce—"

Poker Alice spotted Marlo on the edge of her sight. She shifted her wheelchair with an angry jerk simply to glare hotly at the girl for a second, then jerked back to continue her conversation.

"—your new teacher's aide."

In behind Poker Alice walked a stocky, big-boned girl with eyes set a few millimeters too far apart and with the flared nostrils of a snorting bull. Like the other girls, she wore an oversized grandma sweatshirt, hers reading, WRINKLED WAS NOT ONE OF THE THINGS I WANTED TO BE WHEN I GREW UP.

There was something familiar and instantly dislikable about the girl, Marlo thought. By her furtive glances, it looked as if she recognized Marlo as well but was trying to hide the fact.

"Meet Amandi Firofnu," Poker Alice said with a slight smirk.

The girl blew a strand of blond hair from her face and smiled. "Hello, girls," Amandi said huskily.

Marlo shivered. The girls looked at each other, bewildered.

"Velcome to our little family, *bubeleh*," Ms. Mandelbaum said as she gestured to a small desk next to hers.

The girls winced as Amandi's bulk tested the tiny chair's structural integrity.

Ms. Mandelbaum wrote Amandi's name on the chalkboard, then waddled to her desk with crinkly squeaks.

"It's nice to zee such a healthy young woman for a change. I'm sure with such a large, accommodating frame comes a large, accommodating mind, yes?"

"Oh yeah. Right," Amandi replied, swallowing a tiny lump beneath the high, bunched collar of her sweatshirt. "I know a lot about"—she looked past the teacher's shoulder at the chalkboard—"necroeconomics."

The teacher stared at her expectantly.

"Um," Amandi continued, "it's like . . . regular economics, only . . . *necro*. Deader. Not alive at all."

Ms. Mandelbaum nodded faintly. "So"—she hesitated—"you're zaying that the underworld economy is dictated *by* and supported *through* a vast network of exchanges, most of vich occur beneath ze surface?"

Amandi bobbed her squarish head in agreement. "*Exactly*. Well said, Ms. Mandelbaum."

"Call me *Marm*." The teacher grinned. Appeased, Ms. Mandelbaum walked over to the chalkboard. "Finally, a *maidel* with some *saichel* between her ears," she said while grabbing a stack of papers from her desk. "I was ze upper crust of the lower order, *bubeleh*, back on ze Surface. I helped many young ladies like yourself off ze streets and into other people's wallets—"

"It sounds like you were a veritable *Marm* Teresa," Marlo said, her sarcasm level set dangerously high.

The teacher stormed angrily toward Marlo's desk, like a hippo with hemorrhoids.

Amandi stood up suddenly. "Ms. Mandelbaum . . . *Marm*," she interjected, "don't let this little, um . . . *maidel* waste your time when you have so much knowledge to share with us."

The steam went out of Ms. Mandelbaum's kettle. She fidgeted, rustling in her plastic wrap like a restless slab of deli meat.

"Why don't you tell us about being a"—Amandi looked at the blackboard—"*fence*. Isn't that about hiding precious things like, say, jewels until the heat's off? Where would one hide something of incredible value down here in Heck? Hypothetically, of course."

The teacher arched her penciled eyebrow at Amandi.

"*Hypothetically,*" Ms. Mandelbaum continued with caution, "Sadia vould be a logical choice, because it vould be like breaking into a prison . . . and who in zere right mind would vant to break *into* a prison?"

Sadia, Marlo scribbled in the margin of her notebook. *Perfect hiding place for diamonds.*

Ms. Mandelbaum hastily grabbed a stack of papers from her desk and tossed them to Amandi.

"But enough of hypotheticals," she grumbled. "Pass these tests out and let us see exactly vat ve have to verk with here. And I vant to hear the sounds of happy pencils dancing all 'Hava Nagila' across test papers."

As Amandi distributed the papers, she leaned over Marlo and winked knowingly. Why was this freakishly familiar teacher's aide being nice to her? Marlo wondered as she looked down at her test paper.

1. A stimulative meta-fiscal policy combined with a restrictive monetary policy will necessarily cause:

(A) gross domestic product to increase.

(B) *totally* gross domestic product to, like, *decrease.*

(C) interest rates to fall.

All Marlo knew was that her own personal interest rate couldn't possibly fall any lower. Next to the question, she wrote the name of the new teacher's aide:

AMANDI FIROFNU.

She started playing around with the letters, like they were the word puzzles her mother did on Sunday mornings.

MAN>iA RoFihuf.

I wonder if she still does those dumb puzzles? Marlo thought, still scribbling on her paper.

DiAhAm RiFFuoh.

When you think of all the stuff Mom could have been doing, solving really important puzzles, like how she got stuck living in Kansas raising two creepy kids . . .

Marlo's pencil fell from her hand and rolled gently off her desk and onto the floor. She looked up at the new teacher's aide. "Amandi" looked up from her reading. She grinned—a smile that, in its feigned warmth, became so cold it made Marlo shiver—then gave a dainty wave.

DAmiAh RuFFiho.

25 · CROSSING JORDAN

ACROSS THE STREET from the Barry M. Deepe Funeral Parlor, Milton fidgeted. His hands, balled into fists, burrowed deep inside the pockets of his navy blue Windbreaker.

Why am I doing this? he wondered anxiously. *This doesn't feel right at all. But I've got to get that stupid package.*

"Milton!" Necia called from across the street.

Milton could feel Lucky rustling around nervously in his new backpack. It typically took Lucky weeks to break in a new backpack, achieving that perfect ferrety musk-to-hairball ratio, but this bout of agitation was unusual even for his normally high-strung pet.

"What is it?" Milton asked, peering inside. Lucky wriggled out of the bag.

"Lucky!" Milton shouted as his ferret scurried behind a nearby tree. "I don't have time for this."

He knelt down to his apprehensive pet.

"What gives?"

Lucky hissed and spun in place several times before lying down in a tight, unyielding coil.

"Milton!" Necia yelled. "C'mon! They're waiting for us!"

Lucky's nostrils flared in rapid pulses, tasting the air wafting from the funeral home and not liking its flavor.

"So I take it you're staying," Milton said to Lucky, who—in polecat protest—had succeeded in becoming a dense, immovable object.

Milton sighed, took off his jacket, and laid it over Lucky.

"I'll be back in a flash," he murmured comfortingly. "Promise."

Milton rose, took a deep breath of crisp evening air, and crossed Jordan Avenue to the other side.

Necia grabbed Milton tightly by the hand, smiling fervently into his face. "I knew you'd come." She grinned triumphantly. "It's destiny."

"It's blackmail," Milton snapped back. "So, I'm here. Can I have my package now?"

Necia smelled of bleach, lemons, and hospital astringent. She jutted out her sharp chin. Her smile became faraway and cold.

"No, silly," she said with a dismissive shake of her head. "You don't get it back *that* easy."

She tugged him toward an alley on the side of the

funeral parlor. Beyond an overflowing Dumpster was a purple door with gold lettering: KOOKs DOWN BELOW.

"You've got to come down for a visit first," she squeaked. "We're dying to lead them . . . I mean, *they're dying to meet you!*"

Milton cocked his eyebrow at the sign. "KOOKs?" he asked.

"The Knights of the Omniversalist Order Kinship," Necia replied while yanking him through the door. "The subordinate chapter of the lower Midwest sect."

"How fitting," Milton commented dryly as they descended a dark, narrow staircase. Each tread of his sneakers and Necia's hard leather hospital shoes caused the wooden steps to groan in complaint.

A man wearing a blue robe and a stern expression guarded another door. The gold star on his lapel featured a pair of crossed swords. The man's most prominent fashion accessory, however, was his bloodstained butcher's apron.

"Greetings, Junior Knight Necia," the man said.

Milton's eyes widened, fixated on the man's grisly smock. Necia let go of Milton's hand and stared at the brown-red splotches.

"Did I miss something?" she said weakly. "I thought I was supposed to bring the sacri—" Necia looked over at Milton with discretion. "The guest," she concluded.

The man looked down at his apron. "Oh, this?" he said, stretching the blood-blotched fabric. "We just got a shipment of Rhode Island Reds at work. Good, meaty birds. I had to hurry, chop-chop, to get here on time."

Necia smiled and clasped the guard's hands.

"Greetings, Sentinel Shane," she replied as the two raised their arms together, like a bridge.

Together, they chanted, *"Life is but a passage, a bridge forged of breath . . ."* They bowed their heads and released one another's grasp. *". . . but it was made to pass through us; each span shall fall in death."*

Their arms hung limp at their sides. Milton felt that he should have chosen this moment to flee, but he was entranced by this creepy rendition of "London Bridge Is Falling Down."

"They are waiting for you," Sentinel Shane said. He stepped aside and opened the door for the two children. The harsh, reflected echoes of amateur singing stumbled out of the basement, as if each note were desperately rushing away from the others.

"Though darkness be over me, my rest a stone, in my dreams I'll be, nearer, my lord, to thee," the Knights of the Omniversalist Order Kinship warbled as one. *"I run across the overpass that cleaves the sky, suspended by sacrifice, all to be, nearer, my lord, to thee, nearer to . . ."*

The congregation's song screeched to a halt as all twenty-six eyes were trained on the two children who crept into the basement.

The church smelled of warm candle wax, pungent incense, and years of accumulated dust and mold. It also reeked of vinegar and sweat, like someone had been cooking up a batch of fish and chips in an old sneaker.

"Welcome, Junior Knight Necia," a sharp-featured man said, standing stiffly at the altar and extending the billowing arms of his robe outward in greeting. "And welcome, Milton, to our hallowed temple."

A whisper spread across the congregation, traded in hushes and gasps. The word whispered was "bridge."

"Who . . . who are—" Milton stammered. He stopped suddenly. "How do you know my name?"

The man at the altar smirked. "I am the Guiding Knight," he answered, straightening his purple velvet scarf affectedly. "And all of us here know the name of he who will hasten the Last Days and lead us over his back to our rightful place."

"So may it ever be," murmured the small congregation of hooded acolytes crowding the basement church.

Milton furrowed his brow and looked from knight to knight in hopes of catching the faintest glimmer of sanity.

26 · SACRiFiCES MUST BE MADE

"YOUR CHURCH, YOUR religion . . . what does it mean?" Milton spluttered. "Why am I here?" He looked over at Necia, who grinned like a fisherman holding her day's prize catch. *"For real."*

The Guiding Knight stepped off the dais. The congregation parted as he floated across the scuffed wooden floor to Milton.

"Life is a labyrinth through which we would wander blindly were it not for an all-powerful hand that guides us on our way," the Guiding Knight explained, offering words unencumbered by practical meaning. "This hand belongs to a supreme being that makes and manages the Omniverse, where everything is possible—for the 14,217 people who believe in it, that is. The Knights of the Omniversalist Order Kinship is founded on the belief in the existence of the everlasting everyplace and that life is but the appetizer for the sumptuous feast that is death. For death is an all-you-can-eat buffet of interminable joy for the righteous, a place where all answers lay . . ."

"*Lie*," corrected Milton. "And believe me, the only thing death holds is more questions. Plus, there's no feast, unless you like undercooked liver and overcooked brussels sprouts."

The blue sea of robes rustled nervously, as if an ill, foreboding wind had whispered across it.

"Well," the Guiding Knight said flatly, "it doesn't matter so much whether you believe in us but whether we believe in *you*. And we do. Because you're the Bridge to the other side. And you're going to help prepare our paradise, turn down the sheets of the Omniverse that awaits, uncork the champagne, and put metaphoric mints on the pillows."

Milton stared at the congregation, aghast. "You're all a bunch of kooks," he murmured.

"Exactly," the Guiding Knight replied.

Milton backed into a tall, dark knight, standing just behind him.

"Don't try it, dude," the knight said, placing his bronzed hands on Milton's shoulders. "You're, like, our ticket out of this gnarly dump and to the totally bodacious place beyond."

The Guiding Knight nodded his head toward the dais. "Warder Chango," he ordered. "Take the Bridge to the altar."

Necia followed closely, nervous and excited. It was then that Milton saw the marble altar. It was like a Stone Age twin bed, with a pillow at either end, one in the upper left-hand corner, and the other at the lower right-hand corner. Next to the altar was a nightstand supporting two obsidian knives. Milton had a feeling that this bed's purpose wasn't for spontaneous catnaps.

The Guiding Knight joined him at the dais.

"You have entered our portals, therefore submitting to your destiny," the man said as he rolled up his robe's billowy blue sleeves. "Trust your guide and she will lead you safely through."

Necia joined Milton's side. "It's okay, Milton," she said, interlacing her bony fingers with his. "We'll travel to death together, hand in hand, and prepare the Omniverse for the End of the Last Days and the Beginning of the Next Time."

Milton shot her a filthy sideways glance and tore loose from her grip. *"Trust your guide,"* he spat. "Like how I trusted you when you were all fake-nice and blackmailed me here, knowing it was a one-way trip."

Necia turned to Milton, quivering with crazed conviction.

"But you're the Bridge!" she yelped. "The One! Our Savior!"

Milton shook his head with disgust. "I'm not a bridge, a savior, or the one," he said, his eyes bugging out behind his thick glasses. "I'm just a socially awkward eleven-year-old who died, spent some time in the underworld, and came back by harnessing lost souls in a big balloon made of shirts and pants. You're just a bunch of losers who can't cut it in this world, so you think you're going to be all that and a bag of chips in the next. Believe me, I've seen death, and it sucks. *Bigtime.* And you'll *still* be losers."

There was a profound, awkward silence, like when someone farts in an elevator.

"Junior Knight Necia," the Guiding Knight uttered. "Do you merit the honor we confer, and are you worthy of the trust with which we are about to invest you?"

Necia crouched and bowed before him, her forehead nearly touching her pointy white-stockinged knee. "Yes, Guiding Knight," she murmured. "I will do all within my power to add to our order."

The Guiding Knight turned and grasped the knives, hefting them in his hands to gauge their weight. He cleared his throat. "O, may the Golden Bridge thus be lengthened, becoming the brighter for these two spans, and be strengthened for the great work we strive to do," he declared as he lifted the two knives into the air above his blue silk hood.

He nodded to Necia, who rose, took off her long wool coat, and straightened her candy-striper jumper.

"Junior Knight Necia," he said, "as the scriptures state, you and the Bridge shall cross together, he offering the means for you to travel back and forth, to alert us that paradise awaits."

"It doesn't work that way," Milton protested, as Warder Chango's strong hands pressed down onto his trembling shoulders. "Death is serious. It's not an amusement park where you get your hand stamped and come back whenever you want. I was a mistake. . . ."

"Nothing is a mistake," the Guiding Knight replied with flecks of foam on his tight, quivering lips. "Everything happens as it should. Warder, the time is nigh."

Warder Chango looked at the clock on the wall. "Actually, it's only a quarter till."

The Guiding Knight sighed with the supreme frustration that only the leader of a death cult can fully know. "Warder Chango . . . *dude* . . . what I meant was . . ."

Just behind the Guiding Knight, Milton saw the gift that he had come here to get in the first place, on a table draped with velvet and sitting between two long purple candles. Without thinking, Milton stamped the foot of the warder behind him with all his might.

"Oww!!" Warder Chango yelled. "I'm *totally* gonna lose that nail again!"

Milton rushed to the table, grabbed his gift, knocked over the candles, and leapt off the dais. He charged through the robed congregation—who were paralyzed like tranquilized sheep—and to the basement door.

"Milton!" screamed Necia, seated on the altar. "Stop it! You're ruining everything!"

Just as Milton's hand touched the doorknob, the door flung open. On the other side stood Sentinel Shane, all six feet six of him, glowering down at Milton.

Milton staggered backward. The room spun into streaking snapshots. Stunned, lost faces. Glittering gold badges. Purple velvet sashes. And the smell of incense and burning velvet.

"Fire!" screamed a woman waggling her finger at the burning velvet table.

The congregation churned in confusion. The Guiding Knight stepped to the edge of the dais, extended his arms, palms outstretched, and addressed his panicked flock.

"In the world where death comes not, may we realize the happiness of serving thee forever," he bellowed. "Now someone grab that miserable little boy so I can lie him out and slice him open!!"

Lay, Milton thought as he searched the hot, cramped basement for a way out.

"So may it ever be," chanted the congregation as they circled Milton. Then, to the left of the dais, Milton saw a door, slightly ajar. He dashed toward it. Someone

grabbed his backpack, stopping him cold, his sneakers squeaking on the floor.

A small Filipino knight held tight. "Be a good boy and sacrifice yourself!" the man scolded.

"Don't let him go, Chaplain Charlie!" a willowy woman screeched.

Milton tried to jab him with his elbows, but the chaplain held him at arm's length. *Lucky for Lucky,* Milton thought, *he had the good sense to stay put. I should have listened to him.*

Tucking the gift under his arm, Milton wormed himself free of his backpack's straps.

Chaplain Charlie flew back onto the ground, clutching the backpack that, a half-second before, had been worn by the boy known to him as the Bridge, the supposed key to the man's everlasting soul.

27 · BRiDGE iN TROUBLED WATER

MILTON SNAKED ACROSS the basement floor, darting and
dodging the various knights with frenetic ferret energy.
He ducked into the church's dimly lit antechamber and
locked the door behind him. Scanning the cheerless
room, he noticed an elderly female knight crumpled on
a faded yellow chesterfield, snoring softly. He padded
carefully across the floor, gently pressed open another
door on the opposite end of the room, and peeked into
the adjoining hallway. He could hear Sentinel Shane
and Warder Chango talking.

"Dude," Warder Chango said, "the Guiding Knight
wants us to check out the antechamber. The little
Bridge dude locked the door on the other side. I'd join

you but my foot, man, is axed. I just know my nail is, like, totally . . ."

Milton could hear someone slamming against the other door, trying to break it down. He stole down the hallway, away from the voices, his back sliding against the dingy velvet wallpaper.

Bronze light fixtures on the ceiling cast dim, golden circles down the hallway. Milton followed them around the corner to a pair of metal doors, surrounded by potted palms. He pushed the doors open as the voices behind him gained in volume and clarity.

The doors swung open with a sluggish squeak. Inside the dark, grim room were crates, a conveyor belt leading to a crackling furnace, flowers—orchids and lilies, mostly—bags of popcorn, cases of generic soda, and . . . *a casket*.

A-TISKET, A-TASKET, A GREEN AND YELLOW CASKET™ read the sticker on the side. *A sticker?* Milton thought with distaste. *How tacky!* By the looks of it, though, the sticker was the only thing holding it together. As advertised, the casket was bright, bile green and hornet yellow. It looked like something Batman would use to hastily bury a supervillain's lesser henchman. It was made of plywood, with simulated brass handles that weren't even on completely straight.

Milton shivered and stepped cautiously toward the casket. He needed to look inside. He had no idea why. It was as if the casket were at the bottom of some crater, with Milton standing on the edge, unable to resist its subtle, sloping incline. Part of it, truth be told, was his obsessive-compulsive disorder—the beckoning lure of the sticker's slightly peeling corner was too powerful for him to resist picking at.

He stopped before the casket. Milton ignored the overwhelming urge to peel the sticker; instead, he grasped the lid tentatively and lifted it. A blast of pungent vapor that reminded him of biology class hit him in the face. The smell made his eyes tear up and gave him an instant headache. Through the blur of tears, he saw a husky boy in a cheap navy blue blazer and red striped clip-on tie. The boy's cruel features were slathered with thick orange makeup. His lip was curled into a sneer. Of course Milton would be in this mortuary basement, looking down into the face of the boy he had helped put here.

Damian.

28 · FRIENDS IN LOW PLACES

THE RAPACIA ASSEMBLY was teeming with whispering girls and snickering boys. Up on the auditorium stage were a half dozen male and female teachers shifting uncomfortably on beige metal chairs, save for Poker Alice, whose metal chair had wheels.

"What do you think this is all about?" Norm asked Marlo.

Marlo shrugged. "Got me," she replied. "All I know is that it's taking away from my valuable robbery planning time."

Norm looked at Marlo, her eyes wide with concern. "What if they know?"

Marlo chewed the place on her lip that her mother wouldn't let her pierce.

"Then we're between a screwdriver and a piece of wood," she murmured. "You know, royally—"

A pair of hooves clacked across the gleaming mahogany stage. Marlo's mouth went dry. A hush washed across the crowd like thick, suffocating syrup. A musky odor like that of a wet goat that had rolled in its own dung wafted from the stage, forcing its way into Marlo's nostrils before collecting at the back of her throat.

Bea "Elsa" Bubb gripped the sides of the lectern, her claws wrenching the sides until the wood screamed.

"Girls, boys, teachers, and assorted demons," Principal Bubb said, her voice crackling over the public-address system. "You're here today so that I can make one thing perfectly clear: *Nothing*"—her double-barrel-shotgun eyes fixed on Marlo—"and *no one* is going to interfere with Mallvana Day, where the Grabbit is to cut the ribbon—as much as it can, having no hands—to open a new wing of the afterlife's most prodigious shopping experience: Debtopia. *This is a very big deal.* It's part of the Eternal Quality Unification Adherence Law, where the Powers That Be and the Powers That Be Evil grudgingly work together to assure a strong, stable afterlife."

The side of Marlo's face began to tingle. Sure enough, the creepy new teacher's aide, Amandi Firofnu—aka Damian, she was sure of it—was staring at her.

"She" was the spitting image of Damian, the bane

of both her brother's existence and his *non*existence. But why would he be here, in drag, in Rapacia? It didn't make any sense. It's not like the Powers That Be Evil needed to send in moles to dig up dirt on people. It had never seemed particularly shy about the direct approach. Until she knew more, Marlo intended to just play along, hiding her knowledge of Amandi's true identity like an ace up her sleeve. (*Great,* Marlo thought, *now Poker Alice has* me *thinking in gambling metaphors.*)

Marlo's other cheek began to prickle. It was that boy she'd seen in the hall, observing her in his surreptitious way a dozen or so rows away. Marlo blushed, which she couldn't stand, because—with her scrupulously maintained pallor—it made her feel like a sunburned snowman. She also hated that her own body had betrayed her, sabotaging her attempt to appear aloof by broadcasting her interest in bright crimson.

Bea "Elsa" Bubb surveyed the crowd of restless youth with obvious disgust.

"Tomorrow, before classes, all children will be herded to Mallvana to attend the ceremony."

The children twittered with excitement. The principal did her best to dampen this wave of enthusiasm as quickly as possible.

"All of you will be held on a very tight leash," she added. "Some literally. There will be no disruptions, as the eyes of Heck—the entire afterlife, for that matter—will be trained upon us."

The twitters were now replaced by resigned sighs and groans. The girls and boys were still happy they would be spending an hour in Mallvana—highly supervised or not; they just didn't want their teachers to know that. That way, it would *still* be something that the children could whine and moan about. They couldn't take that away.

This development left Marlo precious little time to transform her cracked team of prepubescent dweebs into a crack team of machine-perfect thieves. At least she had worked out the major points of the job, preying upon the "vanity, greed, and weakness" (thank you, Ms. O'Malley) of her soon-to-be dupes. And, since Marlo's ultimate plan depended on Lyon's, she had sketched out a "can't-miss" ploy of nabbing one of the diamonds from Keats, the bird-demon stagecoach driver, and left it on Lyon's chair before the ceremony so that Lyon would think that *she* had one up on Marlo. Playing fellow players was what being a girl was all about.

Principal Bubb drummed her talons atop the walnut podium. When amplified, they sounded like an army of giant ants marching off to battle in wooden clogs.

"Now, it is my extreme displeasure to introduce the next part of our assembly," she announced with a sour scowl. Marlo noticed that just offstage was a tall, elegant yet frumpy old woman wringing her hands nervously. The woman smiled a radiant, bucktoothed grin.

"Please give a tepid welcome for our next manda-
tory speaker—another contractual obligation of the
Galactic Order Department—all the way from . . ."

The principal tasted the words in her mouth, rolling
them around with the look of a child forced to eat some
terrible food and hoping for an opportunity to spit it
out into her napkin and feed it to the family dog.

". . . *up there*. Ms. Roosevelt."

Bea "Elsa" Bubb waddled to her seat while Ms.
Mandelbaum and Poker Alice rolled their eyes in deri-
sion. The auditorium filled with awkward applause.

Ms. Roosevelt, her white-feathered angel wings jut-
ting out of her dowdy floral-print dress, fluttered onto
the stage. One of the male teachers, a man with a
golden crown and stiff, matching robe, stood up and extended his hand. Ms. Roosevelt briefly considered the
hand, then waggled her finger at the man and grinned.

"Nice try, Mr. Midas," she scolded. The man
shrugged his shoulders and returned to his chair,
which, Marlo noticed, shone like freshly minted gold.

Ms. Roosevelt cleared her throat as she took her
place behind the podium. "I know that your young
selves can only take so much lecturing," she said, her
smile casting a light and a warmth that she spread
across the audience with gentle sweeps of her head.
"Believe it or not, I was once a gangly young thing, impatient to engage with the world, thinking I knew
everything there was to know. But we never know it all,

for there is never enough to know. We grow only by doing what we think we cannot."

The room grew quiet despite itself. Even the teachers seemed to be captivated, albeit reluctantly, by Ms. Roosevelt. No wonder the faculty of Heck seemed loath to allow angels equal stage time. Not only did it set back their agenda of making every child feel ugly, stupid, and worthless, but it was also a painful reminder of a grace they would never know.

"In my lifetime—both on the Stage and *up there,* as Principal Bubb put it—I have learned a few things that could, hopefully, give you a little clarity in these dim times," Ms. Roosevelt said soberly. "It is, after all, better to light one small candle than to curse the darkness."

Okay, that particular piece of fortune-cookie wisdom went way over Marlo's head, but the angel's presence— her soothing sparkle—was enough to drive the message home nonetheless.

"Charity is a subject that is very close to my heart," Ms. Roosevelt relayed with tenderness. "It starts with being generous *with yourself.* Being your own friend. Because, unless you are, you can't expect to be friends with anyone else."

The angel took a quick breath. In that momentary pause, Marlo could hear Lyon's voice—that sugary, breathy yet sharp inflection, like a pink Hello Kitty razor blade—pierce the silence.

"Sounds like what ugly girls tell themselves when they can't make friends."

Bordeaux—the living punctuation to whatever Lyon said—snickered predictably. Lyon looked back at Marlo and smiled slyly, clutching Marlo's note in her hand.

The bait has been taken, Marlo thought with self-satisfaction.

"This place, Rapacia, holds with it opportunity," the angel continued. "Nothing is set in stone. So in this realm of greed and selfishness, I will leave you with a parting thought—"

"Don't let the saloon door hit you in the hiney," Poker Alice quipped to Ms. Mandelbaum out of the corner of her wrinkled, tobacco-stained mouth.

"Shhh!" scolded Ms. O'Malley.

Marlo was liking her swashbuckling pirate of a teacher more and more.

"When you cease to make a contribution, you begin to die," Ms. Roosevelt said in a voice dripping with certainty. "*Really* die. So, in this way, when you give to others, you're really giving to yourself: the gift of eternal life."

Ms. Roosevelt paused, looked out into the audience, searching the faces with eyes leaking tears, and beamed.

"Thank you."

And, just like that, the angel glided off the stage in

one long sweeping gesture, as if she were signing her name with her whole body in a great, cursive flourish. She was gone.

The crowd was speechless. Marlo realized in that moment that most of her life had been spent swinging from one criminal act to another. Just a skinny ape in secondhand clothing avoiding herself, stealing moments, always in motion, either plotting the future or running from the past.

I've got a job to do, and I can't let some old hag with a halo screw that up, Marlo told herself as she wiped away the tears stinging her eyes. *I've got to do it. For the Grabbit. For the girls. For myself.*

Norm patted her on the back comfortingly.

Marlo had indeed made a friend down here. But she still felt that she was a long way from—as Ms. Roosevelt had put it—being her *own* friend.

Just then, a blast of stale breath puffed into Marlo's ear.

"Hello, girls."

Startled, Marlo and Norm turned. There was Amandi, with her arms folded on the back of the two girls' chairs. Creepy, Marlo thought, how she snuck up on them like that.

"What do you want?" Marlo asked suspiciously.

Up on the stage, Principal Bubb prodded Amandi with her eyes.

"Nothing," Amandi said unconvincingly. "Just a little chat. Just us girls." She scooted her chair closer. "Do you ever miss anyone? Like . . . *family*? Wish you could, you know, get in touch with them somehow?"

Marlo and Norm raised their eyebrows at one another as if to say, "This girl is both crazy ugly *and* ugly crazy."

Onstage, the teachers who could rise from their chairs did, while Poker Alice urged her metal throne forward in fitful, labored bursts. Principal Bubb clacked offstage, her burning gaze flaring with every hoof-fall.

Amandi's eyes darted nervously back and forth between the stage and the two stone-faced girls in front of her. The stocky girl sighed.

"This isn't working," Amandi muttered to herself. She cleared her throat with all the prim femininity of a jellyfish being fed down a garbage disposal and leaned in close to Marlo. "I know about the robbery," she whispered.

Marlo's stomach and heart traded places. She fought to tame her budding freak-out in hopes that it remained a freak-*in*.

"What *are* you talking about?" Marlo finally managed.

Amandi smirked. "I overheard a certain airhead

heiress talking about it," she replied, nodding toward Bordeaux, who was staring out at the exit stairwell.

"The escalator is broken," Bordeaux informed a passing demon.

Marlo took a deep breath to steady her nerves. "Look, I don't know what Flintstones vitamins you're both on," she said, "so why don't you just—"

"Here's how it's going down," Amandi interrupted. She sat back in her metal chair smugly. It screamed under the sudden shift in weight. "I'm on your team," she said flatly. "You have no choice. Not with what I know."

Marlo sighed with resignation. Poker Alice wheeled back onstage, chuffing and wheezing like a decommissioned steam engine. She grabbed Midas's golden chair with one arm, while wheeling herself away with the other.

Marlo rubbed her temples. She needed to contain Amandi before she spilled the jelly beans. She had no idea what Amandi/Damian's deal was, but she knew one thing: if Amandi was an enemy, then she would be exactly where Marlo wanted her . . . *close.*

29 · POPPING OFF

MILTON WAS TRANSFIXED by Damian's peaceful expression. It wasn't "peaceful" in the sense that it would bring peace to others. Far from it. It was more like he was at peace with how uncomfortable everyone else was around him.

Milton looked around the basement and its maze of crates. There didn't seem to be another way out. Crawling out through a roaring furnace wasn't an option, unless Milton wanted to escape as smoke. What was that weird conveyor belt about, anyway? He noticed a little motorized trolley thing leading to the furnace, which had a bunch of controls on the front. The Barry M. Deepe Funeral Parlor must be very fussy about maintaining a specific temperature, he thought as he surveyed the temperature gauge, the needle of which hovered at a toasty seven-hundred degrees Celsius.

Milton heard voices from outside the door.

"Put some hustle in your disco, Dominic."

"Don't be dissing my disco, Marco."

His heart in his throat and a slick coat of cold sweat trickling down his back, Milton searched for a place to hide. A few crates away from Damian's coffin was the Get Butter Soon costume he had left in the hospital parking lot and that—obviously—had been scooped up by Necia in some weird "saving-his-butt-while-simultaneously-blackmailing-said-butt" way. The crate that it was leaning against was open. Milton removed the lid and climbed inside. It was full of unpopped popcorn. Milton scooted his way down into the quicksand of kernels until just his face peeked above the surface. He gently reached for the lid and slid it closed.

Milton heard a series of wet, explosive coughs.

"Hey, what was that . . . a coffin fit? Get it?"

"Yeah, I got it, Marco," Dominic replied in a low grunt. "It's this embalming fluid they use. I'm allergic to the stuff in a big way. They'll probably have to cremate *me*, for fear of me sneezing and coughing at my own wake!"

Milton could hear the men wheeling in some more crates, then carelessly depositing them with thumps, scrapes, and crashes. A rush of footsteps spilled into the room.

"Holy and merciful God," the Guiding Knight declared with breathless grandiosity, "who answerest prayer and . . . where *is* that little runt?"

"I *so know* I saw him go in here, Guiding Dude," Warder Chango said.

"I think you've been in the sun too long and your brain has wiped out," Sentinel Shane added with disgust. "Why does a surfer even *live* in Kansas?"

The Guiding Knight cleared his throat and addressed the two mortuary workers. "Have you two . . . *gentlemen* . . . seen a boy?"

"Yes," Dominic answered, "I've seen a boy before. This morning, in fact, right before I came to work. He asked me for his allowance."

Marco and Dominic burst into laughter.

Milton breathed a sigh of relief from inside the crate. More footsteps followed.

"Where is he?" Necia whined. "I've got to cross the bridge and guide us to tomorrow before bedtime, or else I'll get in trouble."

Milton had never encountered anyone so eager to be ritualistically murdered. If Necia and the other KOOKs had any clue as to how incredibly boring and irritating death was, they might enjoy their lives more—while they could.

"Brothers and sisters," the Guiding Knight said, "let us not be dismayed, for our heavenly father has promised to strengthen and uphold us by the right hand of his power—"

There was a prolonged pause.

"—so let's look somewhere else."

The KOOKs murmured to one another and filed out of the furnace room. After a moment, Milton could hear more shuffling.

"Well, Marco," Dominic said, "this job can be dirty and hard, but it's never dull."

"You said it, Disco Man," Marco replied.

"I swear, you take your old lady out dancing one night and you get a reputation," Dominic said. "Which reminds me, I got to get a move on, or I'll get an earful."

"Yep, and that dead kid's tightwad stepdad wants more popcorn. Always with the popcorn. Says it was the deceased's favorite. Personally, I just think he's saving his change for a new car. I mean, look at this casket."

"We don't have time to pop the rest . . . unless—"

"Unless what?"

Milton could hear footsteps coming closer.

"Help me with this," Dominic said.

After the shuffle of more footsteps and the squeal of an old dolly, Milton was suddenly tilted sharply to one side and wheeled across the room.

"Hey, Disco Inferno," Marco said. "Not a bad idea."

Milton wasn't quite sure what was going on, but since he was in a crate of unpopped popcorn, he assumed he was going up to the kitchen. Next, he was hoisted up and placed on something mechanical, maybe a dumbwaiter. Once he was in the kitchen,

Milton plotted, he could burst out of the crate and make good his escape. Relief washed over him. And to think he had almost been, you know, *killed*. And what a stupid way to go: at the hands of some dorky death cult. Milton clutched the gift tightly. Well, at least he had managed to steal back the present and avoid getting into hot water.

Milton started to perspire. Maybe he had a fever. He hadn't been sleeping or eating much lately, after all. The second he got home, he'd have a nice, cool bottle of E-Cola—maybe two, phew, he was hot—and something to settle his stomach, perhaps some Jiffy Pop.

Jiffy Pop.

Then it hit Milton, but—unfortunately—by then, it was far too late. His crate, his temporary refuge, had traveled the length of the conveyor belt until it was pitched into the furnace—or, in funeral-home-speak, the crematory. Milton's last thought was of something his British uncle Benny had told him during one of his visits, about how when an old English guy died, his friends would comically refer to his passing as "popping his clogs." And here was Milton, popping a lot more than his clogs, in an event that he would later refer to as getting *Redenbachered.*

30 · MAKING UP IS HARD TO DO

BEA "ELSA" BUBB preened in front of the cracked vanity in the bathroom of her not-so-secret lair. She took a grimy powder puff and tapped it in a marble bowl full of ground pony bones. Next, she thumped the puff across her face until she was the eye of a seething powder hurricane.

"Doesn't Mommy look pwetty for her big day?" she chirped as she nuzzled Cerberus's left head, the neediest of the three.

"You don't have to answer that without a lawyer present," Lilith quipped from the doorway.

Bea "Elsa" Bubb turned suddenly. Cerberus growled and twisted loose from the principal's grasp.

The two females stared at one another, exchanging the same contemptuous gaze.

"Well?" the principal said finally. "Why are you here?"

Lilith smirked. "I hate to intrude upon your beauty regimen," she replied. "Badness knows you need it. But intrude I must. I need you to go to Rapacia now and prepare the staging area for my arrival."

"And you can't prepare it yourself because . . . ?" Principal Bubb grumbled.

"Someone of my stature can't be too careful," Lilith replied. "I could be a target."

Bea "Elsa" Bubb snorted. "Why would anyone view you as a target?" she asked. "I mean, someone who didn't personally know you, of course?"

Lilith put her hand on her waist so that her arm formed a sharp, bony triangle. A curtain of blond hair fell into her face as she glowered down on Bea "Elsa" Bubb, leaving exposed a fierce green eye.

"As you well know, I am indispensable to the Big Guy Downstairs," she said with brittle hostility. "I possess a wealth of information vital to the underworld, not to mention a diverse modeling portfolio!"

Lilith took a deep breath. Bea "Elsa" Bubb could see the creature's ribs poking through her tailored business suit.

"Bottom line," she said calmly, "the Big Guy

Downstairs can't afford to take any chances now, and if I were to come to harm, it would look bad."

"*Fine,*" Bea "Elsa" Bubb said wearily. "I'll do my part. For *him.* Not for you."

She looked at Lilith's gleaming hooves, then down at her own drab, cracked ones. She rubbed them together quickly, buffing them clean.

"What if there are new arrivals?" the principal asked. "Who will—"

"*I* will," Lilith said as she turned to leave. "Before I leave. How hard can it be?"

"But you'll need to assess them and tell them where to—"

"Go. You. *Now,*" Lilith interrupted, glowering at the principal. "You don't have time to dilly, or even dally, for that matter."

Bea "Elsa" Bubb stopped herself. After all, why should she help Lilith?

The devil's advocate glanced at the expensive watch that hung limply on her golden, skeletal wrist. "Your clock is slow," she said, gesturing toward the clock on the wall as she strutted out the door, her tail swishing and sparking behind her.

"It's Limbo, you idiot," Bea "Elsa" Bubb muttered as she swept a collection of toiletries into her old leather bag. "The clocks are all stopped."

She knelt down and gave Cerberus's right head a

scratch. It turned away, punishing its owner for her impending departure. This was, in Bea "Elsa" Bubb's mind, the problem head.

"Aww, sweetums," she said, undeterred. "Don't be that way. Mommy has some business to do, making sure that Rapacia is safe for that bad, bad lady so that she'll be around to thoroughly embarrass when I deliver the diamonds that will be stolen from right under her snooty nose job and fix whatever damage she'll undoubtedly do here."

Bea "Elsa" Bubb teetered upright and gave herself one last once-over in the mirror. She cracked a smile at her reflection. The mirror cracked in kind.

Milton tumbled off the miles-long corkscrew slide and into the kiddie pool full of Ping-Pong balls and garbage. Again.

> "If you've lived a life so bad
> that you drove your parents and teachers mad,
> one day then, perhaps your last,
> you'll have to pay for every disrupted class. . . ."

The lizards performed the sole song of their repertoire, hopping about in their gold lamé suits, on the stage just outside the Gates of Heck.

Milton felt like he was learning a new video game and had just been knocked back to Level One, forced to play the whole thing over again.

The iron gate, festooned with sugared spikes and barbed licorice, squeaked open. Apart from a few somewhat interested toddlers with squirming fingers wedged in their runny noses, no one seemed to even notice Heck's only two-time visitor.

Two other boys plunged down the slide and into the kiddie pool behind him, unfortunately triggering another performance of the official "Unwelcome to Heck" song.

The boys—one, a stocky boy with a bandaged eye, and the other, a gangly Asian boy with a smoldering hand shy an index finger and pinky—had that newbie glaze of disbelief, as if it were all a dream.

If only, Milton thought.

Milton and the boys loitered in silence for several minutes by the YOU MUST BE THIS SHORT TO ENTER HECK sign before a demon guard gathered them, prodding them into the oppressive and depressing Foul Play Ground.

"Welcome to Limbo," the guard sneered, marching the boys along the filthy plastic runner. "Sorry for the wait."

What is going on? Milton wondered. *Where is Principal Bubb?*

The demon guard shoved him and the two other

boys down a hallway and into a room that was frighteningly familiar yet wonderfully devoid of its owner. Here was Milton, once again, in Principal Bubb's not-so-secret lair. Only instead of the lumpy creature he had been dreading to reunite with, he was presented before a slender, sharply dressed woman appraising herself approvingly in front of a full-length mirror. She pouted and posed, hands on her negligible hips, pointing her dainty hooves girlishly. Her smile dimmed as her nose wrinkled at a sudden, disagreeable odor.

The woman turned sharply.

"Excuse the intrusion," the demon guard said meekly. "I was expecting Principal Bubb."

A cold swarm of prickles ran up and down Milton's spine at the sound of the principal's name.

The woman sighed and returned to her reflection, applying a fresh coat of Beriberi to her pursed lips.

"Then I'm sure you're pleasantly surprised," she said. "Blob isn't here right now, so I'm in charge for the next"—she looked down at her watch—"five minutes. So if you're going to disturb me, then be quick about it."

The demon shifted his weight nervously from hoof to hoof. "Right. Sorry. It's just that I have several new arrivals that just passed through the gates."

"Oh," the woman murmured absentmindedly as she preened. "So *that* was what all the noise was about."

Milton was stupefied. Had Limbo changed hands,

or claws, or whatever? Who was this woman who commanded so much fear and deference, yet seemed to know Jack-squat about running an infernal boarding school for postmortem minors? Though the woman was pretty and smelled good, Milton suspected she was like a carnivorous flower that lured insects close with its bright colors and beguiling fragrance before chomping down on them and digesting them slowly.

The woman turned and appraised Milton and the two other young prisoners. Her body shuddered.

"Ugh . . . those dreary, pathetic faces," she said with revulsion. "They positively *reek* of the Surface. The hopelessness, the inefficiency, the blatant disregard for authority . . ."

"Yes," the demon continued, rubbing a scar on his dull gray cheek. "Usually—actually, always—Principal Bubb personally greets the arrivals, and has them assessed, processed, and sent to the circle of Heck best suited for—"

The woman spun around. "No wonder this place is in the state it's in!" she barked. "It's smothered by process! We need a leaner, meaner machine down here, led by someone with enough guts to make knee-jerk decisions, unencumbered by proven methods and procedures."

Wow, Milton thought. *This woman is like a boa constrictor eating her own tail:* totally full of herself.

"Um . . . okay," the demon said after a pause. "So what should I do with . . ."

"Send them off to Sadia on the next stagecoach," she said coolly.

Milton felt as if the air had been knocked out of him.

The demon's face crinkled in surprise. "Without even looking at their files?" he croaked.

The woman smiled, exposing every one of her pearly, pointy teeth. "Look, they are down here in Heck: where the bad kids go," she clarified. "If they didn't want to end up in the worst, mostly beastly circle imaginable, then they should have thought about that up on the Stage." She clapped her hands in three sharp swipes. "See," she added. "Swift, efficient injustice delivered in record time. Now, if you'll excuse me, I've got a ceremony to monopolize."

"*But that's not fair!*" Milton cried out. "We're supposed to have our souls weighed and assessed first! I demand to see—*oww!*"

The demon guard had clopped Milton hard on the ear. Aghast, the woman eyed Milton as if he were a piece of dog poop suddenly gifted with the power of speech. She prodded the demon guard with burning eyes.

"Do something about . . . *that,*" she said, waving her finger at Milton.

The demon blinked his dull eyes. "Of course," he replied before riffling through a bulging gunnysack strapped across his shoulder. He pulled out a filthy kerchief. "Ah," he hissed as he stuffed it into Milton's mouth. "Just your size."

The kerchief tasted like a hobo's boxer shorts.

The demon seized the boys and pitched them into the hallway.

"I've got plenty of spring left in my spork, troublemaker!" he roared. The demon's voice—now a wicked, commanding baritone—exploded and reverberated through the hallway like a clap of thunder. The woman tucked her purse underneath her arm and strode into the hall behind them. Milton could hear her mumble to herself.

"Is someone making popcorn?" the woman murmured.

The demon pitched Milton forward.

"All right, you miserable wretches!" he barked as he herded the boys away. "Next stop: Sadia!"

31 · A STROKE OF LUCKY

LUCKY STIRRED AWAKE across the street from the Barry M. Deepe Funeral Parlor. The sky was darker. The street was still. The smell of humans was faint.

He sniffed his makeshift bed, Milton's navy blue Windbreaker, and yearned for its owner.

Lucky had dreamt of hot, stale, enclosed spaces. And fear. He knew his master was in trouble.

His pink eyes winced at the harsh yellow radiance of the streetlight. Lucky wriggled across Jordan Avenue like a swift white caterpillar.

Outside the funeral parlor, Lucky stood on his fuzzy haunches and sniffed in the night air with his moist pink nose. He could taste Milton's smell, faintly, in the back of his throat. It was different. The odors told a story, and the ending stunk. Like burnt popcorn.

His nostrils drank in an invisible trail of scent, leading

him to the side of the building in an alley full of strong, biting smells that made the ferret hungry.

There was a door. It was closed. Lucky sniffed the door's metal jamb. There was a narrow piece of rotten weather stripping at the bottom. Lucky tugged at it with his teeth and soon made a small gap, just large enough for him to squeeze through.

The ferret spilled down the steps, untying the knot of odors with his expert nose. He followed the loops of smells down a hallway soft with grass-green carpet, stopping at a pair of metal doors bookended by potted palms.

The doors were open, but two men in blue robes stood barring the entrance, looking inside the room. Lucky's nose was temporarily distracted by the smell of chicken blood on the front of one of the men's robe. The ferret caught his master's scent again and squirmed past them.

"What the—?" Sentinel Shane exclaimed as he backed away from the fuzzy white creature darting past his feet.

A number of men circled a charred crate that was more ash than wood. A ring of burnt popcorn cinders surrounded it. The smell slapped Lucky dead in the face. He recoiled from its intensity. It confused him. It smelled like his master, but it wasn't. At least not anymore.

"That's Milton's ferret!" yelped Necia, her face streaked with dried tears.

The Guiding Knight broke the circle around Milton's remains. "Grab that thing," he ordered Warder Chango and Sentinel Shane, aiming his long bony finger at Lucky.

Lucky stopped and sniffed the air. He hissed. There was something about the spindly, ratlike girl he didn't like. She smelled like two people instead of just one. Lucky turned and fled toward a large plywood box.

Again, another familiar yet less-than-comforting smell assaulted his delicate senses. He jumped onto the box's handles and pressed his nose beneath the lid. A cruel boy who had devoted much of his waking life to tormenting his missing master lay sleeping in the box. Lucky hissed.

"Shoo!" Chaplain Charlie said as he stepped toward Damian's casket. "Get away from there!"

Lucky breathed in the blast of his master's smell that was slung across the strange man's back. Milton's knapsack! Lucky leapt toward it.

"No bite!" the man yelped.

Chaplain Charlie dropped the knapsack to the ground. Lucky had dug his claws into its fabric and was now coiling himself inside this nest of comforting, reassuring smells.

"What's this?" the Guiding Knight inquired as he knelt to the ground, his blue robe bunching up to reveal black socks and sandals. He picked up a stack of papers that had fallen out of Milton's knapsack.

"The Subtle Energies Commission?" he murmured as he pored through Milton's notes. "Etheric energy trap . . . life force . . . *reanimation?*"

The skeletal man licked his thin lips and gazed at Damian's casket. He opened the lid and stared inside at the sneering boy in his cheap navy blue blazer. The Guiding Knight rubbed his chin until he, too, was sneering.

"Sentinel Shane," the Guiding Knight said after a prolonged pause. "I have an idea and will need your help in carrying it out."

"Of course," the man with the weather-beaten cowboy face replied. "Anything you wish."

Necia appeared at the Guiding Knight's side, eyeing him quizzically as he leafed through the stack of papers in his hands.

"What is it, O honorific one?" she asked humbly.

A smile broke across the Guiding Knight's drawn face, like the arctic sun peeking through the clouds, teasing, before retreating for several months of blizzards.

"If a bridge goes out," he said mysteriously, "you simply take a detour."

32 · WARREN PEACE

MARLO RACED PAST the dissipating paintings, sculptures, and glasswork that lined the hallway leading to the Grabbit's warren. As she ran, she left small explosions of plaster dust with each footfall. Marlo was caked with the stuff, a sleepless, punch-drunk powdered doughnut in stirrup pants, her head nearly cracking with schemes restless to hatch.

She wanted to tell the Grabbit all about the perfect heist she was just about to execute. It involved all the essentials for a classic caper: dupes, disguise, psychological profiling, and brazen brinksmanship. Marlo wasn't even completely sure what that last word meant, but it sounded smart and confident in her head.

As she made the turn leading to the Grabbit's golden door, she nearly ran smack into the bionic bunny as three straining demons wheeled it down the hall on a massive bronze dolly.

The Grabbit's leer had grown wider ever since the twin atom smashers had been attached to the creature's sides, like coiling tentacles spiraling inward.

"Oh, hello, Grabbit," Marlo said, jarred by seeing the vice principal outside of its warren. It was like seeing a mountain going out for a leisurely drive. "I just wanted to tell you about . . . you know . . . our *little job*."

The demons grunted as they heaved the Grabbit forward. Marlo trotted at their side.

"It's actually happening right now," she continued with pride. "My part is just about to—"

"We don't have time for your babbling," one demon with a gold sash tied across his heavily muscled chest growled. "If we stopped for every Chatty Cathy who wanted to suck up to the Grabbit, it would be late for its own ceremony."

"So scram!" yelled another burly demon, wincing with exertion as it lurched the Grabbit onward.

Lately, Marlo reflected, everyone seemed on edge. Tempers flared, emotions ran high . . . the entire Rapacian population was restless, seeking some kind of relief. It didn't help that, with the exotic fur carpet outside the Grabbit's lair, every step built up a charge of static electricity that either nested within you like a swarm of hornets or nearly electrocuted anyone you touched.

"Don't get your togas in a bunch," she called out,

watching the demons wheel the Grabbit around the bend. As each beam of fluorescent light grazed the Grabbit's metal skin, hidden grooves and crevices were illuminated, turning its cheerful smoothness into something ancient and malevolent. It was like watching someone's fake smile fade when they thought no one was looking.

The Grabbit sang—if you could call it that—as it was carted away:

> *"What's yours is mine,*
> *what's mine is yours,*
> *and that's just fine and dandy. . . .*
> *But more's divine,*
> *and time ensures . . ."*

Marlo shrugged her dusty shoulders and began to walk away. She paused, a mischievous grin spreading across her chalky face as she looked behind her at the Grabbit's warren. The golden door had been left open. Marlo trotted into the Grabbit's warren for one brief glimpse of Mallvana to give her the electric tingle she needed to pull off her part of the heist.

The warren was deathly still. Spotlights sliced through the dark in languid sweeps, spilling down from Mallvana through the bronze ceiling grate. Marlo crept across, scraped the Smash 'n' Flash Atom Cannon crates across the floor, then clambered atop them to peer through the grate.

She could just make out some activity in the main concourse. There was a stage, some scaffolding, and a large screen. Even though the sharp angle made it difficult to fully discern, Marlo thought that—if she squinted her eyes just right—she could make out Yojuanna on the screen, jabbing her elbows out to her sides and bobbing her head back and forth. She sang into her pearlescent microphone headpiece.

"But more's divine,
and time ensures,
I'll soon have all your candy!"

Marlo could see two demons in overalls working beneath the screen, securing aluminum supports and railings to a platform on the stage.

Yojuanna jerked in fits and starts. Her face was a scrolling menu of expressions—joy, determination, sultriness, despair, and mania. She also had a disturbing tendency to burst into static when she clapped her hands together.

One of the demons tapped a microphone with his finger. "Testing, testing," he repeated dully.

Yojuanna waved her hands in the air as if she just didn't care. She pumped her fists in front of her, sparring with an imaginary foe. Then, the pop screen saver began to lose herself entirely.

"Ugh," the demon said to his partner with a shrug

of his bony shoulders. "Before, at least she had a good beat and was easy to dance to. Now she just creeps me out with all that hopping and depressing gibberish."

The digital diva continued to degrade as she lapsed into a blur of tiny jagged squares. Then, suddenly, the collection of blurry boxes that was Yojuanna just winked out of existence, leaving behind a small, hot-white throb of light that dimmed nearly imperceptibly. The demon sighed as he knelt for a rope by the microphone stand.

"Good riddance . . . help me with this, will you?"

The other demon worker scrambled up onto the rostrum. The two yanked ropes through pulleys mounted on the ceiling until a bright green banner rose above the stage: WELCOME TO MALLVANA DAY: EVERYTHING MUST GO!

"They must be having one heck of a sale," Marlo murmured. "Everything must go . . ."

She glanced down at an antique great-great-grandfather clock in the corner. Its face read half past VII, which Marlo assumed meant seven.

"Everything must go . . . *including me!*"

She hopped down from the crates and saw a huge painting in another corner covered by a billowing gray drop cloth. The exposed corner revealed a brilliant green . . . *rabbit's foot.*

Curious, Marlo tugged the cloth free. She gasped. Before her was a nearly life-sized portrait of the Grabbit, ancient by the looks of it—cracked paint, chipped varnish, and canvas peeling out of its intricately carved silver-leaf frame. Marlo's exhaustion-rimmed eyes narrowed.

"Perfect," she purred.

She knelt beneath the towering portrait and worried the peeling flaps of the canvas with her fingers until she had freed the entire painting.

"I might just pull a rabbit out of a hat after all," she snickered as she rolled the canvas up tightly, bundled it in her arms, and hurried down the deserted hallway.

33 · POETIC INJUSTICE

MILTON COULD BARELY breathe inside the scratchy burlap sack the demon guard had pulled over his head. Through a slight tear in the fabric, he could make out the walls of a tunnel, which were the color of bruises and contusions. Sporadic flashes of electricity made the tunnel seem somehow alive, creating a horrible confusion of trembling shadows.

"Owwwrrmphh!" Milton protested through the gag in his mouth as the guard shoved him into a gleaming black stagecoach with the two other boys.

"What's wrong with *him?*" the stagecoach driver asked the demon guard. "Speech impediment?"

"No, Byron. Just mouthy."

"It's *Lord* Byron!" the driver snapped. "And if being mouthy were a crime, half the employees here would have scarves in their gobs!"

Lord Byron peeled Milton's chin free of the sack and untied his kerchief. Milton stretched his aching jaws. His mouth felt like a lint trap after drying a dozen wool sweaters.

"Thanks," Milton managed through cracked, dried lips.

"I assure you," Lord Byron replied, "it has nothing to do with kindness. It's just that, as a lover of words, I cannot tolerate them being muffled. Language must be allowed to run free, like a stallion."

Lord Byron cracked a whip over his skittish horse's albino head. "Get a move on, Leucous!" the veiny red demon shouted.

The stagecoach lurched forward. The three captive passengers were slammed to the back of the carriage.

"Ouch!" one boy yelped from beneath his burlap hood.

I need to figure a way out of this, Milton thought desperately. *A kid like me wouldn't last a second in Sadia. It's full of bullies . . . big, bad bullies . . . bullies like . . .*

Milton gulped.

Damian. Of course. *He's dead, which means he's here, which means that—being the baron of barbarity—he has to be in Sadia. They've probably already put his face on all their money. I'm doomed.* Milton tried to shake his mind clear of anxiety. He had to think of something. . . .

Milton leaned forward. "Lord Byron?" he asked.

"*Byron!*" cackled one of the boys. "What a nerd name!"

"Weren't you a poet?" Milton continued, hoping to establish some rapport with the driver. "Up on the Stage?"

"I was *the* poet!" Lord Byron shot back. "And still am!"

"I'm a poet, too," brayed the donkey boy. *"Here I sit, brokenhearted . . ."*

"I will have *no* lavatory doggerel in my carriage!" Lord Byron ordered.

The demon stagecoach driver turned to Milton and smiled: a jagged fence of exposed teeth with lips curled on the inside. "Would you like to hear one of my poems?"

Of all the questions in the universe, "Would you like to hear one of my poems?" is the hardest, as there is no good way of answering it.

Milton sighed. "Yeah, sure."

"While it's not yet fully refined," the demon went on, "it is evidence that my Byronic mastery of the English language did not expire upon my death."

He coughed, clearing a throat that Milton could plainly hear was clear to begin with.

"Bunnies will go to France,
and they will look up teachers' underpants,
then do the latest bunny dance—"

Laughter exploded from beneath the burlap hoods of the two other boys.

"Underpants!" they chortled in unison.

Lord Byron stiffened. "It's experimental," he said

defensively. "I obviously don't literally mean *under-pants*, per se, but instead the feelings that we all keep hidden away—"

"I think I know one of your poems," Milton interrupted. "One of your *old* ones."

Lord Byron puffed out his exposed chest until the ribs stuck out like a batting cage.

"How flattering," he said in a sorry excuse for false modesty.

Milton dredged his mind for scraps of remembered poetry until a verse surfaced.

"A thing of beauty is a joy forever . . . ," Milton said.

"KEATS!!" Lord Byron bellowed. *"THAT WAS KEATS!!"*

"Byron! Byron! Face like a moron!" the two hooded boys chanted.

"THAT ISN'T EVEN A PROPER RHYME!" the peeved poet screeched.

Lord Byron slowed his horse's canter down to a trot and reached behind his seat.

"I'll teach you shabby scapegraces that words are a privilege, not a right!"

He stopped his horse. Then he pulled out a handful of rags, jumped down from the driver's box, and proceeded to gag the two hooded boys.

"It astes ike oogers and not," one boy groused.

"You should be so lucky," Lord Byron muttered as he stuffed Milton's kerchief back into his mouth.

Lord Byron climbed back onto the driver's box. He snapped the reins, bringing his draw-and-quarter horse to a full gallop.

"A thing of beauty is a joy for no one," he grumbled. "It's just nature showing off. *Keats* . . . that birdbrained, winged wannabe, he couldn't tell a good poem from a cuttlebone . . . *wait.*"

Lord Byron looked down from the stagecoach at the mottled red and purple channel. The way was blocked by a series of bright orange cones.

"I need this like I need an X-ray," the driver groaned.

A large, handmade sign hung on the wall, with an arrow pointing to a branch of the channel: SADISTIC CHANNEL REPAIR UNDER WAY. SHORTCUT TO SADIA.

The pulsating meat demon flicked the reins, and the stagecoach veered down the bypass. They soon arrived at a grand foyer, carpeted in blood-red shag and flanked by two huge Gothic columns. A paper banner hung from the ceiling of the channel: UNWELCOME TO NORTH SADIA. A tall, black-robed figure emerged from the foyer and staggered shakily to meet the demon and his cargo.

"Whoa, Leucous!" Lord Byron called to his nervous horse. The stagecoach came to a squeaky halt.

Milton's eyelashes brushed the lens of his glasses as he pressed his eye against the gash in the hood.

The demon grabbed a burgundy pouch next to him. The disgustingly visible veins of his arms bulged from the strain, though the pouch seemed no bigger than a change purse. Lord Byron hopped out onto the ground. Milton rubbed his burlap hood against the glass of the stagecoach window until the slit aligned perfectly with his right lens.

"So," the teetering figure said in a higher-than-expected voice, "you have what we are waiting for?"

"What?" Lord Byron said. "Oh yes. Atrocious grammar."

He patted the velvet pouch he held in his trembling hand. "I'd like to take it inside myself, if you don't mind."

The robed entity paused, swaying like a tree in a storm.

"Of course," it said finally. "As you wish. Only, I thought you might want to hurry to Rapacia and deliver poem for ceremony."

"Poem?" Lord Byron said, smiling. "Really?"

"Yes," the figure replied. "Grabbit wants poem for end of Mallvana ceremony. But if you want to deliver diamond personally, I am sure Keats can give poem."

"Keats!" Lord Byron screeched. The veins and arteries laced across his skin pumped with fury. It was as if he were having a heart attack on the outside.

Milton leaned against the stagecoach door to give himself a better view.

"Yes." The robed figure nodded. "He was just here. He is very excited about giving poem."

Lord Byron flushed all over, darkening from red straight to purple, ignoring fuchsia in the process.

"I'll pluck that preening parakeet with my poetic prowess!" the bright red demon alliterated as he turned on his exposed heel. The robed figure coughed for his attention. He swung around, his red-rimmed eyes quivering with impatience. The figure held out its tiny hand.

"Oh, right," Lord Byron said vaguely. "Of course."

He wrested a larger-than-normal diamond from the sack and dropped it into the figure's hand. The weight of it made the robed figure wobble and lurch.

"Thank you," the figure replied. "You do your job good."

"*Well*," corrected Lord Byron as he ran back to his black coach. He stopped suddenly by the carriage door. "I almost forgot . . ."

The wooden door swung open. Milton tumbled onto the ground. Through the slit, he could see Lord Byron grabbing the other two boys with his slimy meat hooks and flinging them out of the stagecoach.

The demon climbed onto the driver's box. Leucous reared into the air, whinnying, his muzzle flecked with foam.

With a snap of a whip, Lord Byron and his unsettling draw-and-quarter horse charged into the swollen darkness of the tunnel of bruises.

The looming, listing figure stood silent. Its black

robe billowed in the rippling gust of sour wind from down the channel. In the crook of its arms, it held the dense, despairing, and dazzling diamond. The figure shook off its hood, freeing its pink hair.

"All clear," the Japanese girl said as she tousled her cotton-candy bob.

From behind a column emerged a squat girl with a haircut that was either really, really bad or the latest thing; Milton couldn't be sure. The girl looked down the Sadistic Channel nervously.

"You think he's really gone?" the girl asked.

A voice as thick and dark as a smoker's chest X-ray gurgled from beneath the Japanese girl. "Norm, can you get Tokyo off of me?"

"It is *Takara*," the Japanese girl replied as the girl with the hacked-up hair—named Norm, apparently—helped her off the shoulders of another person: a hulking, big-boned tank of a girl who had served as the robed figure's sturdy trunk. The frail Japanese girl cupped the diamond in her trembling hands. Norm and the big, creepy girl peered down, mouths slack with awe, at the glittering jewel.

"It is so heavy!" Takara said. "But so small. It looks like tear."

Behind them, a Gothic column flanking the grand foyer tilted, then slammed into the other. Both pillars smashed into shards of paper and dust as they tumbled to the blood-red-carpeted floor.

"Good thing veiny poet demon gone!" Takara said.

Norm looked over at the damage. "Yeah," she replied. "No wonder the drama department was going to throw them out."

The beefy girl—*Where have I seen her before?* Milton thought as he eyed the scene from the ground—blew her blond bangs out of her face. Her wide-set eyes twinkled with greed as she gazed down upon the diamond. "Let me see it."

Norm looked up at the strange girl's squared head and thick features with distrust. "You *are* seeing it, Amandi."

"You know what I mean," the hefty girl snapped.

Norm and Takara looked at one another. Takara shrugged and rolled the diamond into Amandi's palm. Amandi—*What a weird name,* Milton thought—was the only human so far who didn't struggle with the diamond's surprising weight.

"It's . . . *perfect,*" she said as she licked beads of sweat from her fuzzy upper lip.

The girls looked at Amandi suspiciously.

"So what next?" Takara asked.

Norm smirked, shaking her head. "Well, I guess that's up to Marlo," she replied with a shrug. "Wherever she is."

"Marlo!" Milton yelped with surprise, though to the diamond-distracted girls beyond him, it sounded more like a muffled, "Mlow!"

34 · UNDERNEATH iT MALL

THE THREE GIRLS led Milton and the other boys from the stagecoach through a dark, dusty tunnel that smelled of mold and cobwebs. Barely able to make out any light sources through the small tear in his burlap sack, Milton was forced to rely on an endless stream of bickering and chattering to find his way.

"This place is creepy," Norm commented as she crept cautiously in the dim light.

"And water is wet," the larger girl, Amandi, answered, in a voice that seemed strangely familiar to Milton. "Thanks for the update."

The girls tromped through the catacomb. Broken glass crunched beneath their shoes.

Amandi squinted back at Norm. "Nice hair, by the way," she said. "Where did you get it done, Stupor Cuts?"

"Actually," Norm replied defensively, patting her

fiercely uneven hair, "I was a compulsive hair chewer—
before. I'd always chomp on the ends of my hair when I
was nervous, which was a lot. And, one day in my after-
school hairdressing class—"

"*Hairdressing class,*" Amandi repeated with disbelief.
"That's priceless! Couldn't the school afford mirrors?
And *scissors*? I've heard of bad hair days, but you're hav-
ing a bad hair *eternity*!"

"So tell me, Norm," Takara, the Japanese girl,
chirped, wedging herself between the two fuming
girls, "how did you die?"

"*Like I was saying,*" Norm continued, "one day after
class, I just fainted and was taken to the hospital. I kind
of went in and out of consciousness, but I heard my
doctor talking about how the stomach can't digest hair
and that mine was plugged up, like a big hair clog in a
drain. The nurse said the clog looked like a dead rat."

After a long pause, Takara added soothingly, "That
is very interesting way to go, Norm."

Amandi snorted. "Yeah, fascinating," she said dryly.
"In a 'hair today, gone tomorrow' kind of way."

"Well, then, *Amandi,*" Norm replied in a huff, blowing away strands of nonexistent bangs from her eyes, "I
bet I know what killed you."

"What?"

"Your face . . . because it's sure killing me."

"Shhh," Takara interrupted. "I hear something."

Footsteps plodded nearby in the darkness ahead.

Sharp voices, slapping against the stone and mortar walls, filled the stifling air around them.

"That was, like, *so major cool*! The way he just crashed right into the mirror! He must've been all, 'Oh snap!' "

"What did I tell yeh, Bordeaux, 'bout saying 'snap'?!"

"*Whatever.* That demon with the pretty blue feathers, the one driving the stagecoach, reminded me of a blue parakeet I used to have, Papa Smurf."

"Papa Smurf?"

"Yeah, he used to peck at himself in the mirror all day."

"Lyon, I thought yeh were jess a glaikit skinny dip. How did ye know that daft demon would crash inta the mirror like that?"

"Well, I did a little research, and I knew the driver was, like, *super* vain and would think his reflection was another demon trying to challenge him."

"Research? But I thought you, like, totally got the idea from that weird note you found on your chair—?"

"*Zip it, Bordeaux.*"

In the dim light of the tunnel, just beyond a network of large dripping pipes, Milton could see three figures: two looked like skinny blond cheerleaders on their day off, while the other reminded Milton of a brooding storm cloud stuffed into an ugly sweat suit.

"Lyon!" Takara smiled as the three girls walked into view. "You made it!"

"Where's Marlo?" Lyon said with a scowl. "Did she run away again?"

"Mowlo," Milton inadvertently gurgled through his filthy, spit-soaked kerchief. *We must be close to Rapacia,* he surmised.

"She's going to meet us later to help get the diamonds to the Grabbit," Norm explained.

"I don't believe it," Lyon said with disgust and dismay. "Actually, I *do* believe it. We're down here doing all the dirty work while she waits all safe and cozy up in Mallvana to take the credit."

Bordeaux gestured to the three hooded boys. "Who are they?" she asked.

"Forget them," Amandi said. "They were on the stagecoach."

"Oh," Bordeaux replied with a faraway look. "We just, like, left ours. Whoopsie . . . *our bad!* Were we supposed to take them? What'll we do with them?"

"We'll dump them off to Bubb when we're through," Amandi interrupted.

Principal Bubb! Milton groaned to himself. The high spirits he had at the mention of his sister's name came plummeting down so fast that his nose began to bleed.

Amandi galumphed toward Lyon and Bordeaux across the floor of broken glass. There was something about the blocky hulk-of-a-girl that made the hair on the back of Milton's neck do the Wave.

"Do you have it?" Amandi asked.

"If anyone has got it, Wide Load, it's me," Lyon replied with a defiant smirk.

After a brief stare down, Lyon relented and held out a dismal yet dazzling gem cupped in both hands, straining to hold it out. "If you mean 'did we get the diamond,'" Lyon said through gritted teeth, "then, yeah, we totally did."

Amandi leered at the sight of the jewel.

The smile, Milton thought. *It's so awful . . . so familiar. So awfully familiar.*

Lyon narrowed her eyes in the murkiness. She placed the diamond into a leather saddlebag she wore across her chest. "Now it's your turn to show and tell," she said.

Amandi took one big, crunchy step toward Lyon. Lyon looked the large, charmless girl up and down with distaste.

"I'll do more than show you this *sin-sational* diamond," Amandi smirked. She handed the heavy gem to Lyon. "I'll give it to you."

"*What?!*" screamed Norm.

"It was not yours to give!" Takara yelped.

Lyon glanced over at the two enraged girls, smiled a wide, nasty grin, and snatched the gem from Amandi's outstretched hand. Unfortunately, the heavy diamond—

and Lyon with it—tumbled to the floor. With much effort, Lyon lifted the diamond with her skinny, trembling arms and placed it in her saddlebag with its mate.

Jordie glared at Amandi suspiciously.

"Now, why would ye pinch yer own mates like that?" she asked.

"Because," Amandi replied matter-of-factly, "I want to be on the winning team. And now we've got both Hopeless Diamonds, don't we, *team?*"

Bordeaux, Lyon, and Jordie jumped in the air, whooping and high-fiving one another.

Lyon gave Norm and Takara a look packed tight with mock pity. "Now, now, enough with the long faces," she said. "You look horsey enough as it is. C'mon . . . the Grabbit is waiting for us. And I have a feelin' he'll be *hoppy* to see us."

She stared at the expressionless girls.

"Get it?" Lyon asked.

"Yeah, we got it," Norm said bitterly.

The group of girls and hooded hostages skirted around the leaking pipes into the darkness beyond. The smothering heat clung tight to them until there was no difference between their hot breath and the stale air around them.

Through the labored panting, crunching glass, and echoing drips, new sounds emerged from above: the murmur of a crowd and the thrum of footsteps.

"There!" Jordie shouted, pointing at a trapdoor in the ceiling. She strained to touch it with the tip of her finger, but the hatch was several inches out of reach.

Amandi's eyes darted from side to side before settling her creepy, familiar gaze on Milton and the other two boys. *Who* is *this bruiser of a girl?* thought Milton just before Amandi lurched forward, grabbing the other, bigger boys by the scruffs of their necks and throwing them to the ground.

"This whole thing is *so* unfair," Norm whispered to Takara.

Takara shook her head. Her bangs rippled like pink fringe.

"Marlo is not going to like this," Takara whispered back, "wherever she is."

"Marlo will come through," Norm faltered. *"I hope."*

Amandi looked over at Jordie. "Scary British girls first," she said, holding out her arms in mock graciousness.

Jordie shrugged, climbed on top of the groaning boys on the floor, then pushed open the trapdoor and clambered through.

One by one, the girls climbed through the trapdoor. At first, it seemed to Milton as if the girls had abandoned the bound boys in the passageway. But Amandi popped her square head back through the portal in the ceiling, grabbed Milton by the shoulders, and hoisted him up through the trapdoor.

Milton tumbled on concrete before stopping himself with his elbow. He rubbed the sack on the ground until the slit again aligned with his lens. It looked as if they were in a huge underground parking structure.

Amandi brusquely and with undisguised relish pulled the other boys through the portal. She surveyed the gargantuan garage crowded with every imaginable make and model of car.

"We've got a problem," Amandi said, pointing at the front of a snaking line of people and demons.

"What?" Lyon asked, joining the thick-featured girl.

"They've got a booty-load of security up there," Amandi said grimly. "I don't see how we could sneak past something as . . . as—"

"—conspicuously heavy?" offered Norm.

"Yeah, *conspicuously heavy* as the Hopeless Diamonds."

"What do we do?" asked Bordeaux.

"If only there was some way to smuggle them past security," Amandi mused, rubbing her chin and giving a sideways glance at Lyon and Bordeaux. "But the detector would be bound to pick up extra weight, you know, from a heavier-than-normal girl."

"I got it!" Lyon declared with her fists balled up against her hips.

Amandi smiled furtively.

"I was counting on it," Milton heard the linebacker-sized girl murmur darkly to herself.

Lyon held Bordeaux's hand. "Remember, at Bart Hammond's big party, where you did that really cool trick?" Lyon said, her pale blue eyes locked on the pale blue eyes of her best friend.

"The one with the cell phone?" Bordeaux replied.

"Yes!" Lyon gushed. "You swallowed it and I called, pretending to be your stomach: 'Hello, I'm Bordeaux's stomach and I'd really like a Triple Bypass Burger, no bun, and a Diet Mountain Don't.' "

"Right!" Bordeaux giggled, her eyes bugging out. "That was totally funny! But what does it have to do with—"

"*Everything,*" Lyon interrupted. "You're, like, the totally skinniest person here . . . maybe anywhere."

Bordeaux blushed. "You're, like, so sweet! Like Splenda!" she said, clutching her friend's hand tightly.

"If we did that cell-phone trick, only with the Hopeless Diamonds, we could *totally* get past security," Lyon said. "They'd just think we were, like"—Lyon's face soured, as if she were chewing aspirin—"*average* girls."

Bordeaux and Lyon scowled as one.

The line crept forward as security demons fed the anxious spectators through a battery of detection machines.

Lyon lifted one of the Hopeless Diamonds out of her saddlebag, her arm trembling under the strain, and handed it to her friend. Bordeaux tucked her gleaming platinum hair behind her ears and took the diamond with both hands. She sighed and closed her eyes.

"First, I have to clear my mind," Bordeaux said. "Okay, done."

She tilted her head back and swallowed the diamond. The small yet dense gem traveled down Bordeaux's slender throat. She looked like an anaconda digesting a baby caribou.

"Ugh," Bordeaux complained as the Hopeless Diamond settled into her stomach. "I feel so fat!"

Lyon hoisted the other diamond out of her saddlebag, set the gem on her tongue, gagged until her eyes bulged, then gulped it down.

She grimaced and clutched her throat. "It's going down wrong," Lyon whined. "It's like swallowing a tiny bowling ball."

Lyon coughed and the diamond fell into her stomach. The girl doubled over. "Oh my gawd!" she yelped. "That, like, hurt so much!"

Several old women and demons ahead of them in line looked back suspiciously. A security demon with a long crooked neck that jutted out like a bent knee beckoned the girls with a curl of its claw.

"Next!" he called to Lyon.

Lyon parted the black drapes and stared at the huge security machine, an enclosed electronic vestibule with a conveyor belt walkway. She shuffled forward. Each step was a painful lurch as she struggled to maintain her balance, her body now nearly twenty pounds heavier right around the stomach region. The security tunnel buzzed and hummed. A demon resembling a plump, slimy leech helped her off the moving sidewalk, holding out a claw encased in a rubber glove.

"What about Buffy here?" the obese demon wheezed.

"Average," the scrawny demon answered.

Lyon winced.

"As if," she muttered under her breath as she staggered through the curtains into Mallvana.

One by one, the girls passed through the curtain. Amandi herded Milton and the two other hooded boys along.

"Wait," the fat demon gurgled. "What's the deal with the three little-dead-riding-hoods here?"

Amandi fought to lock eyes with those of the demon's, whose dull gaze was concealed beneath drooping eyelids.

"Principal Bubb told me to torment them with the splendors of Mallvana before sentencing them to the unspeakable anguish of Sadia," Amandi declared.

The demon chuckled, which caused his chins to ripple like someone shuffling a deck of cold cuts.

"That Bubb, always taking punishment to the next level," the demon replied before waving Amandi and her gaggle of prisoners forward.

"Demons are *so* gullible," Amandi sneered to herself while shoving the three boys through the curtains.

Lyon, Bordeaux, Norm, Jordie, and Takara had congregated by a towering Madagascar dragon tree just inside the mall. Amandi looked over at Lyon and Bordeaux, whose faces were as green as grass stains on new white jeans.

"Time to cough up the goods," Amandi ordered. "We've got a date with a diamond-hungry bunny."

Lyon and Bordeaux nodded and waddled into a nearby women's rest (in peace) room. An assortment of retches, gags, and coughs ricocheted from inside the tiled lavatory.

"I hope those two glaikit chippies wash them diamonds orf before they give 'em to the Grabbit," Jordie said.

Lyon and Bordeaux emerged, wiping their pouty mouths. Lyon smiled and patted her saddlebag.

"The only thing wrong with this moment," Lyon gloated, "is that Marlo isn't here to see it."

"This way," Amandi said, striding toward the Express Escalator to the SkyDeck.

"But everyone else is going to concourse," Takara said with a mystified slant of her eyebrows.

Amandi stopped and turned to Takara. The pink-haired Japanese girl pointed to a snaking line of people boarding the spiral escalator bound for the concourse level.

"The Grabbit wanted us to make the drop at the staging area, up on the SkyDeck," she answered. "After it gets the diamonds, then it'll be hop-hop-hoppin' back down."

Lyon cocked her eyebrow. "And how do you know so much about the Grabbit's business?" she asked suspiciously.

Amandi's mouth curled into a sly smile. "Why, Lyon," she asked, "didn't you get the memo?"

Lyon's golden face flushed pink around the edges. "Oh, right. *That*," she replied uneasily. "I must have forgotten, what with the excitement of getting both diamonds and all."

The girls followed Amandi up the Express Escalator, with the three hostages keeping up the rear. A perfumed wind blew in the dazed girls' hair as they were whizzed at breakneck speed to the SkyDeck.

Milton clutched the handrail tightly as he scanned the bustling mall with one eye for any sign of Marlo.

"I can't believe Marlo would bail on us like this," Norm mumbled from behind to Takara, eerily as if reading Milton's thoughts. "I thought we were friends!"

With a sudden heave, Milton and the other passengers tumbled off the faster-than-necessary escalator and onto the SkyDeck. He slid across the slick, white marble floor until stopping with a painful thud at a brass railing.

The girls rose to their feet, rubbing sore knees and elbows while Milton and the boys—their arms tied behind their backs—staggered and squirmed upright.

"I don't see—" said Lyon before her observation was cut short by a hollow, booming voice from one of the abandoned offices on the other side of the dizzyingly high span.

"So long I have been waiting
for all you silly fools,
but instead of us debating,
just show me my new jewels."

35 · FUNNY BUNNY

MILTON STRAINED THROUGH the tear in his hood to discern the source of the odd, toneless voice. The confused girls looked across the SkyBridge, which gleamed in the simulated morning light pouring through the glass ceiling.

"This doesn't make sense," Lyon said, folding her golden arms. "It didn't even really sound like—"

"We don't have time for this," Amandi complained in a voice as thick and inelegant as her body. "The Grabbit needs the Hopeless Diamonds before its ceremony."

"Hey," Bordeaux said, "look at the funny shadow in that office!"

Through the slats of the venetian blinds that covered the glass wall of a nearby office, Milton could make out a monstrous silhouette—two large ears and twin coiled arms that unfurled like party favors.

"It's too quiet," Norm said suspiciously as she cased out the SkyDeck. "Where's security?"

"The bluebottles must all be downstairs, preparin' for the big party," Jordie surmised.

Amandi shoved Milton and the other boys across the SkyBridge to the office. Lyon pushed herself ahead and poked her flawless face into the room.

"Hello, Mr. Grabbit?" she asked nervously. "I've got . . . *oh gawd.*"

In the back of the office was a bulky, hulking shape standing motionless in front of a plate-glass wall, looking down upon the mall concourse below. The creature was dimly illuminated by a small desk lamp, which cast it with a sickly jaundiced glow. Smoky incense filled the room with pungent, sooty tendrils. The effect was disorienting and intimidating, like a school dance.

"Hello, little miss,
so frail, so young.
Is something amiss?
Has a cat got your tongue?"

So that's a . . . Grabbit, thought Milton. *Looks like a lumpy, overgrown, white chocolate Easter bunny.*

Bordeaux and the other girls joined Lyon in the doorway.

"No, I just," Lyon stammered, "you just seem . . . different."

"It sounds like it has a cold," Norm whispered to Takara.

"Well, Grabbit," Lyon said as she fumbled through her saddlebag, "before I give you the diamonds—which Bordeaux, Jordie, and I stole, by the way—I want to know what we're going to get. My team, that is, not Marlo's, because she totally flaked and—"

> "Enough of Marlo Fauster, please,
> a girl of grace and expertise.
> It just so happens that I was gonna
> give your team this place, Mallvana."

Lyon's jaw dropped. Bordeaux and Jordie gasped. After a moment of shock, the three girls jumped up and down, squealing with delight. Bordeaux clutched Lyon tight, like a designer handbag. Norm, indignant, stormed up to the Grabbit.

"This is *not fair!*" she complained. "We stole one of the Hopeless Diamonds; then Amandi double-crossed us and gave it to their stupid team!"

> "Now that all the drama's done,
> let's get back to my own rules.
> See, it doesn't matter which girl won;
> just give me now my jewels."

Norm wiped away her indignant tears and joined Takara at the back of the room. Lyon slipped from Bordeaux's embrace, straightened her awful WHAT HAPPENS AT GRANDMA'S *STAYS* AT GRANDMA'S sweatshirt, and marched back to the Grabbit. Lyon took out the two diamonds, one in each trembling hand.

That weird voice, thought Milton. *It's like when you order fast food at a drive-through and struggle to untangle the crackling voice of a fiberglass clown.*

"Where . . . do you . . . want . . . them?" Lyon muttered under clenched teeth as she strained to hold the Hopeless Diamonds with her superficially toned arms.

> *"Perfect, flawless, like a tear,*
> *two sad and glistening charms.*
> *Hurry, while the coast is clear,*
> *and drop them in my, um . . . swirly arms."*

Lyon nodded as perspiration began to bead on her forehead. She heaved a diamond into a hole at the top of one of the Grabbit's coiling arms. The dense gem rattled and rocked its way down into the robotic rabbit's torso, landing with a great *plunk.* Then, with a pained grunt, she deposited the last Hopeless Diamond into her school's vice principal.

Lyon squinted through the dim light and thick smoke. "Wait a second," she muttered. "You're . . . *disappearing.*"

The Grabbit's cartoonish features and festive colors began to fade, revealing a pale, rabbit-shaped lump underneath. It was as if someone had projected the image of a rabbit onto a mammoth snow-bunny and the projector's bulb was dying.

"Thank you, miss, for your donation.
Relax, I'm sure you're tuckered.
But don't expect your compensation,
because you have been suckered!"

The Grabbit shook furiously until its belly burst in an explosion of canvas and plaster. Milton, his eye bulging beneath the tear in his hood, struggled to make sense of what was happening. The girls surrounding him screamed and stumbled back in shock. Out tumbled a figure, chalky white with dust.

"Didya miss me?" Marlo asked as she rose to her feet, brushing off chunks of papier-mâché and torn pieces of the Grabbit's vanishing portrait. She grinned so wide it looked as if her face were about to split in two. Marlo's dark eyes twinkled at Lyon as she patted her bulging fanny pack.

"Oh, and, like, thanks for the diamonds." She giggled. "You are, like, my bestest friend *ever.*"

"Marlo!" shrieked Norm as she ran to embrace her. "I knew you hadn't run away!"

Milton, meanwhile, was dumbstruck at the surreal

sight of his sister tumbling out of a jumbo-sized bunny tummy. It was thrilling, disturbing, and surprising in how unsurprising it was—Marlo at the center of some convoluted plot.

"Mlow!" Milton called out through his gag. "Mlow!"

Marlo noticed the three hostage boys in the doorway. "Who are *they*?" she asked. "Demon cats or something?"

Milton vibrated like a toddler after too much apple juice.

"Boys," Norm explained. "They were on the stage-coach, on the way to Sadia."

Lyon shoved her way past Norm. Her eyes were hot blue flames aching to burn. "You totally cheated!" she screeched. "This won't count!"

Bordeaux trembled by Amandi's side. She wrapped her skinny arms around herself as she stared at the piles of torn paper and plaster with a traumatized expression on her face.

"How did you get the Grabbit to eat you?" she said with distress.

Marlo threw back her head and laughed. Flecks of the crumbling portrait she had stolen from the Grab-bit's warren flew from her mouth. It was like there was a parade inside her, celebrating her victory with joyful blasts of confetti.

Norm gawked at her friend with open admiration.

"But how did you know that Amandi would give the Hopeless Diamonds to—"

She leveled her gaze at Amandi hovering at the back of the office. Despite the girlish grin, she still resembled a Bulgarian wrestler with wildly fluctuating hormone levels.

Norm smiled.

"Ooh, you guys are good!"

Lyon pushed Norm out of her way and got in Marlo's face.

"Fine, you and Uggs played us, but why go through all this trouble?" she said, waving at the huge, busted bunny piñata in the corner.

Marlo brushed dust off the front of her tacky sweatshirt, which only made its innate tackiness shine through.

"It's easy, but I'll speak slowly so you can follow along," Marlo explained. "We knew it would be hard to get these heavy Hopeless wonders past security," she said, patting her fanny pack with satisfaction. "We pretty much figured the only way to get them through undetected was by swallowing them, and since you and Bordeaux are to body fat what reality TV is to actual reality, you were the best candidates."

"But why all the barney rubble of dressin' as the big bunn?" Jordie asked, still a little angry yet grudgingly impressed.

"Well, Lyon here may be dumb, but she's not stupid," Marlo clarified. "We knew the only way to get her greedy mitts off those diamonds was to trick her into thinking she was delivering them straight to the Grabbit itself. And, boy, did I!"

Amandi stepped forward in two hulking stomps.

"We'd better get the Hopeless Diamonds to the Grabbit now," the stocky girl said. "The real one."

Amandi looked Marlo up and down.

"You're kind of a mess . . . *nothing personal*," she observed. "You might arouse suspicion."

Marlo straightened her hair, causing a small avalanche of plaster dust to rain down onto her face and shoulders.

"I should take the diamonds down to the Grabbit," Amandi continued.

Milton fidgeted in a spastic fit, trying to free himself from his bonds.

Marlo peered beyond Amandi's beefy shoulder at Milton. "They seem uncomfortable," she commented. "Especially that little one . . ."

"Nah, they love it," Amandi replied.

She stepped in front of the boys.

"Whoever wants to be untied, raise their hand," she asked.

The boys writhed and moaned.

"See," Amandi said, turning to Marlo and puffing up menacingly. "Now hand over the diamonds, before it's too—"

"What's with the hoods?" Marlo persisted. She was fascinated by the bouncing boy in the middle. She stalked toward him, grabbed his canvas hood, and yanked.

Milton's eyes protruded behind his spectacles, and his face shimmered with a sickly, clammy sheen. He was hyperventilating through the kerchief in his mouth.

"Milton!" yelped Marlo.

"Milquetoast," murmured Amandi. She folded her thick arms against her ample A GRANDMA IS A MOM WITH EXTRA FROSTING sweatshirt and glared at Milton, her lip curling with amused malevolence.

Marlo yanked Milton's gag out of his mouth.

"Marlo!" he yelped. "I . . ."

Marlo beamed, hugging her brother, who, with thick twine around his wrists, couldn't hug back.

"What's this?" she asked, noticing a small package tucked into the back of his pants.

"It's nothing," Milton gasped, hungrily breathing in air through his mouth. His eyes rested on Amandi. There was something about the girl that filled Milton's stomach with molten dread. The wide-set, coal-black eyes and coarse features . . .

"Stop squirming," Marlo scolded as she uncoiled the rough twine from her brother's raw wrists. "Did you make it back up to the Surface? If so, how did you get back? I mean, if you escaped, then came back, then how . . ."

Milton smiled as his sister barraged him with questions that she had no intention of letting him answer.

Marlo's nose curled.

"Let me guess," she continued. "It involved a microwave loaded with Kernel Instapop's gourmet popping corn exploding in your face."

"Something like that." Milton grinned. His sister managed to take the sting out of, again, dying in a food-related accident.

"I love family reunions as much as the next guy—uh, *girl*," Amandi said, brushing blond bangs from her short, wide forehead, "but we don't have time. The Grabbit needs those diamonds now, or else all this was just a big waste of time."

The Fauster children stared at Amandi with wide, questioning eyes.

"I'm a teacher's aide," she said after registering the doubt in Milton's and Marlo's faces. "I can slip through security faster and—"

Just then, Amandi's thumb and pinky rang.

The girls traded glances until finally settling on Amandi as she tried to ignore the ringtone emanating from her hand.

Marlo glared at her suspiciously.

"Aren't you going to get that?" she asked.

"What?" Amandi replied with a quaver, her fuzzy lip twitching slightly. "Oh. *This*. No one ever . . . it must be a wrong number."

"Only one way to find out," Norm said flatly.

Amandi sighed. She stuck her thumb in her ear and talked into her pinky.

"Hello?" she answered under her breath, turning away toward the plate-glass wall.

"Damian?" Bea "Elsa" Bubb squawked from the other end of the phone. "Is that—"

"Wrong number," Amandi hissed into her pinky.

A swarm of prickles traveled up Milton's spine as his stomach sagged, like a leaky balloon filled with sour milk and battery acid. His ferret-heightened ears echoed with the wretched name, uttered by a wretched voice. Apparently, his link to Lucky—though now jagged and stuttery, like a bad cell-phone connection— had survived the Transdimensional Power Grid.

"Damian!" Milton yelled. He grabbed Marlo and pulled her close. "And she . . . *he* . . . is talking to Bea 'Elsa' Bubb!"

"So *that's* your game!" Marlo seethed.

Her face crinkled into a dusty white mask, like that of a mischievous baby ghost. Without warning, Marlo ran over to Damian and kicked him full force between the legs. The faux female doubled over in excruciating pain.

"And we've got *your* number, *Damian,*" Marlo sneered. "On speed dial."

She walked back to Milton.

"C'mon, we've got to skedaddle."

Lyon and Bordeaux blocked the door leading back to the SkyBridge. Between their scrawny shoulders, Marlo could see several demon guards stumbling off the Express Escalator and onto the SkyDeck.

"Looks like we're headed off at the pass," Marlo said. Lyon and Bordeaux looked smugly at one another.

Marlo gulped, then took Milton's hand.

"Trust me," she whispered into her brother's ears.

If Milton had a nickel for every bad thing that happened after Marlo uttered the words "trust me," he thought, he would have . . . well . . . *a whole lot of nickels.*

But even a boy as bright as Milton couldn't see a way out, so he'd have to trust that his reckless sister had spotted an exit that he had the good sense not to. He squeezed her hand.

Marlo turned, pulling Milton into position next to her. They faced the wreckage of the ersatz Grabbit, at the feet of which Damian was now writhing and moaning.

Marlo leaned into her brother's ear.

"On the count of three, we run," she whispered, squeezing her brother's hand. "One . . ."

"Where?" Milton asked incredulously.

". . . two . . ."

"Stop!" a demon guard roared as it burst into the office.

". . . *three!*"

Marlo and Milton sprinted straight into the broken hull of the papier-mâché Grabbit, using it as a protective shell as they crashed through the plate-glass wall and tumbled down to the mall below.

36 · FALLING AFOUL

"AAAAAAAEEEEYYYYYAAAAHHHHH!!!" MILTON AND Marlo screamed as they clutched one another inside the free-falling bunny sculpture.

Milton watched the glitter of Mallvana swirl around him, as if someone had filled up a huge washing machine with every possible want and desire and set it on "Heavy Load: Extra Rinse." *What is this place?* he mused. It made him feel anxious and excited, and he *hated* malls. The fact that his last mall outing had ended in a fiery eruption of molten marshmallow could also have fed this aversion. And—as the dazzling jeweled floor of Mallvana's twelfth tier rushed to meet them—his latest trip to the mall didn't bode much better.

The Fausters' papier-mâché shell exploded into vaporized plaster and newspaper shreds as they hit the floor. They rolled out of the chaotic cloud, spinning and shrieking, while terrified shoppers gasped and stumbled back out of harm's way.

Milton and Marlo slammed into the burnished copper railing. The siblings lay panting at the lip of Mallvana's twelfth tier, hundreds of feet above the concourse.

Milton opened his eyes, looked down below, then nearly lost the last lunch he ever ate alive (a grilled-cheese sandwich with peperoncinos and a tapioca pudding cup). He rolled over and stared up at the breathtaking stained-crystal ceiling.

"What is this place?" he asked.

"You have died and gone to Mallvana," Marlo explained.

She rose to her feet, leaned over the railing, and peered down at the mall below. Rivers of people flowed through the shopping Shangri-la, spilling down escalators like human water, heading for the concourse.

"We've got to boogie down," Marlo muttered. She looked up at the SkyDeck. Lyon, Bordeaux, and Damian peered down through the shattered glass wall.

"*And* do the hustle." She gulped.

"I'm fine, by the way," Milton mumbled. He stood up, shaky and dizzy, like a poster boy for inner-ear disorders. "Thanks for asking."

Damian glared at them from above. He ripped off his blond wig, wiped off his smear of bright red lipstick, and then disappeared.

"Uh-oh," Marlo said. "Something ugly this way comes. C'mon."

Marlo ran to the escalator between Sole Salvation and Pearly Gate and Barrel. Milton followed, managing to run and sulk at the same time.

"You mean we're not going to bungee jump without a bungee this time?"

Marlo weaved through the escalator, which was clogged with old women with tiny white wings poking through the backs of their off-white tracksuits and sweaters. Milton, trying to keep up, looked behind him and saw a burly, angry boy in a granny sweatshirt descending the escalator.

Milton swallowed hard. He joined his sister, who had just stumbled off the escalator.

"Damian's coming," Milton panted.

Marlo looked over beyond the Transcendental House of Pancakes at the next down escalator. It had a CLOSED FOR REPAIR. PLEASE USE THE STAIRS WAY OVER THERE sign blocking shoppers from entry. Next to it, throngs of old women—some dragging put-upon old men behind them who were paying for their earthly transgressions by being forced to shop with their wives for all eternity—spilled out of the up escalator into the Angel Food Court.

"Looks like we've got to take the hard way down," she said. "But we're used to swimming against the mainstream, aren't we?"

She grabbed Milton's arm and gave a tug. *Is this my role in death as it was in life?* Milton pondered as he was led to the up escalator. *To be dragged behind my sister in a mall?*

Bea "Elsa" Bubb's yellow goat eyes widened in shock.

"We must have a bad connection," she whispered into her No-Fee Hi-Fi Faux Phone, "because I thought I just heard you say that you were chasing Marlo *and* Milton Fauster. How is that possible? I would have been alerted the second he passed through the gates, unless . . ."

Her eyes darted across the Mallvana security cove—where she and several demons were staring at a bank of closed-circuit televisions—at Lilith, in the corner, on the phone as usual.

". . . unless that skinny, manipulative whippet in a designer dress screwed up somehow."

Bea "Elsa" Bubb grinned at the thought.

"Whatever," Damian said. He stopped, huffing, in front of Hot Dog on a Scepter. A man in an impaled sausage costume greeted him.

"Hot diggity dog," the man said wearily as he waved a sausage pierced by a jeweled staff. "Can I hook you up with an extra-large lanced link?"

Damian grabbed the man's scepter and ran.

"Hey!" the man yelled, shuffling in hot-dog-costume-hobbled pursuit.

"What's going on?" Bea "Elsa" Bubb asked.

"Just picking up a little present for my good friend Milton," Damian said as he sliced through the crowd of senior citizens to the down escalator.

"Why are you wasting time when you should be bringing me my diamonds?" she hissed discreetly, turning away from the other demons in the cloistered cove. "I've got that emaciated she-devil on the ropes, and those diamonds could put her out of my misery and *me* right by Lucifer's side—"

"Is there some trouble, Blubb?" Lilith asked as she sashayed across the security room.

Principal Bubb smiled as sweetly as someone with a face like an open wound can.

"No trouble," she replied. "Though there soon may be for *you* . . . ," she whispered under her bad breath.

"*Do* try to keep on top of things while I receive Mammon," Lilith gloated, her flawless, angular face cast in the glow of the flickering monitors.

"Can I go back to doing my job now?" Damian said. "You know, the one that helps you keep *yours*."

"And no personal phone calls," Lilith added as she left the room.

Bea "Elsa" Bubb gnashed her fangs together with a squeak.

"Fine," she sighed into her pinky. "Point taken."

Damian stomped down the escalator.

"That's the idea," he murmured, testing the keen tip of his stolen scepter on the rear of the unfortunate woman in front of him.

"Nice shirt," an old woman said, pointing at Marlo's sweatshirt. "Where did you ever—"

"Out of my way, Grandma," Marlo grunted with a shove as she descended the ascending escalator.

Several steps behind, trudging against the flow of human traffic, Milton followed in her wake.

"Sorry," he apologized to the flabbergasted biddies. Milton scowled at his sister.

"What if that really *was* our grandma?" he scolded.

Marlo looked back with curiosity at the clot of old women.

"Nah," she said. "Grandma Fauster died in that stampede at the bingo hall. She'd be . . . *flatter.*"

They hopped off the escalator and circled toward the next. Galloping near the banister overlooking the mall commons, Milton looked up while Marlo looked down.

"Maybe we . . . lost . . . *him,*" Milton wheezed.

"Not likely," Marlo replied.

She scanned the floor below. Outside of Halo/Good Buy was a sign: NO SAIL SALE: ALL CANOES, KAYAKS, ROWBOATS, AND DINGHIES MUST GO!

Marlo smirked as she grabbed the velvet handrail of the next escalator.

"What are we even *doing*?" Milton groused. "We have those diamonds. We should use them to buy our way out of this place or something. Why are we giving them to some weird metal rabbit?"

"*Grabbit*," Marlo corrected. "It said if I stole the Hopeless Diamonds for it, this whole place could be sent into some kind of chaos."

"It's hard to imagine this place as anything *but* chaotic," Milton said desperately as he was buffeted about by countless shoulders and hips.

"It also promised me my own circle of Heck."

Milton joined his sister on the mall floor. He straightened his glasses and looked at her incredulously.

"You can't be serious," he said. "First off, it would never do that. Second, why would you want to have your own circle? That's like having your own mental hospital and graveyard wrapped up into one."

"I always wanted to get into management," she said with a grin. "I am, after all, a people person in the worst way. *I can't stand them.*"

Milton's jaw went slack as he stared at his sister.

"C'mon," Marlo ordered, pulling his arm. "A little detour."

She dragged Milton to Halo/Good Buy.

"One that might save us a lot of time in the long run."

Milton looked at the NO SAIL SALE sign and felt his stomach sink into his shoes.

"Oh no . . . ," he murmured.

Marlo turned and gave her brother a look like a dark, frozen one-way street. Her fingers flexed at her sides, as if doing warm-up exercises for some Olympic thieving event, like the hundred-yard snatch.

"Why do I have the feeling that whatever it is you're planning," Milton said, "isn't going to be exactly *covert*?"

37 · ROCKING THE BOAT

"WHAT AM I supposed to do?" Milton asked as he scanned the empty store with nervous sweeps of his eyes. "The coast looks clear."

"Clear?" Marlo said. "Perhaps to the untrained eye, but mine—both of them, in fact—are *highly* trained. An empty store never makes for optimal lifting. On the plus side, though, I don't see any guards. They must be running around doing the big bunny's bidding."

Marlo made her way toward the Sponges, Spoons, and Sporting Goods aisle. Milton followed, as jumpy as a cricket on a hot plate.

"First off, short bus," Marlo said, looking her brother up and down, "stop announcing to the whole world that we're about to steal something. *Relax.* Your role in our little two-kid play is thus: *that of distraction.* You just toddle over yonder to the emergency exits and pull. And if I'm right, pandemonium will ensue. Got it?"

Milton nodded.

"Then get with it."

Milton grimaced, sighed, and skulked away.

"Milton," Marlo called.

Milton turned.

"What?"

"I missed you," she said sweetly. "For real."

Milton smiled despite himself.

"Ditto," he replied before heading toward Corsets, Cosmetics, and Custards.

Marlo strained underneath the bright yellow kayak. She looked like a shaved monkey making off with a gargantuan, genetically modified banana. The blare of alarms flooded the aisles like screaming ghosts.

Milton trotted up next to her, breathing heavily.

"I did it," he said with a blend of pride and terror. "I actually opened the emergency exits, even though there were signs that expressly said *not* to open them!"

"You're a true-blue desperado, little brother," Marlo grunted. "Now how about helping me get this kayak off my back?"

Milton took the bow of the fiberglass kayak and Marlo the stern.

"What is it with you and small nautical vessels?"

Milton asked as they crept as surreptitiously as possible toward the front of the store.

"I don't know." Marlo shrugged. "Must be the call of the sea. Or tides. You know, a girl thing. Like horses."

"And why did I open all of the emergency exits?"

"Because you're a good boy and do what you're told," Marlo explained. "Plus, pretty soon, if I played my cards right—ugh, *poker metaphors!*—a whole bunch of homeless phantoms should come trickling in from the alleyway, tired of Dumpster-diving and hungry for some *real* deals! I know *I* would if I were a POD."

"POD?" Milton asked.

"*PODs,*" Marlo clarified without clarifying.

"PODs!" screamed a girl in a white lab coat, working the cosmetics counter.

Dozens of gaunt spirits pushed their rusted, overflowing shopping carts through the aisles. A man with a cut underneath his eye wheeled past the Fausters. He furrowed his brow briefly at the sight of two children struggling beneath a bright yellow kayak before squeaking away, scrutinizing the items crowding the aisles.

"Perfect," Marlo whispered from beneath the back of the kayak. "Let's make a run for it."

Milton peered out from beneath the boat. He eyed the destitute men and women with awe as they began to form roving packs, cleaning out the shelves with fluid precision.

"Phantoms," he murmured.

"Yeah, Phantoms of the Dispossessed," Marlo replied. "*PODs* for short. All right, here we go."

The harried shopgirls were so preoccupied by the POD people that Milton and Marlo were able to charge unbothered through the automatic doors and into the mall. The two children stopped by the escalators outside of Salvation Armani as old women cascaded around them on either side, caught in their own ceaseless consumerist flow.

"So what's with the kayak?" Milton panted.

"I'll tell you after we've glided down the spiral escalators to the main floor."

"What?!" exclaimed Milton as he set the kayak down. "You're crazy!"

Milton looked up. On the eleventh floor, Damian charged out of Hallowed Grounds, slugging down a quintuple-shot venti espressoccino frappé, no foam. He crushed the cup in his hand and unsheathed a pointy scepter from his sweatpants.

"Maybe it's not such a crazy idea after all," Milton gulped, sitting in the front of the kayak.

"Okay, then," Marlo said as she stood in the back of the boat, one leg still on the mall floor. "Brace yourself. We're in for one wild ride."

With a sharp kick, Marlo sent the boat careening down the up escalator past dozens of frightened, outraged shoppers. The elderly women pressed against the velvet handrails, clutching their bags as the kayak sliced downward. Behind them, the Fausters left a trail of shock, confusion, and quaint cries of "Good heavens!" "Kids today!" and "Oh my stars and garters!"

38 · THE BUCKTOOTH STOPS HERE

MARLO LEANED INTO a turn out of one escalator and down into the next. Milton gritted his teeth, his hands coiled tightly under the lip of the kayak's edge.

Soon the kayak thudded loudly onto yet another floor, skidding past the Out of Body Shop before gliding back into another moving staircase, thanks to the expert rudder that was Marlo's foot.

Milton managed to steal a desperate peek behind him. Clumps of frightened old women fanned themselves outside the escalators. And, in hot pursuit, Damian bounded over the elderly debris just one floor above.

The Fausters slammed into the fourth tier, toppling over a row of wheezing women clutching platinum walkers. Marlo smirked as dozens, perhaps hundreds, of phantoms coursed out of Mallvana's luxurious stores, each pack opening up another emergency exit for their comrades outside. Mayhem was spreading quickly.

Marlo pressed her foot into the bejeweled mall floor. The kayak skidded to a stop just outside of Aberzombie & Flinch.

"What are we doing?" Milton asked.

Marlo hopped out of the kayak and tugged it behind her.

"Nope, don't need any help, thanks for asking," Marlo grunted. "We're about to shoot down the mother of indoor escalator rapids."

Before them lay a majestic helix of escalators lushly upholstered in black velvet, spiraling in near-mechanical free fall to the main concourse below. It made the escalators above seem like bone-dry Slip 'n' Slides. The plunging chute ahead was Niagara Falls by comparison.

Marlo scooted the kayak into position and took in the breathtaking mallscape. "Ah," she said with something bordering on contentment. "What a beautiful day to do something really, really stupid."

Milton ducked his head between his shaking knees while Marlo kicked out behind her like a peevish mule, sending their kayak screaming down the coiling metal slalom.

"Whooo!!" Marlo squealed, waving her arms as if she were back home at the Dunk 'n' Disorderly water park. The speeding yellow kayak buffeted about the escalator violently before hugging the outermost handrail in centrifugal intensity.

Milton's eyes were squeezed shut. His entire digestive system was crackling with a sickening electricity. He felt like he was having a grand mall seizure. The kayak slammed into hard, level ground that did nothing to dampen its amazing momentum.

Suddenly, with a great thud, the boat came to a complete, painful stop. Their bodies lurched forward, apparently receiving the news of their abrupt halt a little late. Milton reached out his hand, touching something cold, something metal, something that tingled in a maddening way that filled him with an almost unbearable anxiety, an itchiness inside that nothing could ever satisfactorily scratch.

His eyes slowly opened and crawled up the hulking metal figure before him, from its painted white paws to its pudgy metal belly to its sickly pink nose until finally resting on a pair of long slender ears.

> "Dear Fausters, here at last,
> fulfill your special role.
> Before more time has passed,
> hand over what you stole . . .
> NOW!"

39 · A HOLE LOT OF NOTHING

"MILTON, GRABBIT," MARLO said, rising to her feet. "Grabbit, Milton."

Milton stood up and surveyed the haunted, full-metal rabbit before him, perched atop a riser in the back of the concourse behind plush, emerald-green curtains. What confused Milton most, though—besides the rhyming rabbit's existence in the first place—were the coiling arms that had been soldered onto its sides. He could just make out stenciled letters painted beneath each arm, spelling out SMASH 'N' FLASH ATOM CANNON. He gulped.

"H-hello . . . Grabbit," Milton managed.

> *"Hello, Milton F.*
> *However did you find us?*
> *Marlo, are you deaf?*
> *I asked you for the diamonds!"*

Marlo's smile faded. The Grabbit seemed so . . . *testy*. No interest in how she had gotten the diamonds, her brilliant plan, the amusing anecdotes collected along the way. The hulking hare just wanted to hop right to the finish line. *Well,* Marlo mused, *rabbits do love carats.*

She sighed, unzipped her fanny pack, and—with hands trembling under the strain—scooped out one of the Hopeless Diamonds and held it up, supporting her shaky arm with the other so that the Grabbit could see her achievement in all its glittering glory.

Behind the stage, pulsating on one of Mallvana's massive plasma screens, was Yojuanna, dancing in jerky spasms, clad in a shimmering electric jumpsuit with lasers for suspenders. Her face was dead white, like a clown's, with black dollar signs painted around her mad eyes. The digital diva's face loomed large as she gazed down at the diamond and sang:

"Diamonds are this girl's best friend.
Gotta, gotta give 'em, give 'em on the double.
But if you don't put 'em in the bunny's hands,
then there's gonna, gonna, gonna be some trouble."

Milton shot his sister a baffled look. "What's with all the rhyming?" he asked.

Marlo shrugged. "You get used to it."

She stepped forward to the Grabbit. Milton

watched as his sister's eyes crawled over the metal creature, transfixed. She shifted from foot to foot. It looked almost like her whole body, her whole soul—everything that she was—had to go to the bathroom, really, really bad. Marlo eyed the openings at the tip of each of the Grabbit's coiling arms.

> *"Yes, you've got it. That's the ticket.*
> *Put the diamonds right in there.*
> *Then I'll have it, why, I'll take it!*
> *Everything in everywhere."*

Marlo stood on her tiptoes, just beneath the Grabbit's right hand, and hoisted up one of the Hopeless Diamonds in her palm. A demon in overalls flicked on a switch, and bright green spotlights flooded the stage. The Grabbit gave off a sickly glow. One of the lights popped, leaving the creature's face in darkness.

"Uh-oh, we lost a light," he shouted to a cohort up on the scaffolding. "And it's just about showtime. See if you can't get a replacement to fill in this black hole."

As the gorgeously glum jewel sparkled in the stage lights, a terrible thought struck Milton: *Atom smasher. Diamonds. Black hole.*

"Wait!" yelped Milton, running to his sister's side. "Black hole!"

Startled by the sound of her brother's yelp, Marlo jumped. The diamond rolled out of her palm and into the maw of the Grabbit's metal hand, where it dropped with a reverberating *thunk*. The vibration traveled down the Grabbit's arm, making it hum all over.

Marlo was shaking. "What?" she asked. "You scared the bejeebus out of me!"

Milton stared at the smiling metal monster. The coin had dropped, and he waited for the candy to fall.

Marlo backed away from the vibrating Grabbit.

"Black hole? Is that one of your stupid *Battlestar Trek* sci-fi things? What does it have to do with—"

"Black holes are *real*," Milton said. "They're a region of space-time where nothing can escape."

Marlo cocked her nonexistent eyebrow. "Like family game night?"

"Sort of," Milton said. "A black hole is kind of like when you divide by zero. It creates this infinite impossibility that . . ."

Marlo's eyes were dark with incomprehension.

". . . that can suck up and destroy everything around it. And that's what the Grabbit's trying to do."

Marlo folded her arms and scrutinized the Grabbit's indecipherable grin.

"How can a big metal bunny make a black hole out of diamonds?" she asked. "It doesn't make any sense."

"Some scientists were able to do it back up on the Surface," Milton replied, pacing in front of the stage. "They took a particle accelerator and slammed atoms together and made tiny black holes that lasted only a few seconds. But if someone—or some*thing*—slammed together something as dense as the Hopeless Diamonds, they could possibly make one big enough to swallow up . . . *everything.*"

"But why?" Marlo said with frustration.

A withered woman with a puffy cloud of white hair piled on top of her head peeked through the curtain. "It's those terrible children!" she kvetched to a flock of skinny, white-haired women grumbling like a cluster of grouchy Q-tips. Milton parted the curtain and peered out into the concourse. The group of old women and assorted demons slowly transformed into, if not quite an angry mob, a decidedly crotchety one.

The Grabbit's voice sliced through the din growing beyond the curtain.

> *"Don't listen to the boy.*
> *He knows not what he's saying.*
> *I've no plans to destroy.*
> *Now stop all this delaying!"*

Marlo trembled. What if her brother was right? What if all this had been a trick to help the Grabbit with some evil plot? But why would something, even something that wasn't truly alive, want to wipe out everything around it, including itself?

Milton anxiously peered out over the ever-growing crowd. "We've got company," he said.

The woman he had seen in Bea "Elsa" Bubb's not-so-secret lair snaked through the crowd toward the stage.

"Milton," Marlo said, joining him to peek through the curtain, "if I don't give the Grabbit the diamonds, we'll be taken away and sent . . . *somewhere worse*. And who knows what would happen to you. You wouldn't last a second in a place like Sadia, tormented by bullies like—"

"*Damian!*" Milton cried, pointing to the rim of the swelling crowd.

Cutting a swath—literally—through the mob was Damian: half boy, half girl, and all dangerous, swishing his scepter through the air.

Marlo gazed out at the growing mob and fretfully tucked her blue hair behind her ears.

"I have no choice," she said sadly, shaking her head. "We can't run away—there's nowhere *to* run—and if we stay here, they'll just lock us away in some extra-terrible place for stealing the jewels. The only hope we have is that the Grabbit's telling the truth, and it can shake up this place, control the new economy, and make me in charge of a circle where—hopefully—I can pardon you."

Marlo pardon *him*, Milton thought. It was almost funny. *Almost.* But in this upside-down, topsy-turvy place, it would only seem fitting that his sociopathic sister would be in some position of power, absolving Milton of his crimes of common sense.

Marlo walked over to the Grabbit's coiling right limb. She wrapped her shaking hands around the second

Hopeless Diamond and struggled to lift it out of her fanny pack.

"At last I'll sate my greed.
No longer will things taunt.
Don't give me what I need.
Just give me what I want!"

"I'm trying, I'm trying!" grumbled Marlo as, with trembling arms, she lifted the diamond up to the Grabbit's metal paw.

"This isn't right, Marlo!" Milton shouted against the noise of the agitated crowd. "Please! If we stall, something else is bound to present itself. . . ."

Present, Milton thought. He patted himself. Tucked into the back of his singed pants was the small present his mom had given him what seemed like—and in a way *was*—a lifetime ago.

Meanwhile, Yojuanna gyrated herself into a digital frenzy outside on the concourse wall, the screen's plasma cells working hard to keep up with her furious motion. It was as if she were stirring a pot of electricity, with herself as the spoon.

"Goody, goody, goody good.
Give this girl just whatcha should.
Love that shiny, flashy bling,
more than every everything!"

The computer-generated pop star grew warped and distorted. Her once-perfect, expertly coded features were now gruesome and exaggerated. The elderly women in the audience shook their gray heads.

"You call that music?" one woman with painted-on eyebrows said to her friend.

"Shameful," her friend concurred.

40 · A DiAMOND
iN THE BLUFF

FAITH, HOPE, AND Charity strode their synchronized runway strut from Hosanna Republic to the crowd's periphery, meeting Lilith at the edge of the swelling, milling mob.

"Has the Grabbit started without us?" Hope asked, stretching the limits of her satin high-heeled pumps to see the stage. "I hear something going on back there. . . ."

A musical ringtone chirruped from Lilith's thumb. "Excuse me," she said, turning away to answer her No-Fee Hi-Fi Faux Phone. "Hello? Yes, this is . . . *what? Both* stagecoaches? You've got to be kidding . . . of course, I know your jokes are funnier than that but . . . you're sure? No sign of either Hopeless—?" Lilith rubbed her temples. *"Okay,"* she said fretfully. "I'll do what I can here."

Lilith flexed her hand, ending her call, and peered above the murky sea of gray hair. Through a part in the curtain, she saw two children onstage, arguing with one another in front of the Grabbit. The small, twerpy boy with glasses looked familiar.

"I've got a bad feeling about this," she mumbled as she surveyed the concourse. Her biting green eyes rested on Bea "Elsa" Bubb, descending the stairs from the security cove next to the Garden of Eatin' with several security demons. Lilith plunged two of her slender fingers into her mouth and let loose a piercing whistle.

"Blubb!" Lilith shouted. "Over here!"

Principal Bubb grudgingly joined Lilith at the rim of the crowd. "I'm not your dog, by the way," Principal Bubb protested.

"I know . . . my dogs all have *pedigrees*," Lilith said, looking around her nervously and speaking to the principal in hushed tones. "Right now, Fido, I just want to know what you're going to do about *that*." Lilith jabbed a finger at the stage.

Bea "Elsa" Bubb's nostrils flared with anger. There they were, the Fauster children, flaunting their wretchedness up onstage, at the Grabbit's feet, no less. She turned her yolky eyes back at Lilith.

"I *am* doing something about it," she replied. "In fact, I have someone on it right now."

"Let me guess," Lilith said. "The deranged boy wearing makeup and waving the scepter."

Principal Bubb saw Damian, screaming at frightened old women to get out of his way, bounding toward the stage.

"Don't botch this, Blubb," Lilith said with breath like a hot blast of cinnamon. "If this doesn't go down well—"

"—then *you're* going down," Principal Bubb hissed. "That nasty bespectacled nerd onstage is *Milton Fauster*. Now, however did he get here without you knowing it?"

Lilith swallowed hard. Her golden face blanched to tarnished tin. "Well," she continued weakly. "At least Mammon isn't here yet. We still have a little time."

Principal Bubb stared across the throbbing concourse at a disturbed clot of old women, screaming as someone—or some*thing*—entered the gray-haired fray.

"*Very* little, by the looks of it," she mumbled with a mixture of awe and unease.

A stooped, hulking figure sliced its way through the gasping crowd, leaving behind it a jagged scarlike swath. The barrel-chested yet elegant creature— perhaps eight feet tall—twitched its pointy ears to note the various sounds surrounding it, while never once taking its cold green eyes from the stage.

"M-m-mammon," Lilith stammered.

Mammon—a large, brooding man-wolf stuffed into

an expensive power suit—stalked closer to the stage in hungry strides. Lilith elbowed her way through the crowd to staunch the pulsing gush of his progress. Bea "Elsa" Bubb followed in the wake of the desperate devil's advocate, savoring Lilith's panic as if sipping a rare vintage of champagne—slowly so that the bubbles wouldn't tickle her snout.

"Chairman!" Lilith yelped as she sprung into the air, waving her bamboo-thin arm like a drowning praying mantis.

Mammon stopped. His head swiveled with a predator's swift grace. Principal Bubb gulped, yet her throat was so dry that it had nothing to swallow.

The chairman's face was bare, shaved smooth from the top of his forehead to midway down his neck. His features were dusted with dark stubble, save for his smooth, moist snout and thin black lips.

Mammon briefly considered Lilith with his unreadable emerald eyes, then strode over to her. Frightened old women dove out of his way as if he were helming an invisible tanker that displaced gurgling gray water. He stood before Lilith and the principal with the cold, stony silence of an ancient creature that has long outlived social niceties.

Mammon's charcoal pinstripe suit with its squared, draping shoulders made the creature's upper body seem somehow gorilla-like in proportion. The wolf-demon wore the suit like armor, as if every seam and stitch had been engineered to breed submission and uncertainty on the battlefield of a corporate boardroom.

"M-m-mamm," Lilith faltered again, sounding like a sputtering outboard motor.

Mammon set down his briefcase with a grunt—only the grunt didn't come from him. Instead of an elegantly tooled leather attaché case, Mammon sported a living black boar, which the wolf-demon held by a handle attached to leather straps ribbed around the bristly creature's midsection. Striped down its back, an inch to the left of the swine's spine, was a long gold zipper stretching from the nape of its neck to its tail.

"Did you just call me 'ma'am'?" Mammon growled.

This is going to be good, Bea "Elsa" Bubb thought.

Lilith trembled, her gangly limbs rattling like someone rolling dice in a game of Yahtzee. "No," she managed. "Of course not. I . . . I'm just . . . excited to finally meet you. And cold. But that's what I get for having virtually no body fat . . . uh . . . nice briefcase." Lilith snickered, a hyena in a designer dress laughing at her own joke.

"Is everything under control, Miss Couture?" Mammon growled.

Bea "Elsa" Bubb exposed every one of her nasty, yellow teeth in a gracious leer. "Chairman Mammon," the principal said, bolstered by Lilith's lack of composure.

Lilith nudged the principal sharply with the bony

dagger that was her elbow. "Principal, perhaps you should tend to that . . . *situation* we were discussing earlier?"

"Yes," Bea "Elsa" Bubb replied reluctantly. "I wouldn't want *your* situation to affect *our* ceremony."

The principal stormed off toward the stage on an intercept course with Damian, looking over her shoulder to give Lilith one last parting sneer.

"Situation?" Mammon barked. His briefcase sniffed the air with its wet pink snout, then grunted in disapproval. "There, there, my filthy Lucre," Mammon cooed, scratching the beast behind its stiff, pointy ears. "I smell it, too . . . something fishy. Like convenience-store sushi."

Lilith's face muscles tugged, tied, and tamed her grimace into a bright, confident smile. "Fishy? Of course not! It's nothing . . . no big deal. Nothing to concern yourself—"

"No big deal?!" Mammon roared. "I've spent *centuries* inflaming the human heart with greed. And why? To ensure that everything is indeed a *big deal.*"

"No need to be so grumpy, Mr. Chairman," Lilith murmured in a tone as sweet and intoxicating as freshly baked rum cake. "Even if something *were* to happen— which it won't—it's not like you, with all your assets, would ever be hurting for money if a deal were to—"

"I don't make deals for the money," he snorted. "I do it to *do it.* Money is just a way of keeping score."

Lilith shrunk back, crumpling like a corsage on the morning after prom.

"And while your wiles may work on the Big Guy Downstairs," the demon man-wolf continued, patting his bulging breast pocket, "I assure you that the closest thing to my heart is my billfold. All I require from you is the assurance that all will go according to plan."

"Of course," Lilith replied shakily as she gave a sideways glance toward the stage, where the Fauster children debated with each other before the unfathomable robotic rabbit, where a snorting bull-of-a-boy in drag shoved old women out of his way in a mad rush to intercept the siblings, and where Principal Bubb rushed to intercept the interceptor. "What could possibly go wrong?"

41 · THE GiFT OF GRAB

"HERE!" MILTON SAID, pressing the present into his sister's chest.

Marlo lowered her shaking, diamond-burdened arms and stared at the small package wrapped in deep blue foil, tied with a bright red bow.

"Milton, you shouldn't have," she replied. "Really. I'm busy here, and you have yet to give me anything I ever really liked."

The Grabbit quaked anew.

"Stop all of this tiresome stalling.
There's no way you can outfox.
Feed my greed; it's quite appalling,
but first, what's in the box?"

Marlo leaned into Milton and whispered, "What exactly *is* in the box?"

"No clue," Milton answered. "But I have a feeling that won't matter. Give the Grabbit a choice."

"You can't be serious," Marlo countered. "I've got one of the most precious gems *ever*. Whatever's in this box couldn't possibly be anywhere near as good. It barely weighs *anything*."

"Just ask it," Milton replied. "Pretend it's like a game show."

"Hmm," Marlo considered.

She cleared her throat.

"What's in the box, you ask?" she posed to the green metal rabbit before her. "Well, that's for us to know and you to find out, isn't it?"

The Grabbit vibrated so hard that it hummed, a high-pitched frequency that made Milton clap his hands over his ears. The group of old women watching through the parted curtain checked their hearing aids.

"So what's it going to be, bunny?" Marlo taunted. "The diamond or the mysterious secret inside this festively wrapped box?"

The old women pressing against the stage began calling out.

"The diamond!"

"The mysterious box!"

"Diamond!"

"Mysterious box!"

"An exasperating choice you pose.
How I love the precious rocks!
But a mystery I must expose;
show me what's inside the box!"

Marlo plunked the Hopeless Diamond back into her fanny pack, grabbed the gift from Milton, and held it up to the Grabbit's jittery metal limb.

"Now, Grabbit, for your big prize," she announced, *"the mysterious box!"*

Marlo slid the package into the opening of the Grabbit's Smash 'n' Flash Atom Cannon arm. The gift fell in silently, a silence that spilled out across the stage and washed over the crowd. After a hushed moment, a faint whirring emanated from the Grabbit's limbs, gradually gaining momentum, like a washer beginning its spin cycle. The Grabbit began to shake and lurch, as if it were the victim of an unbalanced load, which indeed it was.

"What have you two done?
Is this some kind of prank?
I'm spinning, spunning, spun,
And feeling very . . . blank."

The grinning creature wobbled violently as the Hopeless Diamond in its right arm twisted through the Smash 'n' Flash Atom Cannon's coils, gaining in velocity, while the gift in the left arm did likewise, only with less fanfare. Milton and Marlo stepped back.

"Silly Grabbit," Marlo said. "Tricks are for kids."

With a mighty shudder, the diamond and small, mysterious, gift-wrapped package were thrust into one another with explosive fury. The Grabbit's metal hull cracked in two, splitting along its leering Cheshire grin.

"Duck!" Marlo yelled, throwing her brother to the ground and covering him with her arm.

The Grabbit's metal skin puckered, sucking in from the inside with creaking dents and dimples before exploding outright. The curtain was ripped from the stage and whipped into the air, an angry ghost of flaming velvet.

Yojuanna's image degraded into a collection of low-definition cubes held together by stuttering static. Her face flattened until it was nothing more than a crude sketch comprised of meaningless letters and numbers, a code that no longer had the energy to decipher itself.

"Snap," she said just before the screen burst into a shower of sparks and glass.

A scorched, tattered note floated gently to the stage in front of Milton's outstretched arm, brushing against his hand. He grabbed it and sat down cross-legged on the stage. Hundreds of elderly women and demons screamed, swatting away pieces of flaming metal. Milton adjusted his glasses and at once identified the familiar loops, slants, and meticulous crossing of *t*'s as those of his mother.

Dearest Milton,

There's nothing I can possibly say to help you feel any better about your sister's death or the traumatic experience you had. It was devastating for us all, but especially for you, having been there with her at the time. No one could ever know how you feel—you're probably having trouble figuring out exactly how you feel yourself—and I won't patronize you by pretending I know what you're going through. And believe me, it's hard to not try. You're my precious little boy, and it's my job to protect you against unnecessary pain and suffering. And I've failed. There's nothing I can do to remove the grief and guilt. Nothing.

Which is why I've given you this gift. It's a box full of what you could have done to prevent Marlo's death. It's full of the worries you should have, churning that terrible day over and over in your head. It's full of the resentment your family has toward you for surviving what she didn't. It's full of the responsibility you should bear to somehow make things right.

It's a box full of nothing.

There's nothing you could have done. There is no amount of worry that will bring her back. There is absolutely no resentment harbored by those who love you, nor is there any responsibility you have to those around you in assuaging our grief.

So this is my gift to you, an empty box. A clean slate. A new beginning. Because sometimes the greatest gift of all is the gift of nothing.

All my love,
Mom

Teardrops splashed onto the note, blurring his mother's signature. All this time, he had been carrying this empty box around, a gift that—at the same time— had been full of so much. The best present he had ever gotten, despite the unspeakable hardships he had endured to protect it.

"What's wrong?" Marlo asked, nudging close to him. Milton silently passed her the note. Her dark eyes grew wet. As tears leaked down her cheek, she shook her head and laughed. "No wonder the Grabbit couldn't stomach the box," she said, sniffing back snot. "It didn't have anything in it except love. It gave its fat greedy belly a bad case of indigestion."

Marlo looked around her at the utter chaos of the

stage, weeping with sadness and with joy. She wiped her eyes with her sweatshirt sleeve.

"It's weird," she murmured. "I feel *wonderful*. Like I've been, I don't know . . . *buried*—which I probably am, somewhere—but now I'm suddenly . . . not. It's like I'm free. Totally free. And I didn't even know I wasn't."

Milton grew suddenly feverish. He pressed his face against the cool surface of the stage. His head swirled with vague, dreamlike images. His nose prickled with sharp smells. His ears were like a blender churning with sounds. He was undergoing another attack of "the ferrets."

Milton sniffed the air and raised his head in alarm. Piercing the hot clouds of lavender, rosewater, and talc was the brutal musk of anger. Sure enough, there was Damian, brandishing the scepter that had once held what smelled like bratwurst. Another smell coiled around Damian's, like two serpents braided in a single purpose.

"Mr. Fauster," Principal Bubb said with disgust, her mouth contorting around the disagreeable name. "We meet again."

Cold, liquid dread filled Milton. He tried to stop his shaking, to at least appear that he felt braver than he actually did, but his body, like it had so many times before, betrayed him.

"Don't worry, bro," Marlo consoled with a pat on his back. "We've been through worse."

Milton glared at his sister.

"Well, at least as bad," she added. *"Nearly.* Anyway, there's always some wriggle room in every situation. It's just a matter of sniffing it out."

A parade of sour smells marched through Milton's nostrils, accompanied by the clang of a hundred shopping carts.

"Over there!" several old ladies screamed, their bony fingers waggling at the spiral escalator.

Cascading down the escalator toward the concourse were hundreds of PODs. Their shopping-cart wheels slammed against the moving stairs in their rush to the concourse.

"Principal Bubb!" one of the security demons called.

Bea "Elsa" Bubb turned angrily, not wanting to take her curdled eyes off her prey, quarry that had escaped before and that she would do anything to capture again.

"What?!"

"We've g-g-got a sit-situation," the security demon stammered. "Look!"

The principal eyed the onslaught of phantoms, intent on making the most of their shopping spree. Her head throbbed, especially around where she had had her horns filed and buffed. She locked eyes with Damian, who had just reached the steps leading to the rostrum.

"Mr. Ruffino," Bea "Elsa" Bubb barked. "He's all

yours. But I want him intact, understand? I can't punish pieces."

Damian smirked. "Yes, ma'am," he said, crossing his fingers behind his back. "You can count on me."

Principal Bubb sighed.

"There's a first for everything, I suppose," she said wearily. "Until we meet again, Mr. Fauster," she called behind her as she turned to join the security squad amassing to deal with the POD invasion. "And I can assure you we will."

Marlo stood up defiantly. "Hey, *Amandi*," she shouted as Damian clambered onto the stage. "If you want to just talk things out—"

Marlo sidled up to the wreckage that, until recently, had been the Grabbit and picked up a severed metal ear.

"—I'm all ears."

Marlo lunged toward Damian, slicing the ear through the air like a sword.

"Now, Milton!" she screamed back at her brother. "Run!"

Milton looked out at the chaotic crowd of terrified old women struggling to get past other terrified old women. Then, in a bright flash of insight, Milton could see a path cutting perfectly through the mob, leading to a stream of PODs rippling out of the Virgin Mary Megastore. He turned to his sister. "I'll come back for you," he said. "I promise."

Marlo smiled as she frantically clashed ear against pointy scepter.

"What part of *run* don't you understand?!" she shouted.

Gathering up the full force of his fleeting ferret power, Milton leapt from the stage and sprinted down the path as it disappeared behind him.

"Oh, no, you don't!" Damian yelled, rushing toward Milton.

"Have a nice trip!" Marlo shouted, throwing the metal ear at Damian's legs, sending him tumbling off the stage and into a mosh pit of wrinkles, adult diapers, and plastic hip joints.

Milton rushed to meet the stampede of squealing wheels and tramping work boots. A man with an unruly salt-and-pepper beard considered Milton with cloudy blue eyes, pushing his bursting cart toward the concourse exit.

The herd of phantoms pressed onward toward the security vestibule leading to the underground parking garage. Inside the hallway of high-tech surveillance equipment, the security demons panicked, futilely trying to control a situation that had long since passed controllable. As Milton approached the black curtains, something sliced through his left calf. He screamed, toppling to the ground and rolling out of the ceaseless crush of shopping carts just in time to avoid being flattened by thousands of merciless wheels. Above him stood Damian, glaring down triumphantly. His A GRANDMA IS A MOM WITH EXTRA FROSTING sweatshirt swelled and collapsed as he caught his breath. His mouth was a sneering smear of lipstick. His eyes burned dark and dense, like the black hole that had nearly formed moments ago.

"Well, well, well," Damian clucked. "How clumsy of you."

Milton clutched his aching leg and brought it close to his chest.

"You promised Principal Bubb that you wouldn't hurt me," Milton gasped.

Damian rubbed his chin thoughtfully.

"Did I?" he mused facetiously. "I thought it was more of a suggestion than an outright order. Oh well, no use crying over spilt blood, is there?"

Damian steadily pressed the tip of the sharpened scepter down on Milton's heaving chest.

"Have you ever wondered what happens to dead boys when they die?" he asked.

Frankly, this had never occurred to Milton before. His survival instinct had overridden all of his higher, critical thinking. Still, it was a riddle he was more than happy to never solve.

"What do you say we find out?" Damian continued, squeezing the point gently yet persistently into Milton's chest. "And by 'we,' I mean *you*."

The last time Milton had been on the business end

of a sharp weapon wielded by Damian, he had been able to gain the upper hand by angering him and muddling his thinking.

"You wouldn't dare," Milton dared. "You're too chicken."

Damian's eyes creased into cruel, glimmering slits. His nostrils flared so wide that they resembled twin caves leading deep into darkness.

"You think this chicken won't cock-a-doodle-do it?" Damian sneered. He raised the gleaming scepter over his head. "Well, think again, brainiac. For the last time . . ."

Then, just as he brought the weapon down full force toward Milton's chest, Damian *vanished,* his scepter landing on the floor with a terrible clang

Milton blinked his eyes in disbelief. Damian, in all his cruel, monstrous glory, had been there, just about to dispatch Milton to a third death (not that Milton was counting) and then—*poof*—he was gone.

But Milton had no time to bask in his confounding fortune, as a squad of security demons surged forth, roughly apprehending writhing PODs and confiscating their wares. The guards appeared to be shackled together at the waist, each a link in a sinister, sinewy chain. Milton staggered to his feet, his leg aching brightly, like a blinding lighthouse of pain. He rejoined the tumble of bodies and wheels streaming through the curtains.

A claw grabbed Milton roughly by the shoulder. "Now I've got you!" a security demon roared.

The leathery demon—resembling a macramé project woven haphazardly of rancid meat—tucked its ropy neck to its chest and hissed into its walkie-talkie. "I've secured the Fauster child," it said triumphantly, digging its claws into Principal Bubb's own personal Public Enemy Number One. "No, the little milksop boy."

From his unfortunate vantage point, Milton noticed that the guard and his cohorts were not merely shackled together but that their bodies were *physically* connected, sharing a gnarled cat's cradle of black and red sinews. Dust from one of the captured PODs flew up into the rear guard's face, causing all six of the demons to sneeze in unison.

Milton tried prying himself free of the front demon's grasp, but its claw was as firm and unyielding as petrified wood.

Beyond the cadaverous conga line of guards (*or was it more like one long caterpillar-of-a-guard?* Milton couldn't be sure), a group of children and adults milled about noisily. From their various historical costumes and the masks of sullen defeat each wore, Milton deduced that the adults were teachers futilely attempting to herd their students.

"Quiet!" ordered one of the teachers, a man with a gleaming crown and robe. "Remember: Silence is golden!"

The group parted and Milton could see Marlo in the distance. She gazed past the line of demons, her eyes stopping at Milton. She hopped up and down and waved her arms.

"No!" he could see her mouthing, but her words were lost in the currents and eddies of babbling commotion.

One of the students, a dark-haired boy in penny loafers, noticed Marlo's outburst and—following her gaze—quickly, yet not completely, took in Milton's situation. The boy inexplicably heaved himself against a potted Madagascar dragon tree, which toppled over onto one of the teachers: the man with the golden crown. The teacher staggered and stumbled into the guard at the end of the row as the tree—now a gleaming gold statue—fell to the ground with a clangorous crash.

One by one, the demon guards turned into gold, each of them becoming glinting links in a golden chain leading straight to Milton. Freaking out, he struggled to free himself from the demon guard's firm clutch, but to no avail. Just as the golden row of "demonos" tumbled toward Milton, a shopping cart slammed into the security demon gripping him.

"Take that, ya nasty piece of maggot food!" a POD with a droopy brown mustache yelped triumphantly as the 24-karat guard toppled to the ground.

A new swell of demons oozed from the concourse.

They indifferently eyed the fallen trophies that had been their cohorts as they rushed toward the security vestibule. A demon tugged the struggling POD away from his cart as a woman behind them squealed.

"Let him go!" yelled Hope, the angelic supermodel, as she kicked the guard with her expensive and surprisingly dangerous stiletto heels.

"All he needs is a little compassion!" Faith screamed as she pummeled the guard with her fists.

Milton stared dumbfounded as the throng of demons absorbed the POD that had saved his afterlife.

"Get a move on, boy!" the POD bellowed as he was dragged away.

Milton grabbed the man's shopping cart, slunk down, and pushed it through the security vestibule and into the parking garage, joining the throng of migrating PODs.

The phantoms surged toward the shadows in the back of the garage. Milton wheeled next to a gangly female phantom with a face creased with sadness, pushing a cart loaded with two-liter jugs filled with a glittering, silver liquid.

She eyed Milton with vague curiosity. "Nice ride," she said faintly.

"Where are we going, ma'am?" Milton asked the woman as he limped beside her.

After a moment's hesitation, the woman gave him a warm, toothless grin. "Nowhere," she answered in a craggy voice. "Anywhere. Everywhere. It's all the same. So many places to go, and not one of them home."

Milton nodded mournfully, feeling an instant kinship with this fellow phantom, a restless spirit on a circuitous quest, the destination changing abruptly with every uncertain step.

The line of squeaky carts snaked into the darkness of the sprawling concrete structure, disappearing, swallowed up by shadows.

42 · CHICKEN FREED

"FOR THE LAST time," Damian said, thrusting his arms down; only, his scepter—and Milton—were gone. In fact, the whole mall had disappeared around him. *Vanished*.

Instead, he was in a dark basement full of crates, lying on the ground, surrounded by a half dozen staring lunatics in blue robes.

"What the—?" he exclaimed. As he tried to rise off the ground, his body painfully refused. Every muscle was stiff and sore, as if he were half boy, half statue. He reached around to the back of his head and plucked out what looked like a meat thermometer. A long cable trailed from the bottom of it, leading beyond his field of vision.

Damian looked around the room, or as much as his rigid neck would allow. The basement reeked of burnt popcorn chicken. The floor was, inexplicably, covered with feathers, blood, and the bodies of hens whose lifeless talons pointed up at the ceiling. The bygone birds were connected by a series of electrical wires clipped to their combs.

"Where am I?" he asked, though his voice hardly sounded like his own. His throat was drier than it had ever been, and the sound he made was a strained croak.

A twitchy mouse of a girl with shiny black eyes stepped away from a cheap plywood casket.

How tacky, Damian thought, *I wouldn't be caught dead in that hunk of junk.*

"Hi, Damian," Necia said with a ghoulish smile. "Welcome back."

"Welcome back?" he rasped.

The Guiding Knight approached Damian with a knowing smile. "Yes," the man said imperiously. "Back to the land of the living to lead us."

He turned to Sentinel Shane, whose butcher's apron was caked with fresh blood.

"Nice job, Sentinel," the Guiding Knight congratulated. "We'll compensate you for all these Rhode Island Reds that died valiantly to deliver us our new Bridge."

"Lead us? Bridge?" Damian squawked. "What are you talking about?"

The Guiding Knight smirked.

"The Bridge between this world and the next," he continued matter-of-factly. "We harnessed the subtle energies available to us, in this case contained within poultry, and were able to revive you, our new Chosen One, the once-dead-now-living Bridge destined to guide us to our rightful place . . . *beyond.*"

Damian fought an almost overwhelming urge to peck at the strange man. "Me?" he replied. "The Chosen One?"

The robed nut jobs around him smiled and nodded with reverence. Damian examined their faces and the blind respect that shone from their eyes.

"So you're telling me that I'm your new leader and you have to do what I say because I'm going to show you the way to your own personal paradise?"

The Knights of the Omniversalist Order Kinship again nodded as one. Damian grinned, his orange, overly made-up face creasing into a grotesque mask. He rubbed his hands together and mentally savored the countless, wicked possibilities that his new situation offered.

"Cool," he tried to reply, but instead his comment came out more as a cluck. He cleared his throat. "What I meant to say is, that *brocks!*"

43 · PLAYING THE FOOLS

MARLO SAT ON the edge of the stage with her legs dangling restlessly. Her limbs itched with the urge to flee, but security demons, teachers, and various Netherworld bureaucrats now surrounded her.

Poker Alice wheeled through the disbanding crowd along with Ms. Mandelbaum, Ms. O'Malley, and Principal Bubb. Soon they were swarming about Marlo and the smoldering bunny wreckage strewn about the stage.

"I knew you was at the root of this, ya miserable little sidewinder!" Poker Alice fumed through a thick cloud of cigar smoke.

Marlo looked up through the mall's thirteen tiers to its gorgeous stained-glass ceiling. The intricate geometric patterns dazzled with fierce color. A dopey grin shellacked itself across Marlo's face. Now that she was free from the Grabbit's greedy grip, she felt bigger on the inside than she was on the outside. Then there was the cool, mysterious boy who had helped her to help Milton escape. For some reason, he, too, made her feel big inside. But, regardless of her newfound inner "bigness," Marlo now found herself in some seriously big trouble. In the kaleidoscope of shapes above, she searched for some way out of her predicament.

"Look at me!" Poker Alice bellowed.

Even on the best of days, the last thing Marlo wanted to do was fill her eyes with Poker Alice's wrinkled gunnysack of a face.

"I'm not saying anything without a lawyer present," Marlo said, still hypnotized by the roof. "Except, of course, for what I just said."

Lilith pried her way through the stubborn, grumbling remnants of the mob and reached the stage. "I demand to know what's going on!" she insisted hotly.

"And who might you be," Ms. Mandelbaum asked, sizing Lilith up with an accusatory crinkle, "like you're ze belle of ze ball?"

Lilith shoved her gilded red and gold business card into Ms. Mandelbaum's shiny, plastic-wrapped face, never taking her eyes off the gnarled, twisted heap on the stage.

LILITH COUTURE
Devil's Advocate

Ms. Mandelbaum gulped, nervous as an antelope on a nature show. "Forgive me, ma'am," she said contritely, smoothing out the wrinkles of her polyethylene coating. "I'm a little *meshuggina* with all this. I'm Ms. Mandelbaum, but please, dear, call me *Marm*."

"I'll do no such thing, Ziploc," Lilith snapped. "I need to know where the Hopeless Diamonds are!"

Principal Bubb joined the vicious circle. "The POD situation is under control," Bea "Elsa" Bubb informed Lilith.

"The blazes with the PODs!" Lilith yelled. "I've got to get those diamonds before the NSE opens, or the whole underworld economy will collapse!"

"The Hopeless Diamonds?!" Mammon howled from behind. "Do *not* tell me that the Hopeless Diamonds aren't safe and sound in Sadia!"

The blood drained from Lilith's face as even her corpuscles tried to flee the body they called home.

With detached amusement, Marlo surveyed the freakish assortment of creatures surrounding her. Her situation seemed like a tiny circus car disgorging a thousand clowns, a visual that made her chuckle, clearing her head in the process.

"What's so blasted funny?!" Poker Alice raged.

In that instant, Marlo knew what she had to do. She fished one of the Hopeless Diamonds out of her fanny pack. Mammon's wolf-pupils widened into dark pools of liquid desire. He thrust out his hairy paw. Marlo suppressed the urge to comment, *My, what big teeth you have, Grandmother.* With both arms straining, she handed him the diamond.

Poker Alice wheeled forward, screeching to a stop in front of Marlo's knees. "I'm on to you, Miss Fauster," she snorted bitterly. "There are two Hopeless Diamonds. Nice try . . . thinking you could fool us by giving—"

"It's over there," Marlo said calmly, casually pointing over her right shoulder toward the Grabbit's charred, fractured torso.

Bea "Elsa" Bubb nodded toward the Grabbit's body, sending her security demons shuffling onto the stage, sifting through the wreckage. The principal grabbed Marlo by the arm, sinking her talons painfully into her flesh.

"I trust you about as far as I could order someone to throw you," Bea "Elsa" Bubb muttered suspiciously.

"Here it is," a muscular demon said as he held up the dazzling teardrop-shaped jewel.

Norm, Takara, Lyon, Bordeaux, and Jordie joined the fray just as the demon handed Mammon the precious gem. The chairman of the Netherworld Soul Exchange lifted up his squealing briefcase, unzipped its bristly back, and deposited the two gems into the creature's fabricated pouch. Mammon set the black boar down on its stubby legs.

The principal arched her eyebrow, which looked

like an angry centipede rearing up to attack. "Now, all I want to know is how this happened," she said, releasing Marlo's arm with great reluctance.

"I'll ask the questions around here," Lilith butted in. "Now, all I want to know is how this happened."

Principal Bubb rolled her curdled yellow eyes.

Lyon stepped forward spryly. "*She* stole them!" Lyon said, stretching her arm at Marlo until it reached its full, accusatory length.

Norm looked at Marlo nervously. "That's not entirely—" Norm sputtered.

"Yes," Marlo interrupted, rubbing her sore arm, "that's true. I *did* steal the Hopeless Diamonds."

She looked deeply into Norm's eyes.

"All by myself."

Lilith folded her smooth, tan arms and scowled at the dusty girl on the stage.

"Do you have any idea how much trouble you're in?!" she pronounced with outrage, hoping to divert Mammon's ire. "What would have happened if—"

"—if the Grabbit had gotten the diamonds?" Marlo interjected. "Yes, I do. Which is why I had to stop it."

"What do you mean?" Lilith scowled.

Marlo stood up onstage. It was showtime. The half dozen security demons reached for the bully clubs dangling at their sides. Principal Bubb waved them off with a waggle of her claw.

"What I mean," Marlo continued, "is that the Grabbit enlisted me—*and only me*—to steal the Hopeless Diamonds for it. Why did I agree? Because I knew that if I didn't, it would just get someone else to do it . . . some *lesser* criminal," she added with a contemptuous sniff so subtle that only Lyon would—*and did*—notice. "So I took the job in order to, ultimately and brilliantly, thwart its plan."

"And what *exactly* was this plan?" Mammon posed with a blend of suspicion and intrigue.

Marlo replied as melodramatically as possible.

"To destroy . . . *everything.*"

Poker Alice laughed.

"Ya can't be expectin' us to swallow this steamin' pile o' hooey," she chortled.

"Silence, you ashtray on wheels!" scolded Mammon, clearly fascinated with Marlo. "Go on . . . what was your name?"

"Marlo Fauster. *F-A-U—*"

"We're all familiar with your unfortunate surname," Principal Bubb grumbled.

Marlo paced the edge of the stage in thoughtful strides.

"See, the Grabbit wanted the Hopeless Diamonds to create a black hole that would suck in everything, everywhere, making every molecule, every atom completely its own. Destroying our humble corner of the universe in the process."

"Black hole?" Ms. Mandelbaum exclaimed. "What bupkes are you talking about?"

"A black hole," Bordeaux interjected, "is an object with a gravitational field so powerful that even electromagnetic radiation, such as light, cannot escape its pull. Within the black hole is a singularity, a place where matter is compressed to such a degree that the known laws of physics no longer apply to it."

Lilith eyed Bordeaux as one might scrutinize an unusual bug that had just splattered on the windshield during a cross-country car trip. "And how was the Grabbit going to accomplish this improbable feat?" she asked, returning her attention to Marlo.

Marlo skipped toward the Grabbit's collapsed hull and dragged out one of its severed, corkscrew arms.

"The Hopeless Diamonds are the densest objects known to man," Marlo said. "And I don't have to tell you that if you slam particles together in a particle accelerator fast enough, you can create your very own black hole."

The small crowd turned to Bordeaux.

"Gawd, I don't know." She gaped back. "Stop staring at me already!"

The teachers, bureaucrats, guards, and students returned their gaze to Marlo.

"Well, you can," Marlo continued. "And, with particles like those in the Hopeless Diamonds, you sure could make one black, unholy hole."

"Astounding," murmured Mammon.

Lyon's jaw fell open in disgust as she watched the gullible grown-ups figuratively perched in the palm of Marlo's hand. "She's lying!" she shrieked. "She didn't steal the diamonds! *I stole the diamonds, too!*"

"But I thought you just said that Miss Fauster did?" Lilith inquired.

Mammon shook his head pityingly.

"Oh, young lady," he offered, "that's just sad."

"This is *so* not over!" Lyon huffed as she yanked Bordeaux by the arm and stormed off.

Mammon stalked to the stage and stood before Marlo, bringing with him a cloud of pungent musk. She noticed that the coarse pelt coating his body was gelled into lacquered waves of gleaming fur, cresting in stiff, crisp peaks at the top of his head.

"The name's Mammon," he said with a pointy-toothed grin. "Chairman of the Netherworld Soul Exchange. And we could use a girl like you . . . *down there.* In fact, you rather remind me of . . . *me.* When I was a cub, that is. Someone who isn't satisfied with just making money but who also wants to make a *statement.* Someone who knows that greed is a game and plays that game to win."

Marlo looked down at Mammon's oxblood leather lace-ups with hand-stitched detailing on the toe. They were buffed so meticulously that she could see a budding pimple on her chin in their reflection. She looked up nervously at Ms. O'Malley, who returned her gaze with a sly wink and a grin, filling Marlo with a quiet confidence.

At that moment, John Keats ran to the stage, the bright blue plumage fringing his head and arms rippling in the wind. "Am I too late?" the feathered poet queried as he fluttered to a stop before the teachers.

"Actually, you just missed—" Ms. O'Malley started to reply before Ms. Mandelbaum elbowed her in the ribs.

"Yer right on time, bluebird of happiness," Ms. Mandelbaum said.

Keats's yellow beak of a mouth widened into a smile as he flittered to the stage.

Ms. O'Malley glared at Ms. Mandelbaum while rubbing her aching side. "Why'd ya do that, ya nasty old sandwich bag?"

Ms. Mandelbaum leaned into the Irish pirate's flaming-red mane. "The only thing worse than that bird-brained blowhard's poetry is listening to him kvetch about not getting to recite it," she whispered through her unzipped mouth. "Plus, it will calm down the old biddies."

Keats pecked the microphone.

"Check, check . . ."

He cleared his throat.

"A thing of beauty is a joy for ever:
Its loveliness increases; it will never—"

An assortment of screams rippled through the crowd as droves of old women made room for an angry red blur hemorrhaging toward the stage.

*"Bunnies will go to France,
and they will look up teachers' . . ."*

Lord Byron glared at the plumed poet perched atop the stage. "KEATS!" he bellowed, popping a network of blood vessels on his angry red cheek.

Bea "Elsa" Bubb pressed her claw against Mammon's hunched back. He turned and, upon seeing the principal's face, grimaced, as if he had just passed a bowling ball–sized kidney stone.

"What?" he grumbled.

"It's Ms. Couture," Principal Bubb said earnestly. "She allowed a known fugitive, Milton Fauster, to return to Heck completely undetected. She let the Hopeless Diamonds fall into unauthorized hands. She's completely—"

"Incompetent," he blurted.

Bea "Elsa" Bubb faltered. "Excuse me?" she asked, bewildered.

"I said, she's completely incompetent," Mammon repeated. "And she's about to learn that just because she has powerful friends in low places, she's not coated in procedural Teflon so that nothing bad will stick to her."

He tromped back to the stage with heavy steps.

"Ms. Fauster," he said in thick, oily syllables, as if his tongue were buttering a slice of toast, "we just might have an infernship opening with the Big Guy Downstairs himself. Are you interested?"

Marlo's attention again went up to the dazzling stained-glass ceiling. As she stared, mesmerized by its radiant geometry, she thought about what the angel, Ms. Roosevelt, had said at assembly, about Rapacia holding with it "opportunity": *Nothing is set in stone. . . . True joy comes from giving to others, because, when you give to others, you're really giving to yourself.*

Maybe this was her opportunity to make things right somehow, by working the system from the inside. Perhaps she could insinuate herself into the machine and help Milton, Norm, Takara, and even Ms. O'Malley . . . all the people she knew who deserved better than to waste their afterlives kowtowing before bitter, grasping bureaucrats who abused their tiny scraps of power. And who knows, she'd probably enjoy some way-cool fringe benefits in the process.

"Sure," Marlo said. "That would be cool."

Ms. O'Malley leaned into Marlo briefly. "Just remember, lass," she whispered, "if you lie down with dogs . . . or wolves . . . you'll rise with fleas."

But Marlo wasn't worried about that. Not now. She didn't want to be like these self-consumed, tyrannical blowhards. She just wanted a little power. But Marlo, never having held a position of power, had no clue as to its tendency to corrupt.

Lilith strutted to Mammon's side. "Infernship?" she said quizzically. "I would have heard about a position like that—"

"Now, don't make a scene, Ms. Couture," he remarked with a sneer.

"Make a scene?!" Lilith yelped, causing dozens of gray heads to crane her way. "Someone like me can't help *but* make a scene! What under Earth are you talking about?!"

"You've bungled this whole affair every step of the way," Mammon replied.

Lilith gulped. The light behind her brilliant green eyes dimmed. She glared at Principal Bubb, who was radiating smug self-satisfaction. The demoness hadn't felt *this* good about herself since inventing summer school.

"I can explain," Lilith murmured.

"Don't write a check you can't cash, Ms. Couture," Mammon countered. "You're so concerned with your next step that you never look at what you've stepped in."

Lilith looked down at her perfect hooves. "I'm a self-starting go-getter with phenomenal people skills, you big, bad—"

Mammon gave a low, reverberating growl.

"Don't think you can dig yourself a hole all the way

back down to"—he looked at the young girls staring at him—"*you know where.* Principal Bubb is obviously overtaxed, considering the sorry state of things down here. I mean, look at the poor woman. She's an absolute disaster. . . ."

"Thanks," the principal mumbled under her fetid anchovy breath.

"And with the Grabbit permanently out of commission, Principal Bubb is going to need help here in Rapacia—"

"You have *got* to be kidding me!" Principal Bubb and Lilith fumed in unison. They glared at one another for a heated second, before Lilith split off into her own private tirade.

"You expect someone of my poise and potential to babysit a bunch of ill-bred, two-bit hoodlums as vice principal?" Lilith seethed.

"Of course not," Mammon replied pompously. "I expect Ms. O'Malley to be the new vice principal. I expect *you* to replace her as a teacher."

Lilith's face burned crimson with rage. "This is *so* not over!" she huffed before turning on her well-heeled heels and storming off.

Ms. O'Malley approached Mammon cautiously. "Excuse me . . . sir. Did I hear ye right? Yer makin' *me* the new vice principal?"

The chairman's emerald eyes twinkled mischievously. "Do you smell that?" Mammon said, pressing close to Ms. O'Malley. The teacher's eyes watered from the musk emanating from the chairman. "That aroma is the result of me being stinking rich," he continued, backing away a step. "And I didn't get that way by making bad decisions. Besides, it seems only fitting that Rapacia be in the hands of a pirate," he replied. "Just watch your stern for bilge rats."

He eyed Ms. Mandelbaum and Poker Alice as they fumed, cawing back and forth to one another like angry crows.

"And if this Marlo Fauster girl can help us out downstairs," Mammon added, "then I think we've got ourselves a win-win. Now if you'll excuse me . . ."

He lumbered away through the thinning crowd, not waiting for "permission" to take leave.

Ms. O'Malley looked over at Marlo, who was still perched on the stage—only now she was engaged in a conversation with a dark-haired boy in penny loafers. The teacher smirked as Marlo, dangling her feet off the rim of the stage in nervous, girlish kicks, gave Rapacia's new vice principal a thumbs-up.

Meanwhile, Principal Bubb—riding a wave of supreme self-satisfaction—wandered away, bumping into confused old women in the process, and extended her thumb and pinky.

"All this and Milton Fauster's head on a platter," the

principal mumbled as she jabbed out Damian's number on her No-Fee Hi-Fi Faux Phone. "Figuratively speaking, unfortunately. Damian's sure to have nabbed that little twerp by now."

"We are sorry," a prerecorded voice squawked through Principal Bubb's thumb, *"but your party is well outside of range. Please try your call again, though we can't promise anything. For a menu of other things we're not responsible for, please press—"*

Bea "Elsa" Bubb grumbled as she stretched out her claw and disconnected her call. As she stepped over a long, toppled golden statue that bore a strong resemblance to her special security squad, she sensed, deep down in the depths of her stomach, that all was not well. That pool of dread, though, could very well have been hunger. For the strangest reason, all Principal Bubb could think of right now was fried chicken.

As she boarded the plush, velvet-upholstered escalator to the Earn Your Wings stand up in the Angel Food Court, she ruminated on her next move. The only card she had left to play was Milton, and there was no way she was giving that one up. No way.

Up on the SkyBridge, a man stared down below through his burnished brass spyglass. Through the lens, he noted the lingering crowd loitering about the concourse, as well as the tense post-Grabbit discussions held by various demons, faculty, and key members of the Netherworld political infrastructure.

He collapsed the spyglass with his palms and returned it to the inside breast pocket of his immaculate white suit.

A POD with a long grizzled beard wheeled his cart across the SkyBridge toward the man.

"Excuse me, sir," the phantom rasped. "Could you spare some change?"

The man smiled.

"Change is coming soon, my brother," he replied in a thick, mannered lilt with just a whiff of upper-class Englishman. The man fished out a coin from his pocket and flicked it into the POD's open palm. The phantom nodded his head and wheeled away.

The man fingered his headpiece—a thin band of gleaming gold crowning his head—causing it to hover slightly with a barely perceptible hum. He tilted the rim of it down to his ear.

"Hello, Uriel?" the man asked. "This is Gabriel. It seems to be all over now. I'll give you a full report upon my return, but suffice it to say, it's chaos down here, simply chaos."

The seasoned gentleman scratched his dark, bushy eyebrows and smirked gently.

"Which is another way of saying that everything is going according to plan."

Gabriel straightened his golden hoop and flicked it off, where it nestled back onto his freshly trimmed, salt-and-pepper hair.

He straightened his white silk tie and polished his badge with his thumb. The badge, pinned to his lapel, was a pair of golden wings sprouting from a glowing pyramid with a little eye perched at the tip. Beneath the pyramid were words written in tiny diamonds: GALACTIC ORDER DEPARTMENT (*GOD*).

BACKWORD

If money is, as it is often posited, the root of all evil, then where does that leave greed? Let's do the math: Greed takes up most of your time and most of your money, so therefore greed = time x money. And, as we all know, time = money. Ergo, greed = money x money. So, if money is the square root of all evil, then we are forced to conclude that greed is evil as well, perhaps even more so, in that it forced us to do math.

But when does the desire to simply possess something turn into unchecked greed? That's easy: when the things that you possess start possessing you.

It's something of a paradox, or a pair of socks, if one of those socks was really cool and all your friends were wearing them even though they were scratchy and uncomfortable and the other was warm and sensible but nothing to write home about, unless you were in the habit of writing home about sensible socks, which is sweet and sad—like when your dad starts humming a song by the pop star you were so into last week.

So, by offering to satisfy, this greedy place deep down in Heck left everyone wanting more. People, demons, phantoms, assorted creatures and entities all pining desperately for things: power, prestige, decent toilet paper . . . you name it. But this desperate pining doesn't guarantee happiness. All it guarantees is desperate pining. But rest assured, there are those who are about to get far more than they ever bargained for. Boy howdy. And then some.

For these certain people, demons, phantoms, assorted creatures and entities are about to realize that fate is not cut like the perfect diamond. Rather, like the cracks in a mirror, it takes a multitude of unpredictable paths and can bring with it years and years of bad luck.

ACKNOWLEDGMENTS

THE BOOK THAT is in your hands, or that is dangling from your special reading helmet, or that you had tattooed to the back of a friend sitting in front of you on the bus who lost that big bet you had going, wouldn't have been possible without the complete lack of support of the following persons:

The countless boys and girls who—through inflated senses of self, overindulging parents, or self-loathing projected outward, then trained unfortunately in my direction—made my life a living heck through the rubbing of fancy things in my face (sometimes literally), psychological torment, or gross failure to appreciate the snazzy denim suits my mom would lay out for me each morning.

The teachers, school administrators, and after-school athletic "supervisors" who aided the above group—either knowingly or unwittingly—in their pre-pubescent reign of thuggery, manipulation, and almost surgically precise teasing.

The hungry machine we call society that both feeds off and perpetuates the above behavior.

I'd also like to thank Paul Harrod, with whom I shared many delightfully devilish hours discussing all manner of things fire and brimstone, stoking the flames that would become this book; Jennifer Pidgeon, who, when presented with a list of story ideas I was considering, laughed when I got to Heck; and my mom, who, apart from the aforementioned snazzy denim suits, was an incredibly supportive force through childhood and continues to be to this day.

ABOUT THE AUTHOR

DALE E. BASYE (a subsidiary of his parents) has written stories, screenplays, essays, reviews, and lies for many publications and organizations. He was a film critic, winning several national journalism awards, and published an arts-and-entertainment newspaper called *Tonic.* He was also the driving musical force behind a series of bands, very few of which sported names suitable for a respectable book jacket. To be perfectly frank (or whomever), if any of them had been any good, you would probably be reading this biography on the back of a CD instead.

Here's what Dale E. Basye has to say about his second book:

"There is a time where you don't fully know what you have, though there is no lack of models, celebrities, and the inexplicably famous rubbing your face in what you *don't.* You'd give anything to have what they have, and that yearning gnaws at you from the inside as if you had swallowed a small, vicious shrew—which, to the best of your knowledge, you haven't. Heck is like that. And, no matter what anyone tells you, Heck is real. This story is real. Or as real as anything like this can be."

Dale E. Basye lives in Portland, Oregon, where he must, on a daily basis, wage life-or-death struggles with grizzly bears, nettled beavers, and inconsistent Wi-Fi signals.

BLiMPO

THE THIRD CIRCLE OF HECK

AVAILABLE JULY 2010